RAIN
WILL
COME

RAIN WILL COME

THOMAS HOLGATE

 **THOMAS & MERCER**

Text copyright © 2020 by Thomas Holgate
All rights reserved.

No part of this book may be reproduced, or stored in a retrieval system, or transmitted in any form or by any means, electronic, mechanical, photocopying, recording, or otherwise, without express written permission of the publisher.

Published by Thomas & Mercer, Seattle

www.apub.com

Amazon, the Amazon logo, and Thomas & Mercer are trademarks of Amazon.com, Inc., or its affiliates.

ISBN-13: 9781542005982
ISBN-10: 1542005981

Cover design by Mike Heath | Magnus Creative

Printed in the United States of America

For Nana. I promised you the next one.

Glioblastoma multiforme: the most aggressive of the gliomas; tumors arising from glia or their precursors within the central nervous system. These tumors grow rapidly and commonly spread to nearby brain tissue. Occur most often in the cerebral hemispheres, especially in the frontal and temporal lobes. A devastating cancer that almost always results in death within fifteen months after diagnosis.

—American Association of Neurological Surgeons

In layman's terms, it means you're
fucked.

—Dr. F. Michael Brin, Royal Academy of Neurosciences

ONE

"You're not one of those freaks, are you?"

Candy Darling, also known to her clients as Ecstasy Escorts Girl #73, stopped unbuttoning her shirt right before she revealed any of the huge Celtic cross tattoo that began at her fourth thoracic vertebra and disappeared between her dimples of Venus.

Her name had been chosen by the service. Candy herself had never heard of Andy Warhol, and the only "factory" she knew of was the one from which her deadbeat ex had been laid off six months ago.

"Why would you think that?"

She glanced over her shoulder, eyes eager to please. "To be honest with you, when a client tells me to get undressed but that he doesn't want to touch me, I start to get worried. But I figure, maybe he's got some crazy fear of disease. Or some other hang-up. But when he tells me he doesn't even want me to take off my clothes, that's when I get *real* worried."

He laughed. "I assure you, you have nothing to worry about."

"So you're not some asshole?" she asked, wanting him to reassure her.

Detective Paul Czarcik of the Illinois Bureau of Judicial Enforcement considered the question. He didn't want to lie. The truth was, he had been called far worse by both the cretins he pursued at risk to life and limb and his colleagues in various state and municipal bureaucracies. The consensus was unanimous. Czarcik *was* an asshole. But not in the way that Ecstasy Escorts Girl #73 meant.

Candy leaned over the 1981 Sony Trinitron sitting on the waist-level dresser. By some electronic miracle it was still working. She closed off her left nostril with her index finger and sniffed up the stray cocaine that had settled on top of the ancient picture-tube. Through her thin, translucent top, Czarcik glimpsed the arms of the Celtic cross stretched across her rib cage as if hugging her from behind. He was glad she wasn't naked. He hated ink, as the kids called it. Not because he was of a generation that believed tattoos were reserved for felons, marines, and sideshow performers, but for aesthetic reasons. Even the most intricately designed ones were nothing more than cheap body graffiti. To call them art, or even anything approaching art, was an affront to, well, art. And despite this recreational pursuit, and the erudition of his current companion, Czarcik fancied himself a man who could appreciate art. A sophisticate, he would have said, if it didn't sound so fucking French.

"Listen," Candy began, "dressed or undressed, you're still on the clock. So you wanna tell me what you want?"

"I want to talk to you."

"About what?"

"About you."

Candy stared at him, her anger apparent. "Listen to me, mister. I don't know what your deal is. But here's *my* deal. There's pretty much nothing I won't let you do to me for the right price. But I'm not telling you shit about me. Not for any amount of money."

"I understand," he replied, unfazed. He patted the bed next to him. "Then let's just watch some TV and smoke some cigarettes."

Czarcik sat propped up in bed, leaning against the headboard. Candy lay with her head at the foot of the bed, her face in her hands, watching the tube.

America's Next Top Model was on. Candy's choice. Czarcik preferred *The Twilight Zone* marathon, but Candy swore she couldn't watch a black-and-white TV show, no matter how much—as Czarcik explained to her—its themes still resonated.

"You think I could be on this show?" she asked, pointing to the screen and laughing at the absurdity of the suggestion.

"You're as pretty as any of them," Czarcik replied bluntly. "And probably a lot smarter."

She turned around, hurt in her eyes. "Don't be mean."

"I wasn't. You're an entrepreneur. Most of these girls couldn't string two sentences together."

Candy paused for a moment and then scurried up to the top of the bed, right next to Czarcik. "Promise you won't laugh?" He crossed his heart. "Well, I actually have a modeling shoot tomorrow. For *Château*, not *Vogue*, but still . . ."

"*Château*, that's still around?"

"Yeah. Pay is shit. Three hundred bucks a session. But it covers my monthly cell bill, at least."

"Who buys magazines anymore? Anything you could want to see is only a click away."

Candy shrugged, as if the answer was self-evident. "Guys your age, mostly. If a dude is over sixty-five and if he can still get it up, chances are he has no idea how to *really* use a computer. When I make house calls, you wouldn't believe how many magazine and VHS collections I see."

Czarcik wasn't the least bit offended she might believe he was eligible for social security. Although he was on the wrong side of fifty, he knew that were it not for his salt-and-pepper sideburns and whalebone-colored goatee, he could easily pass for ten years younger. A daily regimen of weightlifting and jogging kept his body as toned and tight as it was the day he graduated from the Chicago Police Academy as a fresh-faced twenty-three-year-old. But inside his body, where Father Time was allowed to wreak havoc unencumbered by efforts made in the spirit of vanity, years of hard living had taken their toll. Common sense, on which Czarcik prided himself, would dictate that thirty years of smoking, heavy drinking, and the occasional (OK, let's be honest here, *frequent*) snort would eventually culminate in one massive coronary. The only question was when. But questions involving his own mortality didn't much interest Paul Czarcik.

The episode ended. Another hopeful model was sixty minutes closer to her lifelong dream. Candy finished her cigarette and said, "Listen, I know you probably didn't get your money's worth, but I have another client."

"No, no. I enjoyed our time together."

Candy stood up and adjusted her miniskirt. She smoothed down her blouse. Her outfit was classy trashy, such that the quintessential strict movie dad might say, "Young lady, you don't think you're going out in *that*?"

She picked up the hundred-dollar bills left on the table near the door. She straightened them out and fanned them, poker-player style, for Czarcik to see.

"It's all there," he assured her.

"No, it's . . . it's way too much."

Czarcik snubbed out his cigarette in the flimsy tin ashtray lying on the bed next to him. That was one thing he loved about the Wishing Well Motor Lodge. Those cheap ashtrays. It reminded him of the good old soot-covered days when he was still forced to work with a partner and a perpetual cloud of tobacco smoke clung to the station's fiberboard ceiling tiles. "You earned it."

Candy held her tongue and pocketed the cash. As much as she wanted to inquire about this unnecessary generosity, she didn't want to anger him, even if he didn't seem like the type to give her a flaccid-penis rating on the Ecstasy Escorts website. If she received too many limp-dick icons, that bitch Charlotte would move her profile to a back page and lower her rate. The last time that happened, the only clients she managed to attract were college kids—who never tipped—and junkies banking on the off chance she carried and was in a sharing mood.

Sometimes Candy thought she should have been a shrink. With little prodding, complete strangers would reveal to her the most intimate details of their lives. She had no illusions. Part of it was just the nature of the job; men became strangely forthcoming between a pair of soft young thighs. But the other part was specific to her, not her vocation. She had a face that engendered trust, sometimes to her detriment. Because if Candy had learned anything, it was that men wanted their vulnerability rewarded. When it wasn't, they usually showed just how mean they could become.

This one was tougher to read, even if she could somehow account for his lack of sexual desire. He wasn't awkward or nervous as so many of them were. On the contrary, sitting there, cigarette dangling from his lips, he oozed arrogance. She remembered an old movie she had once seen called *Risky Business*. Not since she'd watched the antics of the movie's star—with his Ray-Ban sunglasses and megawatt smile—had she seen anyone acting so effortlessly cool.

Czarcik had been reading Candy as well—from the moment he had disengaged the chain and ushered her into the room. Her accent was specific. Appalachia, most likely just west of the Blue Ridge Mountains near the Tennessee state line. She had grown up poor, but not dirt poor, and did not suffer any chronic affliction that would have pointed to her basic nutritional needs not having been met as a child. Although she had had no orthodontic work done (her top canines slightly overlapped her lateral incisors—easy to correct with braces), her cavities had not gone neglected. However, the fillings were silver amalgam, not composite resin, which suggested a free clinic, the only places that continued to use the cheaper, potentially toxic material.

This pervasive habit of Czarcik's was so ingrained, so instinctual, that when Candy had looked at him for the first time, he found himself wondering about her specific brand of disposable contact lenses. He wasn't obsessive or compulsive. Not like that caricature of a detective on that stupid fucking show—what was it called? *Mook? Monks?* He just had one of those brains that was constantly working. Someone attuned to his condition might say this was why he had never married and had few friends. Czarcik himself scoffed at such cheap psychology. He prized self-awareness above all else and would never ascribe his rank misanthropy to a personality quirk. He didn't particularly care for people and preferred to be left alone. Except, like now, when he wanted company. And for this he was prepared to pay well.

There were some benefits. The traits that made him a pariah in polite society rendered him indispensable to the Bureau of Judicial Enforcement.

He worked most frequently with the Chicago Police Department, and although their high-tech forensic center might have determined that the majority of the West Side's smack was cut with an unidentified baking sugar, only Czarcik found it strange that low-level dealers wouldn't just use the cheapest, most common brand available. And only Czarcik was dogged enough to finally track down the particular manufacturer to a family-owned confectionary in Bellagio, Italy, which had exactly one customer in the United States—Buonta & Sons, an authentic Italian grocery store on Grand Avenue, west of the expressway. Buonta was well known for having the best prosciutto this side of the Atlantic. It was less known for being a front for the Argentado family, the closest thing Chicago had to the Corleones. But once the DA initiated an investigation, the whole enterprise collapsed like a house of cards, leading to the biggest organized crime bust since Alphonse Capone had made his home in Cicero.

In recognition of his exemplary service to the public good, Czarcik had received numerous commendations and awards. The district he had been working out of presented him with a framed photo he had taken with the mayor; the mayor mugged for the camera, a shit-eating grin plastered on his face, while his hands smothered Czarcik's own in a debt of gratitude.

The medals and ribbon bars meant nothing to him, tossed away in the back of a desk drawer. The framed photo, well, its surface was good for cutting coke. But the goodwill he accrued, indispensable. The proverbial "Get Out of Jail Free" card that, eventually, Czarcik assumed he would use quite literally. There had always been whispers about his exploits, but never enough to necessitate an internal investigation. One day, however, his luck would run out. His fatalism all but guaranteed it.

Candy was halfway out the door before shouting a perfunctory thank-you. Czarcik didn't respond, his attention now focused on the White Sox game being transmitted in glorious low definition. Baseball was the only sport he watched nowadays. He liked its predictable rhythms, its familiar sounds. The dirt, the cowhide, the fresh-cut grass.

Besides, football brought back too many memories of talent squandered. Not to mention broken fingers, which was one of the reasons Czarcik was never as good a shot as he should have been. Hockey players were notoriously tough, but there was just something about grown men in ice skates that he couldn't get past. Soccer? Come on. He had seen punks on the street take a slug to the torso and go down with less dramatics than those prima donnas in shin guards. And the NBA? He'd liked it in the seventies, when drugs and violence were endemic. Besides, what kind of self-respecting predominately black league would let Steve Nash, a diminutive white point guard, win two consecutive MVPs?

TWO

At the same time that Detective Paul Czarcik was discussing the evolution of pornographic mediums—from magazines to VHS tapes to the internet—with a well-paid and completely dressed escort, almost one thousand miles away, just outside Dallas, in the gated community of Whippoorwill Falls, Judge Jeral Robertson was pulling his Benz into the garage.

Once inside the house, the judge tossed his keys onto the granite countertop in the kitchen. The sound reverberated through his cavernous McMansion.

Judge Robertson lived alone. His wife had left him last year, taking with her the couple's then-fifteen- and eight-year-old daughters.

After the video had gone viral, everything about his life had changed.

The video had been released on a Monday night. By Tuesday morning, it had been viewed over ten thousand times and generated thousands of page views, as his lawyer had explained. Even in a county, and state, not typically sympathetic to children's rights, the clip managed to create a stir. But that was the internet for you. Liberals in New York and California could suddenly weigh in on how God-fearing Americans raised their children.

On the night in question, Judge Robertson had come home after a long day on the bench in family court. Child Protective Services had been a pain in the ass, doing their best to block the return of a six-year-old boy to his parents simply because they believed in regular corporal punishment.

Claire had made tuna casserole for dinner, never one of his favorites. And because his daughter Jenny and her younger sister, Emily, were hungry hours ago, it was now cold. No one could blame him for being in a foul mood.

His wife was leaning over the suds-filled sink, latex gloves pulled up to her elbows, working the pan with a scouring brush. "Want me to warm it up for you, honey?" she asked, with her usual cheerful subservience. Judge Robertson grunted and headed upstairs.

In the first bedroom, Emily was playing with a dollhouse she had received the previous Christmas. He smiled to himself, remembering how Claire had suggested that Emmy was probably a little too old for it. "A girl is never too old for a dollhouse," he'd told her. And it was settled.

"Hi, Daddy," Emily called out upon hearing his footsteps.

"Princess," he replied flatly before continuing down the hallway to Jenny's room.

Judge Robertson opened the door without knocking. Privacy was a privilege, not a right, in the Robertson household. Anything inappropriate for a father to see—meaning anything having to do with the female body—should be taken care of in the bathroom.

Jenny was sitting in her swivel chair, her back to the door, engrossed in something on her computer. Her noise-canceling circumaural headphones—another Christmas gift—muffled her father's entrance.

By the time Jenny could throw her hands up across the screen, he was behind her. And had seen enough.

Judge Robertson was no technophile, but as a family court judge it was incumbent upon him to be knowledgeable about what kids were up to, since more often than not their pastimes brought nothing but strife to an otherwise happy household. Although he didn't understand the particulars of different torrent sites, he grasped the overall concept.

These websites were used to trade stolen content, mainly copyrighted movies and music, although any digital media could be transferred from user to user.

He and Jenny had discussed these kinds of sites before and agreed that they would be off limits, both for legal and ethical reasons.

Judge Robertson didn't wait for an explanation, as none would have been sufficient. He grabbed Jenny's hair, just as a frightened "Dad!" escaped her lips, and jerked her to her feet. Her leg braces screeched against each other—metal kissing metal—an audible reminder of the multiple sclerosis that had plagued her since childhood.

Judge Robertson pushed his daughter over her desk. Her head slammed into the side of her computer, upturning the machine. Her chest crushed the keyboard, sending line upon line of gibberish scrolling frantically across the screen. "Stay," he commanded.

Jenny didn't dare defy him. Even if she had wanted to, she lacked the upper body strength necessary to raise her torso off the desk. She didn't even turn around when she heard the familiar sound of her father removing his belt.

Jenny took the first stroke in silence. Her father held nothing back, but she bit her lip and managed to muffle her cry. A small however futile act of defiance. The second blow practically lifted her off the floor. Again she managed to stifle a scream. The third stroke did the trick, and Jenny let out a long, pitiful wail.

Judge Robertson was unmoved.

He wrapped the belt around his knuckles, redoubling his grip. This lesson had to stick. He had warned her once. What kind of a man was he if he couldn't control his own daughter? And under the very roof he provided.

"Jenny," he said with little emotion. "I want you to lower your jeans."

Jenny closed her eyes tightly and began to cry.

"You have no one to blame but yourself," Judge Robertson reminded her. Then he raised the belt and brought it down over and over again without mercy. Jenny fainted after the twentieth stroke. The beating continued for a good fifteen minutes more—all of it caught on his daughter's webcam.

When all was said and done, Judge Robertson should have considered himself lucky. He was forced to attend counseling—which of course he sailed through by telling the therapist exactly what she wanted to hear—and had to recuse himself from any child welfare cases for one year.

On the home front, things were not so easy. Claire had taken the girls and left him. He blamed the lawyers, those fucking vultures who descended to pick through the carcass of his marriage just as soon as the story hit the wires. After all, Claire never would have had the will to leave him without outside encouragement.

She and the girls had moved into a small apartment on the outskirts of town. Although he was legally barred from ever visiting, the judge considered the place just as much his, thanks to the $5,000 a month in child support he was required to pay.

Still, the situation could have been a lot worse. Bachelorhood suited him better than he had expected, and he got to keep the house and cars.

Judge Robertson was not a man prone to self-reflection. The first time he even considered the possibility that he was in any way responsible for his current predicament was when he came to with the worst headache of his life.

A noise.

That's the last thing he remembered. Along with the unsettling feeling that someone was with him in the house. Then the pain. And then it all went black.

He had no idea how long he had been unconscious. Long enough for whoever had played whack-a-mole with his skull to tie his wrists

11

and ankles to the kitchen chair. Long enough for his fingers and toes to have lost all feeling.

Judge Robertson blinked a few times, clearing out the last of the cobwebs. In front of him, no more than ten feet away, sat a man whom the judge could only assume was his assailant. The man's head was bowed, resting in the cradle between his thumb and forefinger, as if he, too, had suffered some devastating blow. He looked up when he heard the judge stirring.

The two locked eyes, and the man waited until the judge was coherent.

"What kind of a man resigns his family to the poorhouse while he himself lives in the lap of luxury?"

Was this a rhetorical question? When the judge didn't respond, the man answered. "I guess the same kind of man who has no compunction about torturing his disabled daughter."

Judge Robertson stiffened visibly at the word *torturing*. Over the past year, he had endured relentless criticism. Editorials called for his resignation. Talk show hosts questioned his competence. But even his most vociferous opponents had never referred to his well-meaning discipline as *torture*. As if reading his mind, the man continued. "Yes, I chose my words carefully."

The judge prided himself on his ability to size up a person at first glance. It was a skill he had honed from years on the bench, but one he was never supposed to utilize. After all, Lady Justice wore a blindfold for a reason.

Studying the man in front of him, Judge Robertson had never been so sure of his instincts. And he didn't like what he saw. The man had a refined, honest face. He wasn't the kind who made a habit out of breaking and entering. He was here for a reason.

"Please, I have a lot of money in the house safe. Take whatever you want." Even before the words left his lips, the judge knew he had made a mistake.

The man smiled, like a parent disappointed by a child. "We both know why I'm here."

Judge Robertson feigned ignorance, unwilling to give the man any possible psychological advantage. What was still a mystery, what Judge Robertson couldn't possibly comprehend, was the specific chain of events that had led to this moment.

Nearly a year had passed since the beating of Jenny Robertson had gone viral. Although it was the buzziest story for one twenty-four-hour news cycle, with the afternoon freak shows squeezing a little more mileage from it with panels of two-bit shrinks pontificating about the merits of corporal punishment, the rest of the world forgot about the scandal as soon as one of those Kardashian girls popped out another baby.

Jenny still hated him of course. But how the hell would a sheltered sixteen-year-old have the means to enact a complicated revenge plot? This unwelcome visitor was no misguided teenager, the kind who could be enticed, maybe with sexual favors, to mete out some vigilante justice to dear old Dad.

Then there was Claire. The incident had empowered her, no doubt. All her newfound friends and compatriots in that cottage industry of domestic-abuse survivors had enabled her to tap into a hereto unknown reservoir of strength. But she was a victim by nature. When the excitement had died down, all she wanted was to be left alone, to raise her two girls far from the prying eyes of the world. Even if part of her pined for vengeance, she would never have made the slightest move to make her plan operational.

And Emily had just turned nine. Too ludicrous to fathom. The judge chalked that one up to his probable concussion.

Again the man seemed to anticipate his thoughts. "I imagine you must be wondering how this all transpired."

This was bad, the judge thought, unease continuing to settle over him. Two-bit robbers didn't use words like *transpired*.

"That's natural, I suppose," the man conceded, running his fingers through his thick hair, pausing momentarily to massage his temples.

The judge was sure he caught the man trying to suppress a grimace. "But you're asking the wrong question."

Silence. Judge Robertson wasn't going to play into his hands.

The man continued, undeterred. "What you should be asking yourself is, 'How much pain can I endure?'"

For the first time since finding himself a prisoner in his own home, Judge Robertson was legitimately frightened. His captor wasn't some hot-blooded degenerate being ushered out of his courtroom in shackles while screaming hollow threats. This was a man not of words but of deeds, who had already shown himself to be a very capable adversary.

"There's one thing I've wondered about," the man said. "Did you ever regret it?"

Judge Robertson swallowed hard. He tightened his jaw and tried to look earnest. "Yes, every day."

The lie was palpable. "I didn't think so," the man said softly.

Judge Robertson closed his eyes. When he opened them, the man was crying. For a split second, the judge felt a sliver of hope, until he realized the stranger wasn't mourning for him.

"I watched that video a hundred times," the man said, as if recalling a painful memory. "Even when she cried, you continued to beat her. And when her fragile body could take no more . . . you continued." Eyes glazed over, the man looked right through the judge. "Your . . . daughter," he said with incomprehension, as if the word itself was inexplicable.

The stranger remained seated but shuffled his chair across the floor until he was only inches from Judge Robertson. "I want you to do me a favor." The judge was noncommittal, uncertain whether this was a last-minute reprieve or simply delaying the inevitable. "When you scream, I want you to think of her smiling face."

The man reached into the inside pocket of his light jacket.

He withdrew a hunting knife, the kind with a crescent blade, perfect for skinning deer. He pressed it against Judge Robertson's cheek.

And then he began.

THREE

Czarcik was on his third Cutty Sark when he felt the familiar tingle on his thigh. He sighed, hoping it would go away.

The detective drank alone at one of Alsace's outdoor tables. Alsace was the hippest new restaurant in Logan Square, Chicago's neighborhood du jour. What was once ground zero for Latino flea markets was now home to three microbreweries, a rye distillery, and a multimedia collective dedicated to preserving vinyl and VHS.

Czarcik didn't give a shit about what happened to Logan Square, or any other neighborhood for that matter. He had seen them rise and fall.

Just ten years ago, the Near West Side had been a haven for wannabe gangbangers, until restaurants with names written in Cyrillic started muscling out the corner liquor stores and pool halls. A few miles north, Wicker Park, a bohemian mecca for as long as Czarcik could remember, was now home to six Starbucks, one of them in an L station that straddled another of the company's freestanding cafés.

If the city was a living organism—a favorite metaphor of politicians—then neighborhoods were its lymphatic system. Always there, always working. Responding to the influx of foreign interlopers with either hospitality or resistance.

Czarcik understood that he was in the minority. Few people were dispassionate about gentrification. They were either rabidly opposed, convinced it was nothing more than a slow form of genocide against indigenous communities, or fanatically steadfast in their belief that it was integral to a healthy and diverse populace.

This constant tension prompted Czarcik to seek out neighborhoods at the nexus of past and present. Because cops there were hated by both demographics, he was left alone to drink in peace.

If it weren't for that infernal tingling.

When it finally became unbearable, Czarcik reached into his pocket and pulled out his BlackBerry. It didn't bother him that he was the last man on earth to use one. The rest of the Bureau of Judicial Enforcement had migrated to the iPhone platform years ago; the BJE had mandated it, though most officers were all too happy to oblige. Czarcik had refused, one of the conditions of his agreement not to retire. Although the BlackBerry operating system was supposedly more secure than iOS or Android, hackability was not one of Czarcik's concerns. He liked, and needed, the physical keys. His fingers had been mangled on the high school gridiron and any touch screen, no matter how responsive, could never replace the tactile feel of hard plastic.

He looked down at the number on the screen. Headquarters.

The BJE had been Czarcik's home for the better part of the last decade, since it was suggested he take early retirement from Chicago PD.

On the books, the BJE was under the auspices of the Illinois attorney general and answered to Springfield. In reality, the organization answered to no one, but reported to and assisted the many cities, towns, and departments that called on its expertise, expertise that was becoming rarer and rarer now that things like diversity training were taking precedence over basic police work. Every once in a while, when an activist decided to delve into the state's inscrutable budget, the bureau's purpose would be questioned. What was wrong with the existing police departments and county sheriffs? Couldn't the FBI be brought in for especially delicate or complicated cases? Sure, and if you suffered a massive coronary, why not just see a podiatrist instead of a cardiac surgeon? After all, they're both doctors. So when push came to shove, there wasn't much dissent. Almost everybody understood the value of an organization that, in layman's terms, knew how to get shit done.

The BJE employed around one hundred men and women at any given time, the kind of people who could no longer work in traditional channels but who had skills that proved eminently useful to the state government.

People like Barry Esposito, a functional schizophrenic who was legitimately psychic. Unfortunately, his abilities could only be accessed while he was off his meds and in the throes of a self-induced hallucinogenic state. Still, he had pinpointed the exact location of three different kidnap victims, three victims who would have undoubtedly been murdered were it not for his visions.

Corrine Fumagalli, a hacker gone straight who looked like a member of Bikini Kill and could have made a fortune in private industry. At nineteen she had been busted for stealing the social security numbers of the University of Chicago's entire incoming freshman class. She cut a deal with the attorney general, who decided that locking her up and squandering her talent might not be in the best interest of the state.

Mad Dog Marone, a former private detective from Philly who was—

Bzz . . .

It was like holding a rabid housefly.

He took one last swig of Cutty and pressed the green phone icon on the device. "Czarcik." The detective listened intently to the voice on the other end. His eyes showed no trace of the liquor he had savored only seconds before.

It was his boss—at least in name—and the head of the BJE, Eldon Parseghian. Few people had the constitution to run the BJE, and Parseghian was one of them. The product of, as he liked to say, a hillbilly father and an Armenian beauty, who took his mother's name for some mysterious reason. Parseghian was brilliant, dashing, and more than a little crazy. Although he worked the street admirably (and had even lost hearing in his left ear during a shoot-out when he was with the gang unit of Chicago PD), Parseghian had easily segued into his new role as a political animal par excellence. His was an appointed position, and he kept the governor protected from the kinds of things that governors *should* but really didn't *need* to know about. More importantly, he kept his team protected from unnecessary oversight and bureaucracy. Because if there was one thing that Parseghian had recognized from the very moment he took the job, it was that the best thing he could do to support the men and women under his command was to leave them the fuck alone.

"I'm leaving now," Czarcik said, and he pressed the red phone icon and stuffed the BlackBerry back into his pocket.

His tattooed waiter was at an adjacent table, educating a group of young mothers about the particulars of France's cheese-making regions and hoping their schoolgirl giggles translated into a larger tip.

Czarcik couldn't wait for the check. Although he knew what a glass of Cutty *should* cost, he didn't know the markup at this place. Just to be safe, he threw an extra twenty on the table, a small price to pay to avoid unnecessary human contact.

Rogers Park was one of Chicago's most storied neighborhoods. Pushed up against the suburb of Evanston and bordered on the east by Lake Michigan, the area had been home to upwardly mobile Jewish immigrants. Its main thoroughfare, Devon Avenue, had been a menagerie of small, family-owned shops, delicatessens, and art galleries specializing in representations of the Wailing Wall. Now, except for a handful of Hasidim, the old inhabitants were long gone. Cheap electronics distributors alternated with ethnic markets whose windows assured customers the food was halal. One of the city's last great strip clubs, the Quilted Panther, was now bordered by a Syrian grocery on one side and, on the other, a clothing store that sold only traditional Middle Eastern garb.

Czarcik piloted his unmarked Crown Victoria past the boarded-up storefronts and newsprint-covered windows.

As he drove, he listened to Camille Saint-Saëns's "Aquarium." The incongruity between the pastoral music and urban strife outside his window wasn't lost on him. His musical tastes used to be eclectic, but now really only occupied opposite ends of the spectrum: classical and death metal (although Celtic Frost and Holst's *The Planets* had more in common than one might think).

From Devon, Czarcik turned onto North Magnolia. There was no need to check the address. Out front were half-a-dozen cruisers, their lights throwing primary colors all over the facades of the greystones. The area around the property had already been cordoned off with police tape, holding back the curious throngs with their iPhones above their heads, trying to get a photo of god knows what.

Magnolia was zoned for permit parking, and Czarcik found a spot easily. He parked the Crown Vic and hurried up the front steps of the building, flashing his ID at a young officer guarding the main door whom he recognized from one of the nearby districts.

The smell hit him as soon as he entered the apartment.

His stomach rolled over, and he wished he hadn't polished off that final Cutty. When he'd been a child, his grandfather, who had then recently immigrated to America, had bought a dairy farm out near Madison, Wisconsin. By all accounts, Papa Czarcik was a wonderful man, but all his grandson could remember of him was the stench of sour milk.

Only one other time had Czarcik smelled anything this revolting. It was his first year as a beat cop, and he had been called out to investigate a domestic disturbance in Back of the Yards, a neighborhood so named because of its proximity to the Union Stock Yards, Chicago's turn-of-the-century meatpacking district that was responsible for one of the city's early nicknames, "hog butcher to the world." By the time he had arrived at the scene, a sanitation worker named Lincoln Dupree had turned his shotgun on his wife and two children before placing the barrel between his own teeth. It proved nearly impossible to remove the remains of Lincoln from the shag carpet, and the hot blood had stunk to high hell on that midsummer morning.

This time, the bodies were in the basement of the house on Magnolia Street. Forensics was already sweeping the place as Czarcik carefully descended the cellar's rotted wooden staircase.

Czarcik was relieved to find Lieutenant Cappy Walsh in charge. He had worked with Walsh on numerous occasions. He was plainspoken and cared little about department politics, which meant he didn't automatically see Czarcik as a threat to his domain. Plus, it was rumored he had a little gambling problem. Nothing too serious—the ponies mostly. This pleased Czarcik. He trusted men with vices. Especially vices they didn't advertise.

Walsh waved Czarcik over the moment he spotted him. "Thanks for coming so quickly, Paul," Walsh said, dispensing with further pleasantries. He handed Czarcik a pair of latex gloves, which the detective snapped on.

"What do we got, Cappy?"

Walsh took a deep breath. "Name's Marisol Fernandez. Thirty-six years old. She's legal. Grew up in Pilsen. Owned a laundromat on Bryn Mawr with her husband."

The woman was curled up in the fetal position, her elbows pulled tightly into her body, as if warding off blows from some invisible attacker. Both her eyes were black, raccoon-like, and her nose was broken. Her lips were far too swollen to see inside her mouth, but Czarcik was certain she was missing plenty of teeth.

Scattered around the body were a variety of instruments: a metal pipe, a coaxial cable, a wooden sorority paddle devoid of Greek letters.

There was something else. A dead chicken was tied around her neck.

Czarcik pointed to the blood-caked items. "I assume these are what did her in?"

Walsh nodded. "According to the preliminary examination," he confirmed. He then dotted the air over each item with his finger, playing a morbid game of Clue. "The pipe shattered her orbital socket. The paddle busted her lips." He gestured up and down Marisol Fernandez's broken body. "She also has welts all over her legs, from the cable."

"Husband?" Czarcik asked, expecting confirmation. It was one of those truisms every cop learned his first year in the academy: ninety-nine percent of the time, it's the loving spouse.

Walsh shook his head slowly and offered a wry smile, as if holding back the twist of a popular mystery novel most people had already read. He took Czarcik's elbow and led him into a small room off the south wall of the basement. At one time it was probably used to store pickling jars. The Fernandezes had used it to store chemicals for their laundromat. Now somebody had used it to store a body. A headless body.

"Is this him?" asked Czarcik.

Walsh shrugged. "We assume. But without a head, we need to wait for prints or DNA."

The body was naked from the waist up. Cigarette burns, all fresh, dotted the torso like a child's ghoulish art project. There were hundreds of them—tiny eyes, grayish at the rims, open wide in agony, with no mouth from which to scream.

The victim's hands were tied behind his back. The rope then continued down between his legs and around his ankles.

"No one else in the house?" Czarcik asked.

"It's clean."

"Kids?"

Walsh glanced down at his tiny spiral notepad. "According to the neighbor, there were three foster children. But all were removed from the home late last year."

The reason for their removal was relevant but not urgent. Czarcik would come back to that. The condition of the body, on the other hand, was pressing.

Czarcik examined the stump upon which once had sat the head of Luis Fernandez. He reached out and lightly ran his latex-covered finger around the circumference of the wound. Jagged tooth-shaped lacerations pocked the neckline.

Czarcik looked over at Walsh. "Wound's a mess. This guy wasn't decapitated with a single blow. It wasn't an ax. Or a sword or machete. Nothing like that. If I had to guess, I'd say a hacksaw."

Walsh nodded. "That's what forensics thought. But we couldn't find the weapon anywhere." He scratched the side of his cheek. "There had to be a reason he took it with him. With Mrs. Fernandez, he left all his tools. Didn't even make an effort to clean or hide them."

There had to be a reason.

The phrase reverberated in Czarcik's brain. That's what he was here for, after all. Nowadays, even the most preternaturally intuitive detective was at the mercy of forensic science. He remembered the days when he would speculate, postmortem, whether a body had been sexually violated. Now tiny measurements of the capillaries in the vaginal walls could render an absolute verdict. He recalled all the hours he once spent trying to match a single fiber to a specific article of clothing. Now atomic microscopes could break down anything to the fundamental building blocks of matter. Guesswork was moot. Answers definitive.

What a computer with unlimited processing power could never explain, however, was the *why*.

The human condition was nature's last unbreakable code. Against it, even the descendants of Deep Blue were no more than blind men groping at an elephant. It's why men like Czarcik still had jobs. They were modern oracles, the rare few who could still read the tea leaves.

There was something about the whole scene that Czarcik didn't like. It was too imperfectly staged. But staged it was; random it wasn't. Of this he was certain.

Czarcik was far from spiritual, yet he had worked plenty of crime scenes where he had felt a palpable evil. Despite the carnage laid out in front of him, this wasn't one of them. This was something equally unsettling. It was phony.

Walsh intruded on his thoughts. "What do you think, Paul? Some sort of ritual, huh?"

"Could be," Czarcik replied.

"It's got to be. 'Specially with that chicken. Why the hell else would you go to the trouble of tying a dead bird around someone's neck?"

"Voodoo is certainly a possibility," Czarcik suggested. This would satisfy Walsh for the remainder of their time together. Corroborate his suspicions. Give him purpose. All bullshit, of course. Because if there was one thing Czarcik was sure of, it was that this had nothing to do with voodoo.

Czarcik peeled off his latex gloves and balled them up. He was finished for the time being. "I'll need the case file."

"Soon as everything is back from the lab," Walsh promised.

"And the medical examiner's report."

"I'll have his office send it directly to you at the bureau."

Czarcik nodded once and began to walk away.

"Paul," Walsh called out.

The detective stopped at the bottom of the cellar steps and turned around. Walsh approached him; his breath stank of subtle spearmint. *He's trying to stop smoking,* thought Czarcik.

"Listen, Paul," Walsh began, somewhat apprehensively. "I know how you BJE guys like to work. But if you need anything . . . I'm here."

Czarcik considered the offer and concluded that gratitude would be the fastest way to get his colleague to leave him the fuck alone. "Thanks, Cappy. I will."

FOUR

Daniel Langdon lay on the bed in the cheap motel room he had paid for in cash.

His eyes were closed, and he massaged his temples in concentric circles, pressing the first two fingers of each hand against his skull as forcefully as he could endure. As expected, the headaches were becoming much more frequent. He considered an injection of Palladone directly into the vagus nerve but decided against it. The pain wasn't yet agonizing, and he wanted to remain lucid, at least until the task at hand was finished.

He thought back to the initial diagnosis. How the doctor had entered the examination room as solemnly as a pallbearer to deliver the death sentence. From that point, he remembered only bits and pieces. The four lobes of the brain and their impact on memory, speech, cognition, intelligence, emotion, and most of all, behavior. *Behavior.* Because of its size and location, behavioral changes were inevitable. As inevitable as the pain. That's what the good old doc had assured him. But that's also when, for the first time, Daniel decided he might not go quietly into the night.

On the bed next to him, in the same spot where a warm lover once nestled into the contours of his body, was the head of Luis Fernandez sitting atop a plastic drop cloth. Bloodless, gray, and misshapen, it looked more like a well-made movie prop than what was once the control center of a human being.

Daniel popped four Advil and turned on the television. It took him a minute or two of channel surfing through reality shows about Alaska and old public-domain horror films before he stopped on a rerun of *The Brady Bunch*. It was the episode where the Brady children, convinced their house is going to be sold, decide to stage a haunting to scare off prospective buyers. In one completely preposterous scene, Alice comes across the three boys, who are wearing sheets with eyeholes cut out. Despite the amateur costumes, and the fact that all three ghosts are exactly the same height as the Brady boys, Alice mistakes them for actual apparitions and has what would amount to a sanitized nervous breakdown.

This was exactly what Daniel needed. Nothing about which he had to think too hard. Once the ibuprofen kicked in and the pain subsided, he had a lot of work to do.

During his preparations, Daniel had used a Tor web browser to conceal his identity while he researched the best ways to dispose of a human skull. He remembered being both surprised and depressed not only at how easily accessible the information was but at its sheer quantity.

Most of the questionable websites focused on the entire body, so he was forced to take some liberties. He assumed the teeth would be the easiest to get rid of. After prying them from the gumline with an ordinary pair of pliers, he could crush them into a fine powder using a stone mortar and pestle. From there, the dust could be flushed down the bathroom toilet. Even a motel with substandard plumbing would be able to handle the residue.

Hydrochloric acid, which wouldn't harm the ceramic tile of the bathtub, would be used to dissolve the flesh. This would take eight hours or so, which was fine, since Daniel needed a good night's sleep.

When the skin and sinew were reduced to a liquid no more viscous than water, he would use a metal crowbar to lift up the tub's stopper and send the noxious brew swirling down the drain.

The skull was more problematic. He wished he could just donate it to a medical school and be done. Unfortunately, even the most unscrupulous institutions had rules preventing the donation of off-the-street specimens.

Daniel decided the most prudent thing to do would be to wrap the skull up in bath towels to muffle the sound and then pound it into small pieces with a cinder block he had found behind the motel. He would then place the pieces in various fast-food containers, which he would throw away at random rest stops between here and his next destination. It was feasible that a curious sanitation worker might somehow come across the remains, identify them as human, and contact the authorities. But it was much, much more likely that they would remain forever the bedfellows of half-eaten burgers, soggy fries, and congealed milkshakes at the bottom of some garbage dump.

Back on the television, the industrious Bradys had convinced a would-be home buyer that a family who would go through so much trouble to scare off prospective suitors should really be the rightful owners. Daniel smiled to himself, amused by how none of the targets of this elaborate ruse seemed the least bit put off by the shenanigans. He was such a sentimentalist, even if his own life had disabused him of the notion of happy endings.

With the Advil now pulling at the edges of his throbbing headache, Daniel got to work, pouring the first bottle of hydrochloric acid into the tub. There was still a lot to do. *And miles to go before I sleep,* he thought before his mind wandered down those two roads that diverged in a yellow wood. He was slightly troubled that the imagery was taken from two different poems and much more upset that he hadn't realized it until he was back on the road. That was the temporal lobe, no doubt.

Altering his memory. Robbing him of the joy he still derived from even the most simple of pleasures.

The woods were dark and deep, indeed. But not so lovely.

The Illinois Bureau of Judicial Enforcement's current headquarters was carved out of a former cold-storage building on the bank of the South Fork of the Chicago River.

Apparently, its construction was significant. All the tree huggers had gotten hard-ons about the fact that it was the first LEED-certified building in the city. Czarcik didn't know what the fuck any of that meant, but he did know that there was something unnatural about a building with grass growing on its roof.

Czarcik sat at his desk, completely oblivious to the din around him. Whatever the space was designed for, it wasn't privacy. When possible, he preferred to work from home, away from prying eyes. But the reports were coming in today, and he wanted to be here when they arrived. Having them messengered to his home would waste precious hours.

His area was Spartan: a metal filing cabinet, gooseneck lamp, papers, and office supplies strewn across the desktop, at odds with the vibe the architect was going for.

He leaned back in his completely nonergonomic chair and put his feet up on the desk. He chewed on a Rocky Patel cigar, his favorite brand. How that Indian knew how to make such a fine smoke, he didn't know, but goddamned did he ever. Even with Czarcik's unusual dispensations, he couldn't flout the city's no-smoking rule. He distinctly remembered when the ban went into effect. How the chief stood before the local TV cameras and asked hypothetically how many police officers' lives would be saved by eliminating tobacco from the workplace. Czarcik was still a relatively young detective in the Chicago Police Department and didn't think it would be conducive to his career to interrupt the press conference in order to inquire how many additional lives would be saved *by* those police officers for whom tobacco was nothing short of a magical elixir, keeping them motivated and focused on the business of saving lives.

Right now, with the stogie's nicotine being absorbed into his bloodstream, Czarcik was completely focused on the black-and-white photograph of Luis Fernandez's headless body. Besides the absence of a head, the most conspicuous detail was the cigarette burns. They were all fresh, most likely administered hours, or even minutes, before his death. Czarcik searched for a pattern, a purpose to their placement. If he were in a pulp detective thriller, this was the point at which he would nearly tumble out of his chair, having just discovered that the burns formed a pentagram. These, however, didn't form anything.

There was something else peculiar about the body—it had no tattoos. If this were gang related, the corpse would be covered in them. Furthermore, anyone involved in the black arts would have some type of body art, if only to adhere to the cliché. Then again, he was certain none of this was occult related.

Walsh slapped a file down on the desk, startling Czarcik. "I told you I'd send the reports over, but I figured I might as well drop them off myself"—he glanced dramatically around the room—"to see how you BJE guys live."

Czarcik put down the crime scene photos and picked up the file. He began to skim through the contents. "Anything interesting?"

Walsh raised his eyebrows and flopped his head from side to side. Czarcik couldn't tell whether he was being coy or just annoying. "Medical examiner's report came back as expected. The woman, Marisol Fernandez, died from blunt force trauma. Her husband . . . well, he died from getting his fucking head cut off." Czarcik was already halfway through the report when Walsh added, "But there is something very curious . . ."

"The foster kids . . ." Czarcik muttered, mainly to himself, finishing Walsh's sentence.

Walsh ignored him. "Remember when I told you that Family Services had removed them from the home?"

Czarcik didn't answer. He already had all the information he needed. Walsh continued anyway. "Turns out the kids were abused in ways similar to the victims. Social worker interviewed said it was one of the worst cases she had ever seen. These pieces of shit didn't want a family. They were just goddamned leeches. Saw a way to get easy state money for their failing business. Hardly paid attention to the kids and barely gave them enough to eat. If any of them spoke up or asked for more, they'd get the paddle. Or the cable. And if these assholes were really angry, they used the kids as ashtrays."

Walsh paused. Czarcik remained stoic, engrossed in the verbiage of the postmortem. "You get to the part about the chicken yet?" Walsh asked.

Czarcik still didn't look up or acknowledge Walsh's presence. He continued. "Kids were finally saved when a neighbor found the youngest, six years old, crawling around the yard with a dead chicken tied around his neck." It was as if he were reading directly from the report. Which he wasn't.

"According to Mrs. Fernandez, the kid was being punished for 'stealing' a few bites of a chicken nugget," Walsh added.

"What I don't see . . ." Czarcik said as he leafed through a few more pages, "is why these two received such light sentences."

A glimmer of satisfaction passed across Walsh's face. "Kids clammed up. Parents claimed the cigarette burns, not to mention all the other wounds, were self-administered. Suggested they did it to each other. After all, these were violent, fucked-up kids whose real parents had abandoned them. And with the kids not talking, the DA thought a year was the maximum he could get. Only thing the wife would admit to was the chicken. The DA said his hands were tied."

Czarcik was suddenly hit by a familiar feeling, as if his whole body had just recharged itself, shocked by an invisible defibrillator. The first time this happened, when he was a rookie, Czarcik thought he was having a massive heart attack. The second time, that same year, he chalked it up to an equally powerful panic attack.

Now he called it the Rush, and it was the physical manifestation of inspiration.

Years had passed before Czarcik understood this unique ability. He still wasn't sure how it worked. All he knew was that certain images, certain words or phrases, plucked out of the ether by his subconscious, would sporadically cause an acute and powerful physical reaction.

The Rush was never arbitrary, never erroneous. It might take him a while—days, even weeks at the longest—but eventually Czarcik would find the connection between the trigger and his case.

There was nothing paranormal or supernatural about the Rush, although it could certainly seem that way to others. It was simply that he was wired differently from most people, and this difference was extremely fortuitous in his current line of work.

The DA said his hands were tied.

The phrase put his brain into overdrive. Czarcik didn't know why this was so important, but he would chew on it as assiduously as he gnawed on that perfect cylinder of packed tobacco between his lips. Eventually, the answer would come.

Walsh studied the slack expression that had overtaken his colleague's face.

"It's too bad the kids didn't do it," Czarcik said sharply, just to get Walsh to stop staring at him like he was a specimen in a top secret laboratory.

"You think there's any way they could have?" Walsh asked.

"Oldest is thirteen. The next one ten, and the youngest, the one with the chicken, is just seven. Damn near impossible."

Walsh laughed condescendingly. "You've been off the beat awhile. You can't imagine what thirteen-year-olds are capable of nowadays." He shook his head and picked at a hangnail, letting Czarcik process his transparent attempt to bolster his street cred. "I was on a case last year in Englewood. You want me to tell you what a gang of twelve- and thirteen-year-olds can do to an eight-year-old girl?"

Czarcik didn't. He could imagine. He had seen things in the city's darkest corners that would have made Walsh's blood run cold. He just had no desire to play a game of one-upmanship.

"We have to interview them, you know. The kids. Protocol."

"Whatever you need to do," Czarcik replied.

"You want to sit in?" Walsh asked. "Watch from behind the glass?"

Czarcik stood up without answering. He waved the file at Walsh. "This my copy?"

"It's all yours."

The detective, thinking about the DA whose hands were tied, walked away from his desk and headed to the exit.

FIVE

Daniel guided his beloved Lexus GS 350 down a country road, just teasing the speed limit. There were few things he enjoyed more than a long drive with the windows open, and even fewer things that a good warm breeze couldn't fix. The wind carried the scent of fresh pine into the car. Even now, at the height of flowering season, the evergreen reigned supreme.

A black leather carrying case that held hundreds of CDs, all meticulously labeled, rode shotgun. Although the car had come with satellite radio, after the three-month trial period had expired, Daniel never bothered to subscribe to the service. At first, he loved the idea of an all-Springsteen station, until it became obvious that the playlist was mainly from *Born in the U.S.A.* as well as some singles from Southside Johnny and the Asbury Jukes. It hadn't been easy for him to make the move to CDs from vinyl (he had chosen to ignore the cassette revolution altogether), and now there was hardly enough time left to migrate to digital. Because of his technical background, he was one of the few people who could actually understand why music in the form of zeros and ones was sonically superior to any other format, and yet he still preferred analog. But because he couldn't cart his beloved Marantz turntable around with him in the car, compact discs were a poor but necessary alternative.

His tastes were eclectic, at least within the narrowly defined genre of rock. He had every studio release from Led Zeppelin, the Who,

Tom Waits, Leonard Cohen, Simon & Garfunkel, Black Sabbath, the Doors, the Velvet Underground, Meat Loaf, and Billy Joel. And *almost* every release from the Beatles, the Stones, the Eagles, Supertramp, Dire Straits, Jimmy Buffett, and Crosby, Stills & Nash. There was also a smattering of albums from a hundred or so other bands, like Seatrain, Free, King Crimson, and Vanilla Fudge. The only classic-rock outfit not represented was the Steve Miller Band. For reasons not fully understood even by him, Daniel had always hated the group. There was a possible explanation from his childhood. Growing up, there was an older teenager on the block who, for the better part of a year, walked around going, "Some people call me Maurice," and then making that grating wolf whistle. But this couldn't be the sole reason. After all, he had an equally annoying connection to Paul Simon's "You Can Call Me Al," and he still loved *Graceland*.

Curiously, there were no jazz CDs in the case. Curious because when people met Daniel, especially in social situations where it was customary to discuss politics, sports, and the arts, they always assumed he was a jazz connoisseur. Daniel took it as a compliment, since everybody knew that jazz was the domain of the sophisticate. The freethinker. The life lover. All interesting people loved jazz. But Daniel hated it as much as he did the Steve Miller Band.

Right now, however, he cherished the silence. The sound of the breeze, amplified by the car's aerodynamics, was all the road music he needed.

Right off Route 12, at a tobacco outlet that straddled the Illinois-Wisconsin border, Daniel tossed a McDonald's bag into the plastic garbage receptacle out front.

Inside were the three pieces of Luis Fernandez's broken mandible.

He continued on Route 12 into Lake Geneva, Wisconsin. Like most resort towns, Lake Geneva was a hive of activity from early June to mid-August. During the summer months, its streets overflowed with a mixture of shoppers, young families pushing strollers, and lovestruck teenagers sharing ice cream. The downtown was charming, and the picturesque lake, which was its namesake, was ringed by stately mansions built by Chicago's and Milwaukee's old-money families.

One of the town's claims to fame was Big Foot Beach, advertised as the "World's Narrowest Public Beach," a ribbon of sand—less than a foot in some places—that separated the highway from the water. Black lakeweed hitched a ride on the inland tide and tickled the shoreline as a lone gull searched in vain for a stray mussel before retreating to the safety of the sky with a futile wail. Soon the beach would be overrun with families looking to escape the summer heat, but now, just like the rest of the town, it was practically deserted.

Daniel parked in front of one of the many antique stores right off the main drag. He walked down to the waterfront and continued onto the pier, past the handful of docked tour boats that would soon be circling the lake hourly. He sat down on a bench overlooking the water and watched as the gulls identified a particularly generous family who, despite posted signs against it, were treating the birds to a meal of Wonder Bread.

The setting sun painted the lake a deep purple. From behind, he could hear the sounds of children, which always made him smile. Two particularly aggressive moppets begged their parents for a slice of fudge from one of the small snack bars along the pier. *Just let them have it,* Daniel thought. He understood that sometimes a parent had to be firm. You didn't want your kids to grow up to be entitled little brats. But this was the kind of place where spoiling them seemed appropriate. Their childhood memories of sleepy early-summer days would last a lifetime.

As the wine-dark lake settled into dusk, Daniel had a sudden urge for a cigar. He wasn't a big smoker but used to enjoy the occasional stogie. How relaxing it would be to puff away as the horizon swallowed the sun. But now smoking only exacerbated his headaches. Plus, there was a woman holding her newborn in a BabyBjörn who was close enough to smell it if the wind was right. So instead, he closed his eyes and let the sun's ambient warmth wash over him.

As he went about disposing of the remaining pieces of Luis Fernandez's head, he realized he still had plenty of time to choose his next victim. He had a list in the car. The folders (dossiers as he liked to call them) that had created the list remained back in Chicago. He had no need for the folders themselves; he had memorized their contents. Each was filled with documents pertaining to worthy candidates. It was really a question of geography. Where did he want to go next?

Minnesota was a possibility. Although he had lived in the Midwest for most of his life, he hadn't spent much time in the Land of 10,000 Lakes. However, Minnesota was home to the Devil's Kettle, with which he had been fascinated since reading about it in a *National Geographic* supplement years ago. The infernally named geographic feature was a waterfall near the mouth of the Brule River that split into two distinct flows. The eastern arm cascaded down a two-step fifty-foot drop and continued downstream. But the western branch spilled ten feet into a pothole hollowed into the rhyolite cliffs and then . . . disappeared forever. Despite countless attempts, nobody had ever located the outflow point. Researchers had dyed the river, dropped hundreds of ping pong balls, and utilized the best aquatic tracking techniques—all to no avail.

Although it flew in the face of common sense, Daniel imagined the Devil's Kettle was a portal to the center of the earth. Or somewhere even farther. A secret river to the land of the dead. He could be a modern-day Charon, sacrificing himself in the name of science. Unfortunately, there was no way to prevent himself from slamming into the jagged rocks that lined the hole. No way to guess how far down those stone teeth descended into the great maw. Even if he managed to survive the initial plunge, and the falls quickly met up with an underground river, he would most likely drown before reaching the surface.

Of course, he could also throw someone else into the void. Then listen to how long the screams echoed.

Detective Czarcik returned home after a long workout. Aside from the obvious physiological benefits, heavy lifting cleared his head. When he first read about antioxidants, how they purged free radicals from the body, he found the perfect analogy in weightlifting. The intense physical exertion forced all the nonsense from his mind, leaving him in a state of almost euphoric clarity.

Today's workout wasn't great. He had focused on his chest, shoulders, and triceps, a typical routine designed to maximize complementary muscle groups. During a set of military presses, he felt a tweak in his rotator cuff. But he persevered and subconsciously put too much stress on the surrounding tendons, resulting in a dull ache that remained long after he left the gym.

Czarcik never worked out with a trainer. Not only was it completely unnecessary, but he had no interest in the casual companionship one provided. Although he would never admit it, even to himself, he was also secretly terrified that someone would tell him that a man his age shouldn't be lifting such an obscene amount of weight. But in his mind, this was the price he paid to maintain his physique, considering his lifestyle and bad habits.

His alarm wailed for nearly half a minute before Czarcik punched in the code. He dropped his gym bag on the floor by the front door and headed to the bathroom to take a shower. He rarely showered at the gym; the combination of rampant fungus and uncircumcised Russian men was simply too much to bear.

Czarcik's West Loop condo overlooked the Kennedy Expressway. A strange place to live, especially for a cop. Most of the units were owned by either young professionals who wanted to ride the real estate boom as the area developed or empty nesters looking for a cost-effective way back into the city now that their suburban homes, absent of children, felt like mausoleums.

Neighbors were irrelevant to Czarcik since he rarely spoke to them. He simply enjoyed watching the traffic from his bedroom window, captivated as the arteries of the city swelled and contracted at regular interludes.

After drying off and throwing on a clean white T-shirt, Czarcik headed into his office. Most people would have used it for the master bedroom, as it was the larger of the condo's two bedrooms. But Czarcik only needed a bed and a nightstand for sleep, so there was no reason to squander space that could be put to better use.

While his space at the station was stark and minimal, his home office looked as if it could have been built by an ambitious set designer making a movie about a rogue detective.

Crime scene photos, ranging from the unassuming (forest clearings and coastlines) to the ultragraphic (on a rusty stove, a pot of boiling water held a woman's breast), covered almost every inch of wall space. Occasionally these were interrupted by maps dotted with push pins connected by strings.

Case files were strewn not just across the heavy wooden L-shaped desk but all over the floor. Some of the scattered papers were decorated in yellow highlighter, others sported random words and circles in permanent marker. Most had illegible notes in the margins.

There were all the accoutrements of any modern office (a color printer, scanner, cable modem) and one anachronistic touch: a huge brass ashtray, its bottom permanently scarred and stained a sickly gray from decades of use. Perched on the rim was a bald eagle. Regal. Poised to kill or defend.

One item that seemed completely out of place was a small fishbowl that sat at the far end of the desk's L, as if Czarcik had purposely placed it as far away from himself as possible. The glass was filthy and the bowl filled halfway up with a thick, black sludge.

The aquarium had been a gift, given to Czarcik during one of the last cases to which he was officially assigned. It was bequeathed to him by ten-year-old Hailey McDonald, whose sister Vanessa had been the final victim of a serial killer colloquially known as Bad Ronald for his still-not-understood penchant for targeting unrelated victims with the surname McDonald.

Czarcik had uncovered the evidence that eventually led to Bad Ronald's capture. Unfortunately, the killer wasn't found until after he'd had plenty of time alone with Vanessa and a straight razor.

Knowledge of her death, however gruesome, gave the family some much-needed closure five months after her disappearance. To thank Czarcik for his help, Hailey had given him Vanessa's goldfish, which she had kept alive and assiduously fed every day with the hope that her sister would eventually be found safe. At first, Czarcik refused. What the fuck did he want with a fish? But when he saw the faces of his colleagues, aghast at his callous refusal of a young girl's symbolic gift, he acquiesced.

He had planned to flush the thing right down the toilet the second he got home. But distracted, he instead left the tank on the corner of his desk and forgot about it. By the third day or so, the fish was dead. After a few weeks, most of the water had evaporated, leaving the tank in its current state. At this point, Czarcik was simply too lazy to care. He had figured that eventually the putrefying mass would harden, and he could just toss it into the alley behind his building. He never did that either. So now the tank just sat there—the world's nastiest paperweight.

Czarcik put his feet up on the desk and began to flip through the Fernandez file. Even after his workout, he found it hard to concentrate. He knew what he needed. In less than ten minutes, he had picked a petite girl with a black bob from the Ecstasy Escorts website and requested that she meet him at the Lonely Hearts Motel on Archer Avenue.

Czarcik refused to bring a professional girl back to his condominium. As reckless as he was, this one rule was sacred. This was his home sanctuary; it couldn't be compromised.

The Lonely Hearts Motel was the perfect solution. The secrets it held were legion, equal only to the misery it perpetuated.

SIX

The girl with the bob, who introduced herself as Nikki, arrived exactly at the scheduled time. Czarcik said his name was Joe and ushered her into the motel room. He used the same pseudonym all the time, and although it was his father's name, he attached no significance to this. *Joe* was just easy to remember.

Because Nikki was technically an escort, not a prostitute, and Ecstasy Escorts was technically an escort service, not a high-tech pimp, Czarcik was technically paying only for her company. The irony, of course, was that this really was *exactly* what he was paying for. But whatever else went on behind closed doors, between consenting adults, well, that was outside the purview of the original transaction.

Czarcik left an unsealed plain white envelope containing five crisp hundred-dollar bills on the table near the door as Nikki went into the bathroom to prepare.

She returned to the room wearing a black leather miniskirt and black lace bra. She gave a cursory glance at the envelope, just to make sure the corners of the C-notes were visible, as was customary. Czarcik was already sitting on the bed, smoking a cigarette.

"I hope this isn't awkward for you," she began, "but usually we're told ahead of time what the client likes. What he expects. But for some reason, the agency didn't tell me."

"I guess that's because they didn't know *how* to explain it."

Her eyes widened at the thought of a previously unimagined degree of perversity.

"Don't look so worried," he assured her. "I'm sure you'll be OK with it. If a little bored." He patted the bed's infrequently changed sheets. "Come sit down." Still hesitant, she nevertheless obliged. "I would really just like to talk with you."

"Dirty talk?"

"Not the kind you mean."

"OK . . ." She still looked unnerved. "Then what?"

"Just about you. Your background. Your aspirations—"

"My what?"

"Your goals. Things you like, things you don't like . . ." Czarcik remembered Candy, the last escort he had hired. She had had a conniption when he got too personal. "Unless you're not comfortable with that," he added. "Because then we can just talk about whatever."

Czarcik needn't have worried. Nikki burst out laughing. He watched her, amused.

"Honey, for five hundred dollars, you can have it all."

So she told him. Told him her whole life story up to this point. Which, when all was said and done, wasn't particularly riveting.

Her real name was Priscilla. She had grown up in a trailer park in Macomb, Illinois, a little over four hours west of Chicago. She'd never met her father; he left her mother the second he realized he had knocked her up. Good guy.

As a single mom and waitress, Nikki's mother didn't have much time for her. So Nikki found ways to keep herself busy with illegal substances, legal substances she was too young to legally use, and boys. Most of all boys.

After high school, which she somehow managed to graduate, she moved to Chicago and began stripping at Larry's Leisure Lounge, a gentleman's club in the South Loop. While stripping, she found herself having a lot of casual sex for free. Well, not exactly free. She had to put up with the assholes who thought it was their God-given right to harass a stripper as well as those on the opposite end of the spectrum who professed their undying love after a single hand job.

When she found out there was a way to make a couple of grand a night without having to deal with either type, she signed right on the dotted line.

"Now can I ask *you* a question?" He nodded. "You crazy rich or something?"

"No."

"Then why waste all this money? I mean, you're not a bad-looking guy. Kind of old, but some girls like that." Czarcik laughed. "You could go out with a lot of girls for free. And a lot of them would even sleep with you. That is, if you're not impotent or anything."

"Hand me a smoke, please." She tossed him the pack of cigarettes from her side of the bed. "I don't know. Somehow . . . paying for it . . . it just makes it feel more genuine."

Nikki seemed to think about it. She bummed a smoke for herself and looked at him. "You know, you're full of shit. But that'll be our little secret."

Czarcik smiled. He was beginning to like her. "What about you, how much longer you gonna do this for?"

She shrugged. "I'd think about getting out now if I wasn't making so much damn money. I mean, I make more in one month than my mom made in her best year. It's just hard to give that up."

"And you really don't mind everything you have to do?"

"I know you don't want to talk about sex, but if I'm being honest, sometimes I even like it." He nodded. He could understand. "I mean, you do get your freaks. The kind who want to watch you pee. Who want to tie you up and—"

It hit him hard and clean.

The Rush.

If his brain had been an animation in a pharmaceutical commercial, it would have been represented by hundreds of disparate pieces coming together to form a single image.

What surprised him most this time was how simple the connection had been.

The DA said his hands were tied.

It wasn't a metaphor, not an expression or idiom. There was nothing to interpret. No vague images to place within a subjective rubric.

It was literal.

Hands were tied.

Mrs. Fernandez's *hands were tied*. A chicken *was tied* around her neck.

Tied. With rope.

The picture in his mind was as clear as day. Mrs. Fernandez's hands were tied one way; the chicken was tied another. The knots were different. *Why? And why did it matter?* And why did it bother Czarcik so much?

The answer came quickly. The killer had bound her hands and feet—most likely first—and then, for some reason known only to him, had chosen a different way to secure the chicken. Was the act symbolic? Deliberately misleading? Only one woman could help him answer these questions, and she was far from the Lonely Hearts Motel.

Nikki could tell something was wrong. "Is everything OK?"

Like a man possessed, her client hopped off the bed. Began to pace, almost manic.

Nikki's job had long ceased to be surprising. The endless parade of men, even the ones who thought they were the kinkiest SOBs around, were all so routine. But this was something new. Nikki had a few clients who had freaked out on her. Husbands overcome with guilt. Religious nuts overcome with shame. This was different. It was as if he had been struck by . . . what was the word? She remembered it from catechism. Divine something or other.

And then, before she knew it, the madman was gone. For a split second, she was hit with a paralyzing fear that he had absconded with her money. But there it was. Sitting undisturbed on the table. The corners of the bills plainly visible.

Nikki thought hard. She couldn't remember the last time she had earned so much for so little.

SEVEN

To law enforcement agents across the country, the Integrated Database Aggregator was better known by its acronym, IDA. The consensus was unanimous—she was one smart bitch.

Technically, IDA was a massive, cloud-housed database programmed with a top secret algorithm. Police departments were supposed to input every bit of information about a case, no matter how small, and it was then stored securely in a well-guarded server farm. Authorized users could access IDA to identify patterns that would have been impossible to find for even the most diligent and collaborative of departments.

If a rapist in Spokane who forced his victims to first clean themselves with a particular brand of bath soap suddenly moved to Fort Lauderdale and continued his fetishized crimes, IDA made the connection.

When the budding serial killer who dubbed himself Bon Vie scrawled the same Latin phrase on the kitchen wall of two of his victims, in their own blood, over three thousand miles apart, it was IDA who knew almost as soon as the words had dried.

At the academy, new recruits were taught that in investigative work, no detail was too small to overlook. In reality, as the rooks soon learned, even the most important details were often missed or ignored. But not by IDA. She never tired, never erred, and never allowed anything to cloud her judgment.

She was cold and analytical. For Czarcik, it was love at first sight.

Eldon Parseghian—he preferred not to use a title, considering it somewhat déclassé when he rubbed shoulders with the movers and shakers—called Czarcik from his car. "Where are you?"

"I'm heading to the office. I want to run something through IDA."

"This about the murders on Magnolia?"

"Yes."

"A break?"

"Don't know yet."

Parseghian knew better than to push. "I've been thinking about the case all day. Mind making a quick pit stop first?" he asked Czarcik. "Where?"

"I'd like you to pay a visit to Salvatore Cicci."

"Ah, shit."

Salvatore Guido Cicci had an office on the 104th floor of the Willis Tower. Willis Group Holdings, an insurance firm, had negotiated for both the naming rights to the building and for the privilege of having it referred to, by every single person in the country, by its original name, Sears Tower.

Except for Sal Cicci, who believed in fresh starts.

Cicci was the only son of one of Chicago's last remaining Mafia families. Like every mobster, Cicci swore that one day he was going to go straight. The only difference was he meant it. He was already out of narcotics and human trafficking. When asked why he got out of these two extremely profitable revenue streams, he would smile and say—to those he thought would get the joke—"I believe this drug business is going to destroy us in the years to come." The truth was, Cicci had three young daughters whom he loved more than anything. When their friends asked them what their daddy did for a living, he didn't want them to have to answer the same way he had, back in grade school.

His desire for legitimacy did not mean he was going soft. When those he cared about were wronged, he could be ruthless. Two summers before, the daughter of his trusted secretary had been raped as a graduate student at the University of Chicago. The police had dragged their feet finding the perpetrator. Cicci found him first, a gang-affiliated kid who had a shit job at a waste-treatment plant. In a tragic accident, the kid had somehow fallen into one of the facility's massive steel vats. When the medical examiner saw the body, he said it looked as if the victim had been boiled alive.

Parseghian knew that Cicci's family once owned a chain of laundromats. Cash business. Perfect to clean dirty money. Literally laundering.

The Fernandezes owned a laundromat. Maybe one still controlled by Cicci. Parseghian remembered the gangbanger. Maybe Cicci got wind of what the Fernandezes were doing to their own brood and got mad?

But mad enough to do this? The theory was weak, he admitted to Czarcik, but it couldn't hurt to check.

As Czarcik rocketed past the 67th floor of the Willis Tower, his ears popped. By the time he stepped off the elevator onto the 104th floor, he felt like he had just left a Rush concert.

He was met by two large men, identically dressed in dark suits over black T-shirts, who ushered him through the frosted glass doors of Cicci Industries. If Cicci was attempting to change the perception of himself and his enterprise, he was off to a poor start.

Sal Cicci was sitting behind his desk, an imposing slab of marble covered with the tools of any ordinary executive. A few personal touches. Framed photos of his wife and daughters. A small branch—an olive branch—enclosed in Lucite, which probably had some significance to his Sicilian heritage.

He stood to greet Czarcik. "Detective, a pleasure to see you." He motioned to a leather chair across the desk from him. "As I explained to Eldon, I don't know anything about your situation. Didn't even catch it on the news. But of course I'm happy to help if I can." He dismissed his two employees with a casual flick of the wrist.

In the comfort of his office, Cicci was a lot better looking than in the newspaper photos Czarcik had seen, usually taken in front of a courthouse—candid shots snapped at the worst possible time. He smiled naturally and had an easy manner. Czarcik wasn't unfamiliar with mobsters. It was apparent why Cicci should be the face of the family.

Czarcik took a seat and filled Cicci in on the murders, making sure to linger on all the grisly details. The mobster shook his head, looking visibly disgusted at the appropriate times. He listened intently, and when Czarcik was finished, he opened his hands and asked, "Why should I know of this terrible crime?"

Subtlety wasn't Czarcik's strong suit. "It's not exactly a secret that the Cicci family had an interest in laundromats."

Cicci smiled and motioned for Czarcik to come closer. The detective leaned in as Cicci took a spreadsheet from a manila folder and laid it on the desktop. "You see this? These are the options on REIT loans all across the city, coming due in less than six months. You know what that means?" Czarcik shook his head. "Well, neither do I. But I have some very smart people on my payroll telling me that these little pieces of paper are going to be worth millions. So tell me, why would I be messing around with a bunch of losers at some shitty laundromat?"

Czarcik leaned back in his chair. Despite himself, he liked Cicci. With all his artifice, there was also something genuine about him. The detective drummed his fingers on the armrest. "Old habits die hard, I guess?"

Cicci leaned back in his own chair and lightly touched his index finger to the outside of his nostril. He did it so quickly the gesture appeared unintentional. "They do, don't they, Detective?"

Czarcik *still* liked him. He got to his feet and buttoned his sport jacket. "Thank you for your time, Mr. Cicci. Good luck with"—he glanced around the room—"with whatever it is you do here."

When he was nearly to the door, Cicci called out to him. "Detective . . . I'll keep my ears open."

Czarcik nodded and walked out of the office.

It was late when Czarcik arrived back at BJE headquarters. He was already annoyed at Parseghian's detour, so he headed straight to his desk, entered his password, and logged into IDA.

As a detective with the BJE, Czarcik was given a lot of leeway, but accessing IDA was one of the few activities he couldn't do from his home office. A special mainframe supposedly created by some of the best minds in the enterprise-security industry ensured that a person could only access the database from within the physical confines of the building.

A welcome screen nearly entirely black, a remnant of DOS, came up. Those brilliant coders weren't much for design. Czarcik entered his password.

ACCESS DENIED.

He frowned. Shook his head. He entered his password again. Slower, more deliberately this time.

Same result, as if the two words in all caps were mocking him. "Jesus fucking Christ," he muttered to himself.

Czarcik got up from his chair and walked across the office, heading over to the desk of Corrine Fumagalli, the BJE's computer expert and, luckily, one of the few people at HQ he could tolerate. This was curious, since literally *everything* about Corrine should have annoyed him.

She was at her desk typing away, hardly surprising, as she usually worked odd hours. You were as likely to see her wandering around the office kitchen at three in the morning, brewing some kind of exotic tea, as you were to find her walking into the building at nine.

Her hair was pulled back in messy pigtails, and she would occasionally play with one of those fidget spinners marketed to hyperactive children. "Are you going to one of those parties where people dress up as characters from video games?"

Corrine stopped typing and spun around in her chair. "I'd accuse you of insulting me—and lodge a complaint with HR—but you might be stupid enough that that was an actual question."

He smiled. No one else at the BJE would dare speak to him like this. "Human Resources? If they spent fifteen minutes just standing by your desk, they'd have you in sensitivity training for weeks."

She considered it, bobbing her head back and forth. "Eh, you're probably right. So . . . what the fuck do you want?"

"I can't get into IDA."

"No means no, Paul. Didn't anyone ever teach you that?"

He shook his head. "Corrine, one day you're going to make some young man very unhappy."

"Already have." And then with a twinkle in her eye, she added, "And plenty of young women too."

"So, what's with my password?"

Corrine turned back around. "We changed them all last week. Security protocol. Didn't you get the memo?"

"Maybe. But if I did, it went right with all the other memos."

From her pursed lips, he could tell Corrine knew all too well where that was. She sighed, busy typing once again, and said, "Your new password is your last name and then the last four numbers of your social in reverse order."

He gave her a grunt of thanks and began to walk off.

"Paul!"

He stopped and looked back. Her eyes were red. Any hint of playfulness was now gone. "I heard about your case. About the kids."

He nodded.

She looked down and shook her head. "I can't handle kids, and I can't handle animals. If you're asking me, those motherfuckers got what was coming to them."

"I wasn't asking you."

"I know." And then Corrine went back to work.

After only one more failed attempt, Czarcik managed to log in to IDA.

Chicago PD was surprisingly on the ball. The Fernandez case was already in the system. Every piece of evidence, every observation, every relevant thread of inquiry had been fed into the computer.

Czarcik scrolled through the data until he came to the crime scene photo of the chicken tied around Mrs. Fernandez's neck. He zoomed in on the photo and then used an editing tool to isolate the knot. After that, he checked off the requisite boxes and chose the appropriate pull-down menus to make his search as broad as possible. Enter. IDA whirred to life. Her state-of-the-art processor sent billions of electronic pulses flying across an interconnected network of routers, servers, and switches, which could also find you a good deal on khakis or locate the hottest Ethiopian restaurant in East LA. Only now, their purpose was cyberjustice.

The first few hits were for nautical websites displaying various types of boating knots. The knot in question was a constrictor hitch, hardly uncommon, but not something that a layman would quickly tie off. Such work took a bit of time, even for an experienced seaman.

Czarcik didn't believe that the killer's vocation was of importance, so he wasted little time exploring the maritime connection. Instead, he had IDA pull crimes within the last month in which the victim was restrained with a similar knot. If Czarcik wanted to, he could extend the time line even further back, but he had a strong suspicion that if the killer had in fact claimed other victims, it was recently. Nothing about this felt like a garden-variety psycho, the kind of monster who might claim a single victim and then lie in wait for years, maybe even decades, before again sating his bloodlust. No, this was purposeful and deliberate.

IDA returned three hits.

The first was completely irrelevant. A gangland murder in El Paso, just over the border from Ciudad Juárez, statistically the most violent city in Mexico. Aside from the fact that the victim was Latino, like the Fernandezes, there was no obvious connection.

The second was equally useless. In the college town of Gainesville, Florida, where the serial killer Danny Rolling once terrorized coeds as the Gainesville Ripper, a former football star had broken into the home of a girl he met at a party, tied her up using a constrictor hitch, and proceeded to rob her blind. He was arrested, found guilty of aggravated robbery, and sentenced to ten years in prison, where he remained.

The third and final hit also seemed like a long shot. A high-profile Texas judge had been found tied to a chair in his home, flayed alive. This judge had plenty of enemies—as the supporting documentation detailed—but how did this case relate to a murder on the North Side of Chicago?

Czarcik scanned the articles about the murder. The judge had ruled on multiple abuse cases. Interestingly, he had also been a perpetrator in one. This didn't surprise Czarcik. It was Texas, after all. Corporal punishment was still legal in schools. If someone didn't have any compunction about a stranger beating their child, chances were they didn't believe in sparing the rod themselves. Still, he had a family judge who ruled in abuse cases; a family who had lost their foster kids as a result of abuse. There was a connection, however tenuous. At least it warranted a phone call.

He picked up the landline on his desk and dialed the main number for the Gillette County Sheriff's Department, which had jurisdiction over the case. According to the notes supplied, the officer in charge was Detective Lance Ringland.

The desk jockey on duty, a sweet woman with a lovely Texas twang, told Czarcik that Detective Ringland wouldn't be in until the following morning. "But he's an early riser," she offered helpfully. "He usually arrives before seven."

Czarcik glanced at the display on the bottom of his computer. It was just after nine. "Have him paged, please."

In the pregnant pause that followed, Czarcik could tell the dispatcher's first instinct would be to politely repeat her answer. But his direct tone made her reconsider. "I can try, sir. But you may have to wait till morning."

"Do what you can."

Another pause. If the dispatcher, a well-mannered Texan, was waiting for an acknowledgment of thanks, she would be waiting all night. She finally broke the stalemate. "All right. Please give me your number. If Detective Ringland fixes to call you tonight, he will. If not, you'll just have to wait till tomorrow." She spoke the last sentence with an edge.

Czarcik gave the woman his number and returned to his computer screen. Aside from the knot, and a probably unrelated child-abuse link between the victims, the only other similarity between the Dallas and Chicago cases was a conspicuous lack of evidence, other than what the killers wanted investigators to find.

Barely a minute later, Czarcik's desk phone rang.

"Czarcik."

Although thick with sleep, the voice on the other end was friendly and lucid, the voice of a man accustomed to being woken up in the dead of night. "Normally, I'd have my girl take a message, but you must have some urgent situation up there in Chicago."

"Detective, aren't you on Central time?" Czarcik asked.

"That's right."

"Well, it's barely past nine."

"Are you aware of Ben Franklin's famous saying?"

Czarcik was aware, and found it completely ludicrous. His best work was done postmidnight. Either way, he had no desire to play *Founding Fathers Jeopardy*.

"Detective Ringland, my name is Paul Czarcik. I'm with the Illinois Bureau of Judicial Enforcement."

"That's what my girl tells me. That's *all* she tells me. Other than she's got a rude caller on the phone who has no respect for my beauty sleep."

Czarcik smiled to himself. He pictured Ringland, plain as day, sitting across from a suspect in an interrogation room. With some disarming wit and a little homespun charm, he could make a jaywalker admit to murder.

"Well, now that I've disturbed you, I was hoping you could help me."

"Tell me what you need," Detective Ringland said. Now all business.

Czarcik could hear whispers and quiet assurances on the other end of the line. He assumed that Ringland was telling his wife to go back to sleep. That everything was fine. Then some shuffling. The sounds of him getting into his bedside slippers and sneaking off into the hallway to take the call.

"Had a pretty brutal case out here the other day. Man and his wife. Tortured to death. Man's head was cut off and has yet to be recovered."

"Goddamn. That is brutal," Ringland replied without the usual cynicism of a veteran detective.

"Crime scene was clean, and we don't have many leads to go on. But IDA flagged a specific knot, a knot used in the murder. A similar one was used in one of your cases."

"Judge Robertson's case."

"How did you know?"

"This isn't Syria. Gillette County encompasses a few rural towns and some unincorporated spillover from the Dallas sprawl. How many murders do you think we see out here?"

"Then if you wouldn't mind, Detective—"

"Lance."

"If you wouldn't mind, Lance, what can you tell me about the judge's case? I don't mean this to sound insulting, but your boys didn't put too much of the report into IDA."

In reality, Czarcik didn't care how it sounded, but he needed Ringland to be amenable.

"Well, like I said, we seldom deal with cases like this. Not like your backyard . . . least from what I see on the news. Plus, out here, we're not always so fond of putting our information into a federal database."

Czarcik let out an exasperated sigh. He had no love for governments—federal, state, or local. They were run by people. Mostly incompetent people. But what he hated even more were provincial yokels who assumed that the fed's main purpose, its raison d'être, was to invade the privacy of ordinary Americans. If the paranoid set really knew the extent of the government's surveillance activities, they would be far more terrified by its gross incompetence at every level.

"Then what can you tell me, Lance?"

"Well, our crime scene sounds like yours. Victim was tortured to death. Perp left no traces. No traces at all. And we even brought the boys from Dallas in to go over it."

"And no suspects?"

Detective Ringland laughed. "Plenty of suspects."

Czarcik sat up straight in his chair. He opened the top drawer of his desk and took out a tin of Skoal, squeezed off a thick pinch, and placed it between his bottom lip and gum. "How's that?"

"Judge Robertson was a family court judge. Every child he took away from two parents and placed in a foster home . . . that's two suspects for you right there. He also sent a lot of teenagers *back* to their homes. Runaways that had been picked up for petty crimes. Lot of them didn't want to go back. Lot of them had good reasons not to want to. All of them, suspects."

"So how are you handling it, then?" Czarcik asked, sucking hard on the dip. His empty stomach turned over. He should have stopped off for a bite to eat.

"The old-fashioned way. Working backwards. Talking to neighbors, people of interest. Following up on leads. Basically, things that don't rely on a lot of fancy computers." It was nothing more than a friendly little dig, but Czarcik wondered whether Ringland knew just how ignorant he sounded. "We're going over his cases. Identifying folks with recent judgments against them. See if any of them were particularly angry about it."

Although Czarcik was convinced this was an exercise in futility, he figured he'd let Ringland spin his wheels a bit longer. "Would you mind if I joined you?" Czarcik asked. "Sounds like you could use another hand."

"It ain't a myth that we're known for our hospitality down here," Detective Ringland replied eagerly. "In fact, if you foot the bill for your trip, I might be able to wrangle you up a free place to stay. Lot of our motels don't fill up anymore, and folks are usually willing to do the local PD a favor."

"I'd be very grateful, Lance. I'll take a flight out tomorrow morning." Detective Ringland laughed again.

"Mr. . . . Czarcik, is it?" He pronounced the name "ZAR-ick."

"'Tsar-sick.' That's right."

"This hunch of yours. The reason you're coming down here. It's all because of a knot?"

"That's right. A knot used to tie a dead chicken around the neck of my victim was identical to the knots used to restrain Judge Robertson."

Detective Ringland thought for a moment. "Must be a pretty unique knot."

"No, not really."

Silence.

"Anyway, let us know when you arrive," Detective Ringland finally replied. "Very least, give you a chance to taste some *real* barbeque."

EIGHT

Even at 4:13 a.m. there were signs of life at the Walter Mondale Rest Area.

A central location just outside Rochester, Minnesota, made it one of the country's busiest truck stops. The big rigs from the East Coast could reach the destination in one day's time, provided the traffic played along and the driver ignored the federal hours-of-service regulations. From the Pacific it was tougher. But with enough coffee and speed, an ambitious driver could run the route in a single stretch, as long as safety was of no concern.

In the parking lot, eighteen-wheelers were lined up like fallen obelisks, their sleeping pharaohs tucked safely in their cabins. They were silent now, although at any moment they could shake off the night with a mechanical growl.

Daniel Langdon was among them. His Lexus was one of only a few cars in the lot that didn't require a commercial driver's license. He wasn't worried about standing out, even in a Lexus. Truck stops were strange places, and short of strolling around the grounds brandishing a decapitated head, a person was unlikely to attract much attention.

Besides, Daniel had already disposed of the last piece of Luis Fernandez's cranium in the restroom's garbage can.

He sat behind the wheel, shrouded in complete darkness. The engine was off, the dashboard black. He was used to stalking his quarries in broad daylight, but for some reason, he felt unnaturally exposed, even though he was far more inconspicuous than usual.

His keys were in the ignition. He could fire up the engine at a moment's notice.

In the row of trucks right in front of him, three eighteen-wheelers to his left, was a rig with Minnesota plates—LMF393, randomly generated by the Minnesota Department of Public Safety.

Daniel had his man.

Somewhere in the cab of LMF393, Edgar Barnes slept peacefully. But down in Kansas City, pretty much a straight shot down I-35, Carlee Ames could hardly sleep at all. In fact, since the accident, more than two or three hours of uninterrupted slumber was a godsend. As a quadriplegic, whose breathing was aided by a ventilator, she usually conked out in her state-of-the-art wheelchair. Her bed was more comfortable. But Carlee being Carlee, she always felt guilty asking her frail, aging mother to maneuver her onto the mattress. So she would just nod off while watching *The Bachelor*, dreaming about suitors who never came and waking fitfully from nightmares that never ended.

Daniel had read about Carlee Ames in *Reader's Digest*, of all places. He was at the dentist's, waiting to have a crown replaced, and it was the only periodical available. He was so engrossed in the story that the hygienist had to call his name three times before he looked up, eyes red with tears. "Mr. Langdon, are you all right?" she had asked him. He wiped his eyes and mumbled something about allergies before following her into the examination room.

He'd always known there would be a reason to remember the story. That reason was now. It was the kind of thing that should never happen but does happen far too often.

Edgar Barnes had been navigating his truck down a two-lane highway. He had just dropped off a load of discount furniture at the flea market on County Road 11. He had been awake for more than thirty-six hours, reeling from Dexedrine that he chased with a pint of Wild

Turkey to take the edge off. His blood alcohol level was 0.2. Almost three times the legal limit. Or so he was told.

Carlee was coming from the opposite direction, driving her beloved Pontiac Firebird that she had bought used with the money she made that summer working at Falcon's Frozen Custard. She was twenty years old. Her blood alcohol level was 0.0.

Then the laws of physics intervened. Specifically the one that states that no two objects can occupy the same space simultaneously.

It was Barnes's third DUI in as many years. He spent thirty days in jail and had to pay Carlee just under $10,000, an amount that covered exactly six months of payments on her ventilator. Following his release, he was arrested two more times for driving while intoxicated. Because nobody else was injured as a result, he received no prison time.

According to the article, Edgar Barnes had never once visited Carlee. He had never inquired about her condition. Never apologized. At the sentencing, he only responded with a meager affirmation that he understood the charges. When the judge asked whether he wanted to make a statement, he declined.

Mr. Edgar Barnes had gone on with his life, unrepentant, while his collateral damage took her meals through a straw.

And now he would pay.

In the glove compartment of Daniel's Lexus was a syringe filled with 50 mg of succinylcholine. Fast acting and effective. Edgar would be completely incapacitated as Daniel went to work. From his research, Daniel figured he would need about fifteen minutes to cut through the neck, locate the spinal cord, and sever it cleanly. He would then place an anonymous call to the rest stop security office and report that a trucker was ill and had passed out in the front seat of his rig. Otherwise, there was the slim chance that if Barnes wasn't discovered for a few days, he might die of dehydration or blood loss. And Daniel didn't want him to die. He wanted him to live. To live and to suffer. Paralyzed. For the rest of his natural life.

As Daniel was finalizing the plan to gain access to Edgar's cab, he heard a sharp knock on his window.

He jerked in his seat, wrenching his shoulder. He had been so focused on the truck parked diagonally from him that he wasn't paying attention to his immediate surroundings.

The face at his window wore too much makeup. Badly applied. But beneath it was the face of an angel. Just like Carlee Ames. This face was separated from his own by only a thin pane of glass.

Another knock. Gentler, but persistent. She wasn't going away.

Daniel wished his Lexus had manual windows so he could operate in the dark. He sighed and turned the ignition one click. The dashboard lit up. The radio crackled to life with the familiar chords of Black Sabbath's "Paranoid." He slammed his hand on the On-Off knob before any lyrics could be heard.

He regained his composure after a few seconds and located the window controls on the armrest. Daniel pressed the button, and the glass descended into the door with a soft whir.

"Can I help you?"

Without the distortion caused by the glass, Daniel could see how young she really was. He was terrible at judging age, but knew she shouldn't be alone at a truck stop this time of night.

"Are you lost, sweetheart?" he asked. He spoke as if addressing a young child and immediately realized how ridiculous he sounded.

The girl batted her lashes and ran her tongue across her front teeth. Vixen mode. "Lonely, mister?"

Daniel closed his eyes and breathed loudly from his nose, more depressed than annoyed. "No, thank you. I'm just resting here after a long trip."

"I can give you a good deal," she offered, hopeful.

Part of him wanted her gone. He didn't need this shit right now, but he felt guilty abandoning her. He motioned to the empty seat next to him. "Please, come in."

He leaned over and unlocked the passenger-side door. She disappeared into the darkness in front of the car before reappearing in the seat next to him. She offered him her hand, grinning. "Cheri."

Daniel shook it, surprised by how tiny it was. "Pleased to meet you, Cheri."

Inside the car, with their faces illuminated only by the dashboard's glowing light, she was in her element. She reached out and put her hand on his leg. "There's a motel about a mile from here. They rent rooms by the hour."

Daniel shifted away from her. "Sorry, but I . . . I need to stay here."

Cheri nodded. She understood. "OK, well, how about a blow job for fifty bucks?" It was a fair price, and when he didn't respond enthusiastically, she tried a different tack. "Please, mister. I need to eat."

"Oh . . ." Daniel reached into his pocket and took out his wallet. As he withdrew a twenty, the headlights of LMF393 came on. He handed the bill to Cheri, never taking his eyes off the rig.

Cheri took the twenty and suddenly began to cry. Daniel glanced over. His first instinct was to comfort her, but the truck was preparing to leave, and he needed to maintain his focus. "It's . . . it's not for food," she admitted.

The last thing Daniel wanted was to engage her, but then he thought of Carlee. How could he expend so much time and energy avenging one girl he knew virtually nothing about while turning away another so obviously in need of help? Carlee was an abstraction. Just a name in a story he had stumbled upon by sheer coincidence. Here, next to him, was a vulnerable child.

The truck's engine roared to life. Edgar Barnes was preparing to move out.

The one thing Daniel could not do was bring Cheri with him, even if he ultimately delivered her to the proper authorities. What was the technical term? Accessory to murder? Although he was fairly certain the charge would never stick, especially when his whole story had been told, he couldn't burden her with the inevitable fallout. She would need to mount a defense to prove she had met him for the first time in the parking lot. And what happened if an ambitious DA wanted to make headlines? Daniel didn't want to leave that in the hands of some public defender.

"I owe my pimp two hundred bucks," she said. "If I don't have it by tomorrow . . . he won't be happy."

Her ensuing silence allowed Daniel time to imagine the details.

If he had been a professional hitman, he probably could have pivoted on a dime. Left Barnes for later and knocked off the pimp. After all, some scumbag who trafficked young girls was just as deserving of justice as some piece-of-shit drunk driver. But Daniel didn't just pluck his victims out of a hat. He waited, patiently at first, until he read about a case that, for whatever reason, spoke to him. Or rattled him to the core.

Plus, his hits took time. A lot of time. Something that he didn't have much of.

In front of him, he could hear the gears of LMF393. The air brakes hissed. Barnes was pulling out. Thinking about his next delivery. His next meal. Women. Whatever long-haul truckers thought about to pass the time. But he wasn't thinking about Carlee Ames. Of this, Daniel was certain.

He tapped his fingers on the dashboard, thinking quickly. Again he took out his wallet and this time peeled off two fresh hundred-dollar bills. He handed them to Cheri. "Here, please."

Cheri just stared at the money. But instead of taking it, she dropped her face into her hands and wept. "I don't have a pimp!" she yelled between snot-filled sobs. Daniel knew it was over.

All his planning and preparation for naught. He could track down Barnes again, fairly easily in fact. But the other targets in his dossiers were at least as worthy. And he had a schedule to keep.

He watched the truck pull out of the parking lot and turn onto the highway's entrance ramp. Its taillights disappeared over a ridge, two fireflies in the night.

Edgar Barnes was a lucky man indeed. For as long as he lived, he would never know that at one time he was only fifteen minutes and one underage prostitute away from becoming nothing more than a head on a stick. Now Cheri had Daniel's undivided attention. He was about to rub her back, comfort her, and then remembered that victims of abuse don't like to be touched in normal ways. So he sat there awkwardly.

"Shh . . . shh" was all he could think to say as she cried. Finally, she quieted down. "Can I take you home?"

Cheri chewed on her fingernails. Shook her head. "I can't."

"No home?"

"I ran away two months ago." Daniel was silent, allowing her to continue. "My mother's boyfriend . . ."

Daniel smiled as if he understood. "A jerk?"

"He started visiting me . . . in my room, at night."

Daniel expected her to begin sobbing once again. But she was dry-eyed. Stoic.

"You told your mother?"

"I told her." Cheri suddenly looked older. Almost too old. Daniel shuddered.

"But she didn't believe you," Daniel offered, trying to help.

She smiled bitterly. "Oh, she believed me."

"But?"

"I think she was wondering what took him so long to start."

There was nothing he could say to that. There was really nothing anybody could say.

"So what was the money really for?" Daniel finally asked.

She looked at him like he was the crazy one. "What do you think? Food, a place to stay, toothpaste, tampons . . . maybe even a movie if I'm being honest. I really like *The Hunger Games* movies. I read all the books." Daniel fought back a smile. Despite her predicament, and her temporary vocation, she was so . . . *normal*. "But if I tell people I have a dangerous pimp, they take pity on me. The good ones do at least. The ones like you."

With LMF393 now just another license plate on the highway, Daniel was no longer in a rush. He looked deeply into her eyes, the best way he knew to impart seriousness. "Cheri, how much would it take for you to make a new start of it? Not for a night or two, but a clean break."

Cheri stared at the stranger, scarcely believing what she was hearing. She was too shocked to do the actual calculations in her head and was never much good at math anyway, so she blurted out the first number that seemed reasonable. "Five thousand dollars."

She expected him to burst out laughing. Instead, he turned off the engine, took the keys out of the ignition, and got out of the car. She watched him walk around the back of the vehicle, wondering what he was up to. He popped the trunk. It blocked her view.

After a few seconds of rummaging around, he got back into the Lexus and closed the door. "Please take care of yourself and be careful. I can tell you're a special young woman," he said, handing her a stack of bills held together by a wrapper. "It's ten grand."

For the third time that night, for the third time in this very car, Cheri began to sob.

"Who are you?" she asked once she finally regained control. "My guardian angel?"

Daniel blushed. The compliment warmed his heart, even if some people would disagree with her assessment. Would disagree vehemently.

In fact, some people might call him the Angel of Death.

NINE

The toilets at Chicago's O'Hare International Airport were outfitted with an automatic seat protector, giving every new visitor a fresh sheet of plastic on which to sit, making the stalls the most pleasurable and hygienic of any major US airport.

Czarcik sat on the toilet. His pants were pulled up and buttoned. He needed privacy, not relief. Carefully, he tapped out a bump of coke onto the side of his hand and snorted it. Then he tossed the empty baggie between his legs and flushed the toilet.

He subscribed to the maxim that breakfast was indeed the most important meal of the day, whether eaten, drunk, or snorted. It had been a restless night, and he wanted to be sharp for his meeting with Detective Ringland.

To prevent the likelihood of a delay, he had booked the first flight of the day, and as expected, it took off on time.

Czarcik spent the majority of the two and a half hours to Dallas studying the crime scene photos of Luis and Marisol Fernandez. The murders were brutal yet so controlled. A combination rarely seen in the field but all too common in B movies and paperback novels.

A delusional psychotic might be able to pull it off. Somebody who was convinced they were doing God's—or some deity's—work, who wouldn't make mistakes caused by anger or compulsion. But this didn't feel right to Czarcik. The crime scene was clean, not clinical. Done with practical, not obsessive, purpose.

The perpetrator had obviously enjoyed his work. There were touches that seemed personal. Czarcik was still convinced the killer didn't know his victims. But how could something this ritualistic be completely random?

The plane touched down on the tarmac of Dallas/Fort Worth International Airport just as the midmorning sun was breaking through the clouds. Czarcik had been sitting in the same position for hours, and his shirt was already stuck to his back. He desperately needed a shower.

He deplaned without incident and headed out of the airport. The car-rental shuttle miraculously appeared just as he stepped off the curb, whisking him off to the rental office, where he was given whatever passed for a compact car nowadays.

A decal on the bottom left corner of the windshield warned of a $250 cleaning fee for smoking in the vehicle. Czarcik smiled and lit up a cigarette. He blew the smoke into the vents and then crushed the butt on the floor of the parking garage. At the exit, as the agent was checking his paperwork, he sniffed audibly and alerted her to the presence of stale smoke. She apologized profusely and asked him if he wanted a different car. "Don't bother," he assured her. "I'm in a bit of a rush. Just didn't want to be charged for it." The agent nodded and made a note on the rental contract.

It was a half-hour drive to the Gillette County Sheriff's Department, where Detective Ringland had promised to meet Czarcik. He took the bypass around Dallas, both to save time and because the view of sagebrush and rusty oil derricks was more palatable to him than shiny new skyscrapers.

The visitor parking in front of headquarters was practically empty, and Czarcik had his choice of spots. He killed the engine and reached into the back seat for his sport jacket. He wasn't sure if protocol dictated he wear one, and because he wasn't sure if Ringland was a stickler for protocol, he put it on. At least it covered his dripping-wet back.

"Morning. How can I assist you?" the woman behind the reception desk asked as Czarcik entered the building. She might have been the same woman he had spoken to the previous night, or everybody in Texas just might share the dispatcher's disagreeably pleasant disposition.

"My name is Paul Czarcik. I have an appointment to see—"

"Lance Ringland." A large, fleshy man bounded over to Czarcik, his hand outstretched. "Pleasure to meet you."

Czarcik shook what felt more like a bear paw. "Detective. Thank you for seeing me."

Detective Ringland had the body of an oversized varsity lineman and the baby face of a high school freshman. Czarcik would have bet his next drink that this was a man once nicknamed "the Gentle Giant." He was clean shaven with a tight crew cut. Only a smattering of gray around his temples betrayed his real age.

He placed his hand on Czarcik's shoulder collegially. "Judging by how quickly you got down here, I know you're eager to begin, but how 'bout a cold sweet tea to refresh you? Most Yankees aren't accustomed to the Texas heat."

"I appreciate that, Detective Ring—"

"That's twice in twenty-four hours, hoss. It's Lance. We don't stand on ceremony down here."

"I appreciate that, *Lance*. But if it's all the same to you, I'd just as soon get started."

A hint of disappointment flitted across Ringland's face but melted back into his accommodating features just as quickly.

"Come on," he said, heading to the rear of the station and motioning for Czarcik to follow. "We'll get right into it."

The adage was true. Everything *was* bigger in Texas, including Detective Ringland's office.

While even the relatively pampered agents in the BJE had to make do with shared desks and dilapidated cubicles, their counterparts in the Lone Star State had room to spare. Behind Ringland's desk was a window that looked out over a neatly manicured municipal field. Goalposts and backstops could be seen in the distance. It could have been the office of some ritzy park commissioner were it not for the photos of the Robertson crime scene tacked to the wall adjacent to the desk. Ringland pointed to them. "I had these prepared for you."

Czarcik stood in front of the photos, hands on his hips, soaking in every detail. An unlit cigarette hung from his mouth. "May I smoke in here?" he asked without looking at Ringland.

"I'm sorry, no."

Czarcik didn't really hear him. He was overwhelmed by the brutality in the photos. Ringland's description on the phone didn't do it justice. This was the work of some incomprehensibly cruel artist.

Judge Robertson, or what was left of him, was tied to a chair. The flesh had literally been peeled from his face at different depths. A square piece on his cheek revealed the white bone underneath. On his forehead, running horizontally from his temple to the bridge of his nose, hung another strip. This wound reminded Czarcik of his sidewalk, shoveled after the first snowfall.

The one saving grace was that Judge Robertson's face was so badly mangled that it retained little of its human form.

It was easy to forget that the thing in the photograph had once been a living, breathing person.

"No DNA?"

"None," Ringland confirmed. "He must have worn gloves because, according to forensics, the skin wasn't sliced off with a razor or a knife."

"How's that?"

"It was pulled off slowly."

Judge Robertson's torso had suffered similar abuse. The longest fleshless strip began at his shoulder and continued down the back of his arm until it reached the elbow, from where the flap had then been torn off. The exposed purple muscle looked like something hanging in a deli.

All in all, there were about a dozen separate wounds on the body.

"I assume he bled to death," Czarcik observed.

No answer. Czarcik turned around. Ringland was shaking his head. "The son of a bitch never hit a vein, or an artery, if you can believe that. The ME put the cause of death as a heart attack."

"A heart attack?"

Ringland nodded solemnly. "From the pain."

Czarcik turned his attention to the knots. He placed his finger against the glossy photo paper and traced the close-up of the rope's swoops and curves. A constrictor hitch. IDA had flagged it, and she was never wrong.

Ringland moved close to Czarcik and rapped his knuckles on the photo. "Same knot as the one on your vic?"

"Looks that way."

There was no need for Czarcik to explain that only *one* of his knots was identical to the ones used to tie up Judge Robertson.

It was the knot that secured the chicken around Marisol Fernandez's neck.

Czarcik was convinced that the killer had taken his time, as he had with the judge. The complexity of the knots bore this out.

There was another link, which the killer had made absolutely no effort to hide, maybe one that he wasn't even aware of.

The sheer brutality of his crimes.

This was not nearly as subjective as he probably assumed. Sometimes wanton cruelty could be as instructive as a fingerprint or a drop of blood.

"Lance, I think I will take that sweet tea now."

Ringland smiled and pressed the intercom on his phone. "Doris, two teas please, if you wouldn't mind."

After placing the order, Ringland sat down in his soft leather desk chair and motioned for Czarcik to take a seat across the desk from him. Once the drinks were delivered, Ringland detailed the history of the case far more thoroughly than Czarcik expected, including Judge Robertson's reputation as a no-nonsense adjudicator, the numerous enemies he could have made on the bench, the fateful video of him abusing his daughter, and the political fallout.

Czarcik listened politely without interrupting. By the time Ringland was finished, so was the sweet tea. The Texan was right about one thing. It was *damn* fine tea.

"I have something for you," Ringland said, wagging his finger at Czarcik, as if he just now decided to bestow a gift upon his new friend. He pushed himself away from his desk with considerable effort and walked over to a metal filing cabinet against the wall. He pulled out a stack of manila folders, slapped them on the desk in front of Czarcik, and plopped back down into his chair, wiping his brow with the back of his hand.

"Soon as we found him, I had my boys request the judge's most contentious cases. Got some help from the courthouse on this one." Ringland motioned to the files. "About twenty of 'em right here. Have to imagine our man is in there somewhere."

Czarcik was convinced he wasn't. But he didn't want to explain the reason why. This would entail a longer and ultimately futile conversation of which he had no desire to be a part, so he just nodded gratefully.

Meanwhile, he kept going back to one number. Ten thousand. Which was approximately how many people had initially viewed the video of Judge Robertson beating his daughter.

That's who his suspect was. Any one of them.

Before takeoff, Czarcik downed three double 7 and 7s at the airport bar. Following a minor delay, the flight back to Chicago was smooth, and he slept deeply until the wheels of the plane hit the tarmac at O'Hare. He dreamed of three things: a hard workout, a stiff drink, and a break in the case.

He took care of the first one upon landing and the second a few hours after.

Relaxing in bed, he took a few big swigs of Wild Turkey and mentally went over everything he knew about the murders.

The physical evidence was flimsy at best. Even the most conspiratorial investigator would find it a mere coincidence that similar knots—not that uncommon—were found at two different crime scenes in two different states. The victims had no relation to one another—one a shit-kicking Texas judge, the others low-class urbanites. While all of the murders were extremely brutal, the method of execution was different. Judge Robertson had had the flesh peeled from his still-living body. Marisol Fernandez had been bludgeoned to death, and her husband had lost his head.

The one thing all the victims had in common was that they deserved to die.

Czarcik sat up and took another swig, taken aback at his own choice of words. *Deserved.* He slipped a cigarette between his lips but didn't light it.

Deserved. According to whom? In these two cases, the ones most qualified to make this determination were the ones least likely to enact the retribution. A frightened wife and young children.

Besides, avenging angels were for the Bible and comic books. And, at least for now, Paul Czarcik believed in neither.

TEN

Chicago Police Chief Eldridge Watkins sat behind his massive, gleaming mahogany desk, glaring at Czarcik.

He pulled at the corner of his perfectly trimmed gray mustache. Everything about him and his immediate sphere of control was impeccable. His uniform, which he had pressed daily, was impossibly wrinkle free. The buttons running down the front and on the sleeves were so well polished that when the chief moved, the sunlight streaming through the window reflected off them, sending blinding points of light dancing on the wall. He wore his insignias and bars properly and proudly, a visual résumé of his long, distinguished career on the force.

Chief Watkins's office was a further reflection of his personality. Uncompromising order. Two standing flags flanked his desk: Old Glory and the city of Chicago's, with its four red stars sandwiched between two powder-blue stripes. The walls were covered with framed commendations, not unlike Czarcik's, only these were prominently displayed behind glass to enhance their visibility, not used as a convenient surface to cut cocaine. There was the chief's diploma from the Chicago College of Criminal Justice, a photo of him with Bears legend Gale Sayers, and another photo, this one old and water damaged, of what looked to be his parents on their wedding day.

A bookshelf contained bound copies of the department's budget going back to the previous decade, along with various pamphlets from other city services. There was also a leather-bound copy of the King James Bible and a first edition of *The Jungle* by Upton Sinclair.

Chief Watkins had risen quickly through the ranks of the CPD, especially for a black man. Until the new millennium, the department hadn't been known for its progressive employment policies. Watkins had made his bones on the street, walking the beat in some of the city's worst neighborhoods. Every promotion he earned was well deserved—and probably overdue—and he met the challenge of each new position with his inimitable mix of integrity and dedication.

The *Chicago Sun-Times*, the more conservative of the city's two daily papers, extolled his uncompromising approach to justice. In interviews, Watkins was dismissive of what he considered irrelevant justification for the rampant crime endemic in the predominantly black South and West Sides. He was interested in prevention and punishment, not root causes, which were the domain of sociology students.

The left-leaning *Chicago Tribune* wasn't shy about throwing out descriptors like *heavy-handed*, *draconian*, or even *fascist*. In some of the city's more radical black churches, the epithet of Uncle Tom was bandied around. Particularly controversial was Watkins's well-known disdain for diversity quotas, which he viewed as condescending and counterproductive.

To Chief Watkins himself, the opinion of others was just background noise. He had one job to do: protect the city. And if he did this to the best of his ability, as quaint a notion as it might seem, he could sleep well at night.

Even among his detractors, who detested his methods, he engendered near-universal respect.

Except from one man who hated him with a passion. And who just happened to be sitting across the desk from him.

In Czarcik's mind, Chief Watkins's greatest attributes were also his greatest liabilities. Going by the book wasn't a virtue, it was a sure-fire prescription for getting officers killed. All the man's awards and accolades, which Czarcik found incredibly tacky anyway, did little to console a grieving widow who had just lost her husband because of the department's cumbersome rules of engagement. Watkins may have never breached protocol, but Czarcik, for his part, had never killed a completely innocent man. And more importantly, he never had to utter the words, "I could have done more."

Chief Watkins didn't care for Czarcik either, having worked with him many times throughout his career, both when Czarcik was with Chicago PD and in his new role with the BJE. In his eyes, the detective was a maverick, loose cannon, and dinosaur. He had done his best to purge these kinds of officers from his own department and wished he could have done the same at the BJE.

Furthermore, he hated the entire idea of the Bureau of Judicial Enforcement. Chicago was supposed to have the country's most finely tuned police force. That it was required to sometimes work with, and rely on, some quasi-independent state agency infuriated him. If the city thought it needed assistance, it should simply train its own officers better.

Because of this mutual antipathy, Czarcik was thoroughly caught off guard when Watkins, after a painfully long period of reflection, agreed to his unorthodox idea.

"But I'm telling you one thing," Chief Watkins warned. He had stopped pulling at his mustache and now jabbed his finger in the air in Czarcik's direction. "If this doesn't work, I let everyone know—*everyone*—that this was entirely a BJE operation. The city just offered tactical support."

Czarcik smiled. He took the mangled, half-eaten cigar he had been chewing on and tossed it into Watkins's wastebasket, and showed himself out of the office.

Daniel couldn't believe it. This was too ironic. Or too coincidental. He wasn't sure which. The words were often used interchangeably but incorrectly. And English, unlike the hard sciences, and despite his predilection for poetry, was never his strong suit.

He was sure, however, that fate had fucked him yet again.

Daniel had been on his way to rural Indiana. There, in the quaint unincorporated town of Bridgeport, was Miriam Manor.

It billed itself as a boarding school where troubled girls could find spiritual peace. In reality, the manor was a house of horrors.

For over forty years, Reverend Seamus Bradley and his obese wife, Dorothy, along with their brood of grown children and pathologically devoted staff ladies, had abused the girls in their care. The endless beatings, psychological manipulation and humiliation, and alternate bouts of starvation and force-feeding were just the appetizers.

For the main course, a walk-in closet. Former residents recounted identical stories of the rusty gynecological table, the restraints, and the visits from a country "doctor" in greasy overalls.

Inside Daniel's trunk was a secret compartment called a trap, typically used by drug runners and weapons dealers. Traps could be as simple as empty space behind a false panel, with enough room to store a kilo or two, or elaborate feats of engineering that rivaled a high-tech panic room.

Daniel's was somewhere in the middle. He had paid a Latino teenager at some sketchy body shop on the West Side $5,000 to create a false bottom in the trunk. If Daniel held down the defroster and seat warmer while tuning his radio to AM 1000, the bottom would pop open to reveal a fireproof box.

Inside was a 9 mm pistol fitted with a suppressor, a brand new scaling knife, and a pint-sized plastic container of avtur—otherwise known as jet fuel—which burned a lot hotter than ordinary gasoline.

Daniel's plan was straightforward, if overly ambitious. He would enter Miriam Manor around three in the morning. Everybody would be asleep. He would shoot all the Bradley children. He would shoot the staff ladies. Then he would deal with Reverend Bradley and his wife. He had special plans for them.

Unfortunately, these plans would have to wait, as currently Daniel was in the throes of the worst headache of his life. He had never had a migraine, and although he knew sufferers claimed it to be the most painful condition imaginable, he had to believe this was worse. Luckily, he managed to navigate off the highway and found a Best Western less than a mile from the exit.

Once in his room, Daniel took out his small black medicine bag. His hands trembled from the pain as he filled a syringe with 40 mg of Palladone and injected it directly into his temple. The relief was instantaneous. He melted into the cheap mattress. The needle rolled off his fingers onto the carpet as his arm hung limply off the bed. Like an angel. Or an addict. And then he slept.

When he woke up six hours later, the pain was gone. Although he had taken enough narcotics to down a small horse, he felt surprisingly refreshed.

Daniel grabbed the remote and turned on the TV out of habit. He wanted a hot shower and a huge plate of pancakes slathered in syrup with a side of crispy bacon.

But what he saw on WGIU—"your source for breaking news and weather"—made him forget everything.

By all appearances, it was a routine press conference. An ordinary-looking official, identified onscreen as Detective Paul Czarcik, Illinois

Bureau of Judicial Enforcement, was standing at the podium. At the top left corner of the screen were two mug shots, a man and a woman, identified as "Victims." Daniel recognized them as something else and, under less pressing circumstances, would have found humor in this characterization.

The photos were of Luis and Marisol Fernandez.

Opposite them, on the other side of this Czarcik character, was a photo of a man whom Daniel didn't recognize. He looked to be in his midthirties, unkempt and disheveled, with a long nappy beard. Daniel was grateful the television wasn't high def; he could almost see the lice crawling around in the man's forest of hair. His eyes were crazy, like the junkies in those *Faces of Death* videos from the seventies, right before they committed suicide by swan diving from a rooftop, the result of, as an earnest narrator intoned, PCP addiction.

His name was Fenton Oakes, and he was identified as a suspect.

You poor disgusting, unlucky, pathetic innocent man, Daniel thought.

On the television, Detective Paul Czarcik adjusted the microphone. The vultures in the press corps below him buzzed with arms extended. They reminded Daniel of the old Frankenstein movies that used to run on Saturday afternoons, but instead of shovels and pitchforks, this angry mob brandished pens, notepads, and mini digital recorders.

"One at a time, one at a time," Czarcik chastised. He obviously had nothing but contempt for the horde, and although he seemed to be a thoroughly unlikeable person, Daniel couldn't help but identify with him. "I'll take some questions, but let me preface this by saying that although we're confident that Mr. Fenton Oakes is responsible for the deaths of Luis and Marisol Fernandez, at this point he's still a suspect and as such deserves and will receive due process. If Mr. Oakes is ultimately convicted, it will be by a jury of his peers, not in the court of public opinion."

Daniel felt light-headed. Untethered. He hadn't been knocked on his ass by a hangover since graduate school, but he was immediately reminded of the sensation. He pressed on his temples to stem the humming in his ears and waited for the physical manifestations of anxiety to leave him.

On the TV, the questions to Detective Czarcik came fast and furious, from the mundane to the ridiculous.

Did Mr. Oakes have any connection to the victims? What was the evidence that led to his arrest? Can you rule out terrorism? Where is Fenton Oakes from? Does he have a criminal record? Have you searched Mr. Oakes's home? Is this a crime of passion? Where does he get his news from? Were the victims sexually assaulted?

Daniel didn't hear a single one. The words were all one big sonic blur. An unintelligible wall of sound.

And none of it mattered. How this incompetent detective had managed to arrest the wrong man was irrelevant. But he had. Somehow he had.

Daniel had been exceedingly careful, or so he thought. Never had he put more planning and preparation into an endeavor. He had studied and memorized the easiest and most difficult surfaces—from glass to human corneas—from which investigators could pull fingerprints. He had researched the best types of gloves to not only avoid leaving prints but to also avoid trapping sweat, skin flakes, and any other material that contained usable DNA.

He had read voraciously about serial killers, pressing on even when their unspeakable deeds and aberrant desires made him physically ill. He understood which crimes would be associated with which psychopathology and made sure to arrange the crime scenes accordingly.

He knew how to dispose of a body and even how to preserve it, at least temporarily, if need be.

He had learned how to hotwire a car, pick a lock, and trace a phone call—with help from the internet, all far easier than anticipated.

He had taken self-taught crash courses in forensics, pathology, anatomy, pharmacology, and less-savory sciences, passing with flying colors.

He had taken every precaution against underestimating his adversaries. His one mistake was overestimating them.

These imbeciles hadn't just failed to catch him, they had arrested the wrong man. An *innocent* man. As much as Daniel tried to convince himself that the poor bastard on his screen—this Fenton Oakes with his wild hair and wilder eyes—must be guilty of something, down deep he knew this rationalization was a poor attempt to assuage his guilt.

After all, the idea was to speak for those who could not speak for themselves.

Although the idea had been percolating for a while, Daniel remembered exactly when the method for choosing his targets had crystallized. He had been in the waiting room at one of his weekly appointments, waiting to hear which of his lobes was now in the crosshairs, when he picked up the Dr. Seuss book *The Lorax* and began flipping through it, bringing back happy memories of his childhood. He thought about the book and what it meant. And Daniel knew in that moment, he would speak for those with no tongues. With no voice. No hope.

Back at the press conference, Czarcik was sparring with a reporter. She had hard, birdlike features and was dressed in a severe pantsuit. "I think that's a little premature, Judy," he replied to one of her inquiries. "That's completely up to the DA. But"—he looked directly into the camera. There was something about his eyes that unsettled Daniel. Hinting at something he didn't quite understand—"it's just unfortunate we no longer have the death penalty. After all, we can't have monsters like this in our city."

You have no idea what monsters are out there, Daniel thought before turning off the TV, bathing the room in darkness.

ELEVEN

One week had passed since Detective Paul Czarcik had convinced his boss, Eldon Parseghian, who had then persuaded Chicago Police Chief Eldridge Watkins, to allow him to take Jake Schaeffer, a young IT technician, and fit him with a wig and fake beard, along with a little mascara to give him that hollow-eyed junkie look, and then take a few snapshots.

Voilà! Fenton Oakes.

Czarcik had had to ply Schaeffer with a few shots of Jägermeister to get him into the spirit of things. Undercover work wasn't really the kid's bag. But once the liquor started flowing, and Czarcik assured him that even his mother wouldn't recognize him, the kid finally gave in.

Chief Watkins had his own reasons for agreeing to such a harebrained idea. It wasn't going to be long before some enterprising reporter discovered that Fenton Oakes was nothing more than a figment of their collective imagination. Once that happened, the ax would fall. And Watkins was going to make damn sure it fell directly on the neck of Czarcik and, by extension, the entire BJE.

Czarcik wasn't naive. He knew that Watkins detested him and everything he stood for. He had been given just enough rope with which to hang himself, but he was also supremely confident in his own abilities. His plan would work.

Czarcik had promised to have his man within a week—two at the most. Now, as the days passed, his confidence was waning.

Originally, he had been all but certain that this ruse would draw out the killer. Even with only two crime scenes to analyze, he believed his profile was sound. Their killer had targeted Judge Robertson and the Fernandezes only after hearing about their cases in the media. The primary unifying feature was that all three murder victims had abused a vulnerable dependent in their care.

If, as Czarcik eventually surmised, the killer viewed himself as some sort of avenging angel, he would be unable to stand idly by as an innocent man was charged. How far would he go, however, to right this wrong? And would it be enough to give Czarcik a glimpse, or even a clue, into his real identity?

There was also the possibility that the killer hadn't seen or heard about the elaborate press conference staged for his benefit. Czarcik found this unlikely. A man—and Czarcik was positive that it was a man—who had been so careful about avoiding detection, for whom notoriety was inconsequential, would be constantly scouring the media for updates on the crimes. Not for arrogance, but for preservation. The fox had to remain ahead of the hounds.

Following an extralong workout, Czarcik stopped in at McGillvey's Pub, a local watering hole where he could drink without being disturbed. He knocked back a double rye before heading over to the Sunfish Motel for his eight o'clock appointment. This had been his daily routine for the past few days as he considered the possibility that maybe the trail had simply gone cold.

There were still things to do. He could interview all the usual suspects—meaning the Fernandezes' remaining family members and tangential business associates—but knew such gestures would be futile. Only the killer himself could help Czarcik now. While he waited, at least he had his vices.

The escort introduced herself as Bertha, as unappealing a name as there was for a prostitute. Even though there was no sex involved, Czarcik was a traditionalist and preferred the easy, sleazy Candys, Ashleys, Brittanys, and Nikkis. Bertha sounded like somebody's great-aunt.

Bertha was pretty enough, with a smile that turned up at one corner in a way that reminded him of Drew Barrymore. She wasn't much of a conversationalist, however, and spent most of the hour educating Czarcik on the benefits of cupping therapy, a type of Chinese medicinal quackery embraced equally by the very famous and very gullible.

After she was gone, Czarcik turned on the TV. The Sunfish was more upscale than his usual love nests, renting rooms only by the day and not the hour. Since he had already paid and was in no condition to drive, he contemplated staying the night. About a gram of coke was left, along with some really good mezcal that he wanted to savor. He'd watch a movie, maybe take a nap, and then see how he felt.

Although the Sunfish boasted of having cable in all its rooms, the establishment offered only the most basic package and included none of the movie channels. Even so, it was impossible for Czarcik to grow bored. As someone who went through most of his adolescence with a single black-and-white television in the house, he was constantly amazed at the sheer number of shows available. One was about a grizzled family of duck hunters who were inexplicably millionaires. Another featured an angry Brit with terrible acne scars who either ran a restaurant or visited restaurants—Czarcik wasn't sure which—and screamed at staff and patrons alike. And his favorite followed a collector who traveled the country trying to track down and purchase vintage Big Ten memorabilia. That half hour flew by in five minutes.

After some halfhearted channel surfing, he landed on TNT, which was airing *Body Heat*. He loved the movie, which reminded him of the old film noirs he used to watch as a kid on the family's thirteen-channel television set. Films like *Double Indemnity, The Postman Always*

Rings Twice, *In a Lonely Place*, and *Out of the Past*. Films with beautiful women, jaded men, and deadly secrets. Always secrets.

He had come in on the action just as William Hurt and Kathleen Turner were ravishing each other for the first time and was asleep long before Hurt even realized he was being double-crossed.

Czarcik awoke barely half an hour later. His back hurt, and his mouth was like cotton. But his buzz was gone, and he felt good enough to drive home.

He arrived back at his condo at one thirty in the morning. He glanced at the glowing numbers of his digital clock, contemplated some good Scotch to take the edge off, decided against it, and was asleep before his head hit the pillow.

The dream was surreal, enhanced by the chemicals still being metabolized by his body.

A white sand beach unfurled in front of him like a giant ribbon. The sea was calm, lapping at his feet as he strolled along. But as the tide drew back, into the vast ocean, it left behind hundreds of bloody mollusks on the shoreline. When Czarcik kneeled down to inspect them, they turned into hairy arachnids, sprouting nonaquatic appendages and scurrying across the sand. He opened his mouth to scream, but it filled with salt water, and even in the dream, he didn't understand why the sight of unnatural but harmless creatures should fill him with dread. As his sleeping brain tried to process the images, he felt something pulling him out of his slumber, prodding him back to reality.

"Please, wake up." The voice was calm, almost reassuring. Something, probably a finger, poked him in the shoulder. Annoying, but hardly threatening.

At first he assumed it was the escort. *The hell was her name? Bertha.* He couldn't remember where he was, so he assumed he must have fallen asleep next to her. But that had never happened before. And this was the voice of a man, not a woman.

Again the voice said, "Please, wake up."

Once Czarcik was aware that there was actually someone in his home, in his room, tapping him on the shoulder, he shot up in bed, only to find himself staring down the barrel of a handgun. It was so close that, at first, his eyes could only focus on the muzzle.

"Please, just remain calm," the comforting voice warned. "I promise. I'm not going to hurt you."

Experience dictated that if Czarcik was going to make a move, now was the time to catch his adversary off guard. But he had just been awakened from a deep sleep, and he questioned his alertness.

Plus, for some reason, he trusted the voice.

Czarcik's field of vision stabilized. He watched as the man sat down in a chair that he had placed at the foot of the bed. The lamp on the nightstand was turned on. But the room was still fairly dark, and Czarcik found it hard to reconcile what he was seeing.

The man wore thick glasses on top of which sat two caterpillar-like eyebrows. An even bushier mustache underlined a prominent nose. There was something familiar, iconic, about him.

"Groucho Marx," the man said, reading Czarcik's mind. "I bought it at a Halloween store a few states over. Crazy how these holidays are now becoming a yearlong thing. I spent some time in Myrtle Beach a few years back, and they had an entire strip mall devoted to Christmas. Multiple stores, literally. One sold only Christmas trees, another specialized in wrapping paper and Advent calendars. Big business, evidently."

This was a good sign, thought Czarcik. If Groucho was planning to kill him, a disguise would have been unnecessary. Still, he wondered how much stock he could put in the rationality of anyone who showed zero compunction about breaking into the home of a police detective while wearing a Marx Brothers costume.

"This is yours, actually," Groucho said to Czarcik, brandishing the detective's Glock 17. "I'll give it back to you in a minute. But first, you have to listen to me."

Czarcik had no choice, so he remained silent. Unable to read his visitor's face, he knew he was at a distinct disadvantage.

"OK?" Groucho pressed.

"You're the one holding the gun."

Groucho adjusted the oversized plastic glasses on the bridge of his nose. "I appreciate that. Thank you for being so agreeable."

Czarcik waited for him to continue, his heart racing.

"I'm the man you're looking for," Groucho finally said.

"I'm looking for a famous vaudeville comedian?"

The joke seemed to momentarily catch Groucho off guard. Then he laughed. "I appreciate your jokes, Detective. I really do. But right now I need you to hear me. I am the man who killed Luis and Marisol Fernandez. If for whatever reason you have cause to doubt me, I'm happy to furnish you with details of the crimes. Details not released to the press."

"I believe you."

Daniel was impressed by Czarcik's stoicism. He assumed the detective had plenty of experience in precarious situations. But he had also read that longtime drug addiction caused irrevocable damage to various receptors in users' brains, leading to muted or abnormal responses to stimuli—not so unlike his own situation. He had to make sure that Czarcik understood who was in control.

"I'm going to toss you a manila envelope," Daniel said. "Please open it." He bent forward and felt around on the bed, never taking his eyes, or his gun, away from Czarcik. After a few seconds of groping, he found the corner of the envelope, picked it up, and threw it next to Czarcik.

The detective stared at the object as if it were a poisonous snake preparing to strike. Daniel smiled, amused. "Go ahead, it's not going to bite you." And then quieter. "Literally, that is."

Czarcik was mentally going through his options.

He considered feigning a seizure, a messy and generally ineffective ploy that actually had worked once in the past. Czarcik had been called to a South Side chicken shack to find some punk hopped up on PCP, holding up the place. Afraid the gunman was going to accidently discharge his weapon, Czarcik fell to the ground and gave the performance of a lifetime, momentarily confusing the suspect so he could be subdued.

Right now, this was unlikely to work. As accommodating and slightly nervous as Groucho appeared, aggressive action on Czarcik's part might change the dynamic. He had seen rational, seemingly agreeable criminals turn deadly once they were threatened. Although this wasn't a man who seemed prone to impulsivity, Czarcik wasn't taking any chances. The best thing to do, at least for now, was play along. It was Groucho's game; he had the gun.

Czarcik tore open the top of the envelope and tapped out a small pile of eight-by-ten glossies. The photos had all been taken over the course of the past week. The first few showed Czarcik entering his motel room, then leaving his motel room; his escort entering his motel room, and then leaving his motel room. A devious husband might be able to explain them away to a willfully ignorant spouse. *That's not really me. They were taken a long time ago. These pictures have been altered.* Besides, all the photos really showed were Czarcik going in and out of various motel rooms, then provocatively dressed women going in and out of those same rooms. There were no time stamps on the photos, and even if there had been, time stamps were notoriously easy to manipulate.

Less easy to manipulate were the photos of Czarcik in bed. Both he and the escorts were dressed; that wasn't the problem. The problem was his service revolver and the cocaine, both of which were clearly visible on the nightstand. The final photos in the stack were close-ups of the incriminating items.

The photographs had all been taken using a high-powered telephoto lens—through the blinds. Czarcik had taken so many unnecessary precautions but had forgotten to draw the shades completely.

"What are you going to do with these?" he asked.

"I hope nothing," Groucho replied, adjusting his glasses again.

Czarcik gathered up all the photos into a stack and returned them to the envelope. Groucho was studying his every move.

"So what?" Czarcik retorted, full of bluster. "If you would've had the balls to have come inside, instead of skulking around outside, you could have gotten some even better photos. I don't know how long you've been following me. But if it's been a while, I imagine you must know that I couldn't begin to give two shits what anybody thinks of me or how I choose to live my life."

"Is that why you frequent different motels, under different names, paying for different women every time?"

Czarcik smiled. "If you're trying to blackmail me, you're barking up the wrong tree."

Groucho considered the suggestion, nodding. "You're right." He took Czarcik's gun and tossed it to the detective. It bounced once on the bed and came to rest against Czarcik's thigh.

Czarcik stared at the gun. A trick. It had to be. The second he went for his piece, Groucho would . . . but what *could* Groucho do? He couldn't beat Czarcik to the gun, which there was no reason for him to have relinquished in the first place.

The man was clearly out of his mind, the only logical explanation. Of course, Czarcik had a gun within his reach and wasn't using it. So who was the crazy one?

Finally, he picked up the weapon and pointed it at Groucho.

Although he felt the familiar heft and instinctively knew that it was loaded, he half-expected a flag to appear with the word *Boom* written on it, or maybe even a stream of water. Groucho would then twirl his bow tie, breaking into some classic Marx Brothers routine, and skip out of the room, leaving Czarcik to ponder the most realistic dream he had ever had. Down deep, he knew he wasn't so lucky.

Czarcik kept a firm grip on the gun but placed it in his lap and spoke forcefully. "So what's to prevent me from blowing your fucking brains out all over my nice clean sheets? I'd be justified, of course. Breaking and entering. Self-defense by even the strictest definition."

Groucho nodded. "I have no doubt you're right. I'm not up to date on the laws governing the use of deadly force, but I'll take your word for it."

Czarcik lifted the gun. He threaded his finger through the trigger guard. "So I ask again, what's to stop me?"

"Right now, copies of those very same pictures are in three private mailboxes around the Chicagoland area. Only I know their locations. And unless I leave here unharmed, and collect my envelopes before the postman arrives tomorrow, those photos will reach the desk of the attorney general, Commissioner Parseghian, and Chief Watkins, in"—Groucho glanced at his watch—"approximately two to three days. Maybe a little longer. Sad state of the postal service nowadays."

"I already told you, I don't give a fuck what anybody thinks. Least of all Watkins and the AG."

"*Thinks.* No, I know you don't care what anyone thinks. But these photos show at least four or five egregious criminal violations. Felony drug possession. Solicitation. Failure to secure one's weapon. And probably one or two more offenses an ambitious DA could drum up. You'd lose your job and, more importantly, your pension. You'd be left with nothing. Of course, I am aware that the department—specifically, the *Chicago* Police Department—tends to take care of its own. But you're not really one of their own, are you?" He tilted his head to the side, as if considering a thought. "Then again, maybe Chief Watkins isn't that much of a stickler for protocol. He seems like the type who'd put his neck on the line for a fellow law enforcement compadre, no?"

The room felt warmer than usual, almost as if Czarcik's anger had ratcheted up the temperature. He sneered at Groucho. Any amount of respect he once had for the man was gone. He considered calling the comedian's bluff and redecorating the wall with his gray matter. If only he thought Groucho was bluffing.

It was physically painful for Czarcik to get the words out. "What do you want?"

Groucho flinched, his surprise evident by his body language, even if the mask didn't register an expression. "Detective, it couldn't be more obvious." Czarcik didn't take the bait, so Groucho continued. "I want you to leave me alone."

Under different circumstances, Czarcik might have found the whole surreal situation nearly comical. "You know I can't do that," he said finally.

"I wish you could," Groucho said. He hung his head. "I mean, in many ways, I'm doing your job for you."

Czarcik could no longer contain himself. He laughed contemptibly. "Really?"

"Yes, really." Groucho's tone was measured. Serious.

Czarcik knew that the more he kept Groucho talking, the greater his chance of getting him to slip up. Getting him to divulge something that might reveal his identity.

"Indulge me, then."

Daniel sighed. Maybe this detective wasn't as sharp as he thought. After all, he *had* arrested the wrong man. About this, Daniel had given Czarcik the benefit of the doubt; this Oakes fellow must have had some connection to the Fernandezes. But maybe the detective was just incompetent.

"I've been watching you, Detective. Every day since your press conference. I know you like old movies. Cop shows. The good ones. The classics." Daniel assumed that Czarcik was proud of his discriminating taste. "I assume you're familiar with *Taxi Driver*?"

"I am."

"Well, then you remember Travis Bickle's famous line."

Czarcik paused for a moment. "You talkin' to me?"

Behind the mask, Daniel smiled. "Yes, of course. But I was thinking of something more profound. And relevant to our current situation."

Czarcik shrugged. "I'm at a loss."

"It's when we see Travis's apartment for the first time, and he's talking about the scum. You remember?"

"I do."

Daniel leaned forward in his chair, resting his elbows on his knees. Behind the thin plastic of the glasses, his pupils contracted as he neared the light from the bedside lamp. "Well, Detective Paul Czarcik . . . I'm that rain."

Czarcik allowed the words to hang in the air. He spoke. "You're crazy."

Daniel laughed, but it wasn't a cruel and cutting laugh. It was relaxed, almost relieved.

"We both know that's not true, Detective. By any measure. I'm not a paranoid schizophrenic. I don't suffer auditory or visual hallucinations. I know the government isn't out to abduct me—although they probably would like some old parking tickets paid. My thoughts are the furthest thing from being confused or fragmented. In fact, I've actually been accused of *lacking* imagination. As for being a delusional psychotic, I'm not that either. I don't believe God speaks to me and me alone. I don't even believe in God, or any higher power for that matter. So I haven't done what I've done at his behest, to gain his favor. Nor do I actually enjoy murder as some deranged narcissists do. To be honest, the thought of causing pain to others sickens me. Most serial killers—the real deviants—demonstrate antisocial tendencies at a much younger age. You know this, Detective. They usually start with small animals and then work their way up the food chain. Nobody who has these urges waits until they're in their midforties to act upon them. So you see, even by the broadest definition of the term, I'm far from insane."

"Since you're obviously a clinical diagnostician, what would you call somebody who decapitates a man, beats a woman to death, and then ties a dead chicken around her neck?"

Daniel scratched his temple. "That depends on the circumstances."

"Really? In my business, we'd just call them a garden-variety nutjob."

Czarcik didn't really believe this, but it's all he had to work with. He needed to poke and prod, to pull back the bandages and pick at the scabs.

"I trust you read the police report," Groucho countered. "Did you see what those two monsters did?" Czarcik said nothing. "It wasn't a rhetorical question, Detective."

"I did."

"Even under the best circumstances, I can only imagine how terrifying being a foster child must be. To be under the control of virtual strangers. With your entire well-being left in their hands. And let's be honest, we both know how effective the child welfare agencies are. So what do you do when those same parents, the ones who have signed affidavits pledging to protect you, cast off the veneer of humanity? When they reveal their true nature?"

Groucho shook his head, then continued. "The six-year-old had cigarette burns all over his body. Dozens of them. Then, after being slowly starved, his punishment for seeking food—the sustenance of life—was being tied up with a dead chicken around his neck. What evil could do that to a child? What evil could allow it?"

The hint of a frown crept out from beneath Groucho's mustache.

"You and I, we both live in the real world, Detective. You tell me. Was a nominal jail stay a just punishment?"

"How can I be sure you actually killed the Fernandezes?" Czarcik asked, ignoring the question. "Maybe Fenton Oakes really did do it—or maybe he didn't; maybe it was someone else, and you're one of those degenerates who gets a perverse thrill out of taking credit. You know the type I'm talking about. Whenever there's a high-profile crime, from the Tylenol Murders to Dahmer, we're inundated with calls from folks claiming they were responsible. I mean, what proof can you actually show me? Mr. Fernandez's head?"

"I disposed of the head appropriately."

"How convenient."

Until now, it had never occurred to Daniel that Czarcik might not believe him. Would he really have broken into Czarcik's apartment if he were not in fact the killer? Would anybody in their right mind—or even in their wrong mind—do such a thing? After all, it hadn't been easy. This was no Watergate job. It took skill and planning. First there was the reconnaissance necessary to obtain all the photographs. After that, Daniel needed a foolproof way to obtain entry into the apartment at will. He picked a time when he knew Czarcik would be gone for hours. Wearing a utility-worker uniform, he hovered outside the front door to the building for less than five minutes before some blissfully ignorant resident ushered him inside. He smiled and thanked her, not particularly surprised; he had a trustworthy face. He knocked on Czarcik's apartment door, and as he pretended to wait, he forced a fast-hardening liquid epoxy into the lock. From this, a key could be fashioned by any competent locksmith for the right price. And in Chicago, there were plenty of enterprising individuals more than happy to do so.

As for the alarm, cutting the wires or destroying the transformer would only alert the security company. Daniel needed the keypad code. Fortunately, Czarcik often disarmed the system with his door still open. A tiny and extremely sensitive microphone placed flush against the doorframe, out of Czarcik's sight, recorded the distinct electronic beeps. Daniel then ran them through a free computer program that translated them into the corresponding numbers. He found it especially funny that Czarcik's code was 0000. The detective was either fearless or a fool.

"Well, what proof do you need?" Daniel asked, speaking quickly, afraid his voice might crack.

If Czarcik had had time, he could have crafted the perfect answer to trip up Groucho. Something to make him unwittingly reveal his true identity or, at the very least, his next victim. Unfortunately, the toxic cocktail of cocaine, adrenaline, and the last vestiges of sleep wasn't conducive to analytical thought.

"Why don't you tell me about Judge Robertson? Why kill him?"

The moment the question left his lips, Czarcik wished he could have reached into the darkness of the bedroom and yanked it back.

He had fucked up. Royally.

Daniel leaned back in the chair. He felt as if he had just been kicked in the solar plexus.

Until now, he'd had no idea that Czarcik knew about the judge. Why would he? The whole press conference, that patsy Fenton Oakes, their conversation up to this point—it was all about the Fernandez murders.

Daniel tried to stop the panic welling up inside him, even as he searched for a plausible way that Czarcik could have connected the cases. Right now, clairvoyance seemed the most logical explanation.

He played the time line of recent events over in his head. As a BJE detective, Czarcik was assigned to the Fernandez case. *Check*. Through solid police work, however faulty, he and his fellow officers had identified and apprehended a suspect. *Check*. With that suspect in custody, a press conference was scheduled, both out of protocol and for a little chest pounding. *Check*. There was nothing, nothing that could have connected the Fernandezes to Judge Robertson. But that's what they were. Connected.

Maybe this detective was simply a lot smarter than Daniel had given him credit for. But if this were true, surely he wouldn't have mentioned the judge, making such an egregious mistake. And that's what this was. A mistake. Czarcik's expression betrayed him the moment he uttered Robertson's name.

This posed another problem for Daniel. Were he to acknowledge the slip, he would be admitting, however tacitly, that Czarcik was right about the connection. This he wasn't ready to do. Not yet.

"I'm afraid I don't know what you're talking about," Groucho said.

"Doesn't matter. I believe you. I believe you killed the Fernandezes." Czarcik was aware he was lying poorly. And because he had fucked up, there wasn't any reason to continue to play dumb. The effect that Judge Robertson's name had on Groucho was obvious. "But I also believe—hell, I *know*—that you killed Judge Jeral Robertson."

Groucho hesitated. "Assuming I know who that is—and I don't—what makes you think that?"

"DNA." The faster he answered, the more truthful he hoped to appear. Otherwise, it might seem he was making it all up as he went along.

Daniel frowned. It was theoretically possible, of course. Specialists were becoming more and more adept at lifting trace DNA from the most unlikely places. But he believed he had taken all the necessary precautions. He doubted he would have left DNA evidence at even *one* of the crime scenes, much less two, which is what investigators would have needed to connect the cases. And if they really had his DNA, they would have had his identity. APBs would have been sent out across multiple states. There would have been no false arrest. Fenton Oakes would still be a free man.

"We're a couple of bad liars," Daniel admitted, talking to himself but loud enough for Czarcik to hear.

Czarcik could tell Groucho was rattled. Frustrated. This wasn't how he had planned it. Not at all. And thus far, he had been a man who relied on meticulous planning. "We both know you're not a professional killer. You're not some maniac. Just between the two of us, I might not even call you a murderer." Czarcik waited for a reaction and then continued. "You might even be brilliant. But even the most brilliant ones eventually get caught. Slip up. You're no different. But I promise you, turn yourself in now, and it will be better for everyone."

Daniel smiled, his confidence creeping back. "Appealing to my vanity is a fool's errand, Detective. As I have none." He leaned in, again fully engaged. "And if I had contemplated turning myself in, if I had even a shred of doubt about my mission, I never would have found it necessary to pay you this visit."

Daniel's head began to throb. The verbal sparring wasn't helping. Thus far he had held off taking any medication in front of Czarcik. Who knew what the detective might use to identify him? But now the pain was coming back, and unless he addressed it immediately, he feared becoming incapacitated before he had a chance to put a safe distance between himself and Czarcik.

Daniel glanced over at the bedroom window. The sun would soon be up. "I think I need to be leaving now, Detective. As we discussed, my first stop will be the three mailboxes to retrieve those inconvenient photos."

He paused, wanting to make sure that Czarcik appreciated the gravity of the situation. "I hope I don't see you down the line. For your sake."

The outside world, which for both men had ceased to exist for the past hour, began to awaken, the sporadic bleating of car horns on the expressway mixing with the low rumblings of the garbage trucks in an urban symphony.

"I have to come after you. And eventually, I will find you."

Groucho rolled his shoulders, stretching. He pressed his thumb into his temple as if tightening a screw. "You do what you need to do, Detective. I came to you tonight to tell you that you had arrested an innocent man. I, on the other hand, am not innocent. But those I visit, they are far less innocent than I am. I think you know that. And I think you agree with me." As a milky dawn pushed through the shades in Czarcik's bedroom, Groucho got out of his chair. He struggled a bit to get to his feet and placed a hand on the wall. As he reached the door, he turned back around. "In another world, at another time, I think we'd be friends, Detective. I really do. I think I'd enjoy talking with you. And you wouldn't even have to pay for it."

Czarcik's anger bubbled up like a witch's cauldron. "It's not too late for me to put a bullet right above that stupid fucking mustache," he replied, fingering the gun.

Groucho nodded and slipped out of the room, leaving Czarcik staring at the black rectangle of the doorway.

Daniel walked briskly down the street. As he approached his car, he removed the disguise and stuffed it into a plastic bag. He would dispose of it in a far less conspicuous place.

Once he was comfortably behind the wheel and well outside the city limits, he pulled over to the side of the road and began to cry. He wasn't surprised at this release. He loathed confrontation, and his visit with Czarcik had left him physically and emotionally drained, much more than his visits to the judge and the Fernandezes had.

Still, it was a necessary step. He was obligated to warn Detective Czarcik.

But if the detective tried to stop him before his work was complete, he would be obligated to kill him.

TWELVE

Czarcik remained in bed for a long time. He had plenty to think about.

Part of him wished he would have just blown the fucking head off the most talented of the Marx brothers. It was as clear cut a case of self-defense as one could hope for: a perpetrator breaks into a private home, wearing a disguise to avoid identification, and threatens the victim at gunpoint. Even those bastards in Internal Affairs would have to rubber-stamp this one.

But then there was the matter of the photographs. There was little reason for Czarcik to doubt Groucho's sincerity. Somewhere out there, three mailboxes held *Collected Vices of Detective Paul Czarcik*.

But what if he had killed Groucho and the photographs had made their way into the right (or wrong) hands? How detrimental would it have been? After all, a dangerous serial killer would have been liquidated. Surely that would have bought him a little leeway. Maybe he could even use that "Get Out of Jail Free" card? But Czarcik could also picture that punctilious son of a bitch Watkins, sitting behind his imperial desk, saying something condescending and asinine like "Fulfilling our oath to protect and serve the citizens of this fair city doesn't absolve us of our duty to do so within the boundaries of the law." And would Parseghian go out of his way to take on Watkins and defend Czarcik? Parseghian was loyal to his men, but he was as much a politician as a cop and was unlikely to do anything to endanger his future career in glad handing and baby kissing.

Furthermore, Czarcik was still bothered by the way his conversation with Groucho had ended. It wasn't the questioning of his moral compass. It was that of his competence—an insult he couldn't suffer quite as easily.

Groucho had, in essence, dared Czarcik to catch him. His ability to track and kill—or at least capture—his quarry was something in which Czarcik still took an enormous amount of pride. He had yet to be bested in any of his biggest cases, the ones into which he put his heart and soul. Not by the Argentados, those slippery Italians who had thought they could muscle out the black gangs for the heroin market. Nor by Feaster Hand, the pharmaceutical magnate who poisoned his first two wives and would have done the same to the third if Czarcik hadn't found the vial of ricin in the basement of the CEO's vacation home on Mirror Lake.

And certainly not by Groucho Marx.

Groucho's Travis Bickle comparison was accurate, however. He *was* washing the scum off the streets. What bothered Czarcik was that he was doing it on his own terms. Saying "Stay the fuck out of my way." And this wasn't something that Czarcik could simply abide.

He turned his attention back to the window.

The garbage trucks were out in full force. He could hear their metallic concerto as they raised overflowing dumpsters to the heavens before smashing them down, now empty, on the cool concrete not yet warmed by the rising sun. Soon the streets would be teeming with commuters, joggers, meter maids—none aware that a very dangerous game was playing out among them.

Groucho Marx had thrown down the gauntlet. Detective Paul Czarcik was about to pick it up, just as soon as he did another bump and took a shower so hot it was nearly intolerable.

He leaned his head against the tile. The condensation dripped onto his face as the steam rose from his cherry-red shoulders.

He thought about Groucho. And Genevieve Kuzma. It had been a long time since he'd thought of her.

THIRTEEN

1985

Officer Paul Czarcik of the CPD stepped into the gloaming.

His eyes were still red, even though he had stopped crying in the theater. It wouldn't do for a cop to be caught bawling on the street, even a twenty-three-year-old rookie just a few months out of the academy.

He walked through the glass doors of the Esquire Theater where he had just seen *Mask*, a tearjerker about Rocky Dennis, a teenager who suffered from craniodiaphyseal dysplasia, a rare genetic condition that left him horribly disfigured.

The advertising had led Czarcik to believe he was in for a film about motorcycle gangs, not the heartbreaking true story of a modern-day Elephant Man.

It was just after Thanksgiving in Chicago. Czarcik wore his leather police department jacket not because of the weather, but because he was proud of it, even prouder than he had been of his high school letterman jacket.

He crossed over Oak Street, maneuvering through the throngs of well-heeled shoppers, like the shifty tailback he once was. He took a left and headed down Rush, where he had found a free parking spot for his beloved 1977 Pontiac Bonneville. It was the color of diarrhea, had two broken taillights, a door that wouldn't open, and was in need of a new transmission. But as a graduation gift from his parents, it was *his*. All his.

First-generation Polish immigrants, Czarcik's parents had never wanted him to become a cop. His father wanted him to go into banking. As a union millwright, the elder Czarcik knew little about high finance. But he knew of growing up hungry in Eastern Europe, behind the Iron Curtain. As a result, he wanted his only son to make as much money as possible.

His mother harbored more romantic notions of employment. She had hoped that Paul would become an educator at one of the city's great universities, preferably a professor of literature. She came from a family of teachers for whom there was no higher calling than the accumulation and dissemination of knowledge.

She had also inadvertently set her son on the path of law enforcement.

As a child, Paul had been surrounded with books. His mother would read to him for hours every night, dazzling him with tales of Arabian nights and death-defying voyages on the seven seas. Hardly surprising, then, that her son became a voracious reader.

But despite her best efforts to introduce him to the works of Dickens, Tolstoy, and Twain, Paul gravitated to Poe, Agatha Christie, M. R. James, and his favorite, Sir Arthur Conan Doyle, whose fictional resident of 221B Baker Street had an indelible impact on his childhood. When he was an impressionable eleven-year-old, Paul slept an entire month with a chair wedged under his doorknob, convinced the hound of the Baskervilles was pawing at his door during the night.

As he got older, he devoured the great American hard-boiled authors—Chandler, Hammett, Cain—and especially the pulp novels of Mickey Spillane, Fredric Brown, and Cornell Woolrich. In 1972, he dressed as Popeye Doyle for Halloween, earning him plenty of curious looks from the parents of run-of-the-mill vampires, ghosts, and baseball players.

At the moment of truth, he sat his parents down at their kitchen table. This was where anything of importance was discussed. "Mom, Dad, I want to be a cop," an eighteen-year-old Paul declared.

His mother had wept. "But you can make a living—a *good* living—teaching Proust," she pleaded.

Once she had calmed down, his father pointed at him with a gnarled, arthritic finger. "You're sure?" he asked. Paul had nodded. "Then you be the best goddamned cop you can be. You make us proud, you hear me?"

Paul had smiled from ear to ear as his mother continued sobbing.

Czarcik piloted the Bonneville down Lake Shore Drive as the first chords of Starship's "We Built This City" came through the radio, a catchy tune that Czarcik didn't mind. As a classic-rock junkie, however, he found it hard to believe the track came from the remnants of Jefferson Airplane, one of the truly transcendent bands of the sixties. Marconi playing the mamba was hardly as profound as the surrealist musings of a hookah-smoking caterpillar.

Despite the mild weather, the lake looked angry, fixing for a storm. Miniature whitecaps smashed against the concrete rib cage of Navy Pier, the three-thousand-foot eyesore that reached into Lake Michigan, as if it wanted no part of the city. It boggled Czarcik's mind that what should have been the country's most attractive piece of real estate was allowed to remain deserted like a postapocalyptic playground. Then again, he was just a beat cop, not a city planner.

As a rookie, Czarcik was assigned to the night shift. The crazy eights—from eight in the evening until eight in the morning. Even though the shift was supposed to be the least desirable, he didn't mind it. The darkness suited him. He was usually back home and in bed by nine in the morning. If he was up by three in the afternoon, that was a good night's sleep, and he still had a few hours to kill with movies, exercise, or other recreational pursuits before he was required to check in for work at the First District on South State Street.

Darkness had fallen by the time Czarcik pulled into the station. He had time for a quick dinner before his shift began, so he walked over to Galway's, an Irish pub on Wabash just under the L tracks. The place was crowded, and Czarcik saw two cops from his precinct—one he knew, one he only recognized from around the station—drinking in a back booth. He turned to avoid them just as Bill Clemens, his acquaintance, caught his eye and waved him over.

"Paul! Paul, over here," he called out, gesturing frantically. Czarcik pretended to notice Clemens for the first time, lifted his head in recognition, and headed over.

Clemens was perfectly bald and obese. He reminded Czarcik of the wrestler King Kong Bundy, whom he had seen earlier in the year at some newfangled event called WrestleMania. "Hey, Paul," he said, smiling deviously, "how come women have two holes?"

"So when they get drunk you can carry them home like a six pack," Czarcik answered. Clemens looked disappointed. "I heard that in like seventh grade. *Truly Tasteless Jokes.*"

"Well, sit down anyway, you son of a bitch." Clemens opened his hand and gestured to the opposite side of the booth. Even if Czarcik had wanted to sit next to Clemens, there wouldn't have been enough room.

"I'm Paul Czarcik," he said, extending his hand. "I've seen you around the station."

"Bob Tibbett," the other cop said as Czarcik plopped down next to him. He was around the same age as Clemens but good looking, with a full head of dark brown hair. Unlike his colleague, he hadn't allowed his body to resemble that of a beluga whale.

Both cops had whiskey tumblers in front of them, halfway filled with a brown liquid. "Join us?" Clemens asked, pointing to his glass.

Czarcik shook his head. "I'm on nights. Shift starts in less than an hour."

A beat of silence and then Clemens and Tibbett erupted in laughter. Czarcik smiled uneasily.

"He's a rookie," Clemens said to Tibbett.

"I never would have guessed," Tibbett replied.

"Good Christ," Clemens said, still laughing, "the hell you come in here for, then? The ambiance?" He pronounced the word like "ambulance."

"Thought I'd grab a quick bite before my shift."

"Stay with the burgers. They're safe. Avoid any of the Irish food. Trust me," Tibbett warned. "And you're talking to a couple of Micks here."

Clemens nodded, corroborating. "Who they have you partnered with now?" he asked.

"Klein." The two men exchanged a look that Czarcik couldn't quite read.

A waitress came over. "What can I get you, sugar?" she said to Czarcik.

"Uh, just a cheeseburger with bacon, please."

"How 'bout to drink?"

"Water is fine."

"Bring 'im a double rye," Clemens chimed in.

"No, I really—" Czarcik began.

"Don't worry, rookie," Clemens assured him. He dismissed the waitress with a flick of his wrist. "I'll drink it." Then he winked at Czarcik. "But you can still pay."

Again he and Tibbett roared, only stopping for Clemens to ask, "What's the difference between Antarctica and a clitoris?"

Ed Klein had hair like a politician. Thick, graying in all the right places, and held perfectly in place by an invisible force of nature. He was also brutally honest, condescending, unambitious, and hated children. All things considered, he was better as a cop.

He had been Czarcik's partner for the past six months and would be his partner for the next six until he retired at age forty-five with a full pension. After that, he and his wife, who hated children with a vigor equal to his own, planned to purchase a cabin on Lake Superior, where they would live out their years with as little human contact as possible.

Czarcik and Klein were paired up thanks to a departmental initiative that sought to place rookie cops with veteran ones. The idea, of course, was to have the first-year officers soak up the experience of their elders. Learn at their knee, so to speak. What should have been more than evident was that cops closing in on retirement had little interest in any kind of half-assed apprenticeship program. They wanted to avoid two things in the twilight of their careers: getting shot and a charge of police brutality. Furthermore, it wasn't particularly inspiring for the rookies to be constantly exposed to such simmering pessimism.

For all the program's faults, Czarcik and Klein got along well enough. In Czarcik, Klein saw a kid who had gotten into law enforcement for the right reasons; in Klein, Czarcik saw someone who was the antithesis of guys like Clemens and Tibbett.

"Ed?" Czarcik said, looking at his partner. Klein was behind the wheel. He always drove when they went out on a call.

"Hmm?"

"Do a lot of cops go drinking before their shift?"

"Who told you that?"

"I was having dinner at Galway's before work and ran into Clemens and Tibbett. They were off duty, but they offered me a drink."

"Those guys are idiots. Miracle they haven't been killed by now."

"But is it true? You know, that a lot of the guys drink on duty?"

Klein looked at him and frowned. "Yeah, it's true." Czarcik nodded and turned toward the window. Klein glanced at him sideways while keeping his eyes on the road. "You're not a big drinker, are you?"

Czarcik shook his head.

Czarcik and Klein had been on plenty of domestic-disturbance calls together. By now, their roles were fairly consistent. Czarcik was the sympathetic ear who took the victim's statement, and Klein, by virtue of his experience and disposition, made sure the aggressor didn't do anything stupid.

Most of these calls played out the same way. Rarely did they walk in on a Carlo and Connie scenario. The man was usually quiet, embarrassed, almost apologetic, while the woman assured the officers—even as her nose began to swell and her eyes blacken—that it was all one big misunderstanding.

Czarcik hated walking away from these calls empty handed. But he couldn't force someone to file charges.

The two were greeted at the door by a man. It wasn't unheard of for a white family to be living in this area of the South Loop, but it wasn't that common either. His color caught the cops off guard, as did the way he greeted them like old friends.

"Come in, come in," he said as he ushered them into the apartment.

"Mr. Kuzma," Klein said as he looked around the apartment, "we received a call from a female at this residence who claimed to be in some type of physical danger."

"*Doctor* Kuzma," the professor clarified. "I'm a professor at the University of Chicago."

Klein ignored him. "How 'bout you tell me what's going on here."

"Nothing; it was my mistake," said a soft female voice. They all turned around as a woman entered the room from a short hallway. She was small and delicate, wearing a modest nightgown, her hair pulled back in a ponytail. Dressed for bed. Her arms were painfully thin, like taut cables covered in parchment paper. Just below one shoulder, peeking out from under the fabric, was a fading yellow bruise.

"Are you all right, ma'am?" Czarcik asked as she walked over and leaned against her husband. He draped his arm around her. She was so frail she seemed to glide, as if her presence in the home was more spectral than human.

"I called the police," she explained. "Wilson was in one of his moods, and I haven't been sleeping."

Czarcik looked over at Klein. They were used to cockamamy explanations. Coded language. Euphemisms to make abuse seem more palatable.

"So, Officers," said the smarmy professor, "we're supporters of civil servants. We give generously during your pledge drive. But as you can plainly see . . . there's nothing to see here." His smile, which he clearly thought was charming, gave Czarcik the willies. His too-white teeth looked like mini tombstones.

Again Klein ignored him and turned to the wife. "Would you like to file a report, ma'am?"

"Good heavens, no," she said, instinctively pulling her nightgown tighter at the neck and moving deeper into her husband.

Czarcik sensed movement behind him. He dropped his hand to his gun, just brushing the weapon, making sure it was there, as a young girl came into the room. She looked to be around fourteen and had the dazed countenance of someone who had just woken up. She didn't appear particularly surprised or unsettled by the presence of the two strange men in her home.

"Go back to bed, Genevieve," said her father. "Mommy and Daddy have visitors."

The girl turned around and walked back to her room. But as she did, she glanced up at Czarcik.

His knees turned to jelly, and he reached out—inconspicuously, he hoped—against the wall to steady himself.

My God, he's fucking his daughter.

He couldn't explain how he knew, how he knew with absolute certainty. The girl held his gaze, locked in, burning the image into his brain. And then she was gone.

For years after, Czarcik tortured himself by trying to assign meaning to that stare. Was it acquiescence? Capitulation? Defiance? He didn't know. But her eyes. Her eyes were hollow.

"Officer Czarcik?" Klein was saying with some impatience in his voice. Czarcik looked over. The girl was gone, and Klein and her parents were waiting on him.

"Huh?"

"I said, 'We're wrapping up here.'"

He didn't know how long he had been out of it. Couldn't have been more than a few seconds. "Last chance, ma'am. You sure you don't want to file a report?"

She looked at him with pure disdain. They had covered this already.

"You've been very helpful," the professor said as he led the officers out.

"Professor, just one more question," Czarcik said. "Out of curiosity, what do you teach?"

"Philosophy."

"Ah." Czarcik smiled. *"Forsan miseros meliora sequentur."*

Dr. Kuzma frowned. "Gentlemen." He closed the door quickly.

"That was one weird fucking family."

The duo was back in the car, driving up Wabash as the L shrieked above, sending showers of sparks raining down around them.

"We should have stayed. We should have pushed. Gotten her to make a statement," Czarcik said angrily.

Klein looked at his younger partner. "You out of your mind? How many of these domestic calls have you been on now? You weren't going to pry a word out of that woman with a crowbar and thumbscrews."

"Still . . ."

Klein shook his head. "And what the fuck were you doing at the end there? Speaking in tongues?"

"It was Latin. From Virgil. Loosely translated to, 'For those in misery, perhaps better things will follow.'"

Klein seemed to ponder the phrase. He wasn't much of a scholar. "A-fucking-men," he said finally.

Czarcik never mentioned the girl again to Klein or anybody else. Over time he even forgot her name. But he never forgot those eyes.

FOURTEEN

"I'm pulling you off the case."

This was not what Czarcik had been expecting.

He had been planning to make a brief appearance at BJE headquarters, have a few cups of bad coffee, maybe admire the new desk sergeant who had just gotten a breast enhancement. What he wasn't expecting was this shit.

"I'm leaving it in the hands of the very capable Chicago Police Department," said Eldon Parseghian.

He was standing in front of the mirror on the back of his office door, adjusting his navy power tie. Parseghian was dressed in his best Armani suit, preparing for a lunch with the governor to discuss something obviously above Czarcik's pay grade. His back was to Czarcik, who was sitting in a chair in front of his boss's desk.

"I think that's a mistake. A big one."

"I'm sure you do. What I can't really figure out is *why*. I mean, they brought us in to look at the crime scene, determine what the fuck happened. A robbery? A territorial beef? Some weird voodoo shit? I figured you'd give it the once-over and throw it right back at them. But you've been chewing on this like some goddamned junkyard dog. The whole Chicago PD sting. I didn't understand what the fuck that was about. But I wasn't about to question you if we got our man and some good press. At this point, though, we got nothing. Just a drain on resources."

"I'll do it on my own time. I have more than a month of vacation time coming my way."

Parseghian checked himself in the mirror one last time. He pushed a few strands of gray, wet with styling gel, back behind his ear and turned to Czarcik, looking at him like he was crazy. He then went back and sat down behind his desk. "You out of your mind?"

"There's more to this than any of us realize."

"Tell me."

"Not yet."

Parseghian didn't push it. He rarely put the screws to an agent unless he felt the agent was holding out on him. And even then, he trusted the judgment of his best ones.

The two men weren't close—Czarcik wasn't close to anyone—but he could read his boss fairly well. "What aren't you telling me about this?"

Parseghian sighed. He looked like an actor suffering from heartburn in an antacid commercial. "Watkins called me this morning."

"He's an insufferable prick."

"Goes without saying. But that insufferable prick has a lot of pull in Springfield. He kept reminding me that this idea of yours has generated no legitimate leads." Czarcik's jaw tightened. Parseghian continued. "According to Watkins, they got a single confession last week. Off the street. The guy walked right through the front door and turned himself in. Callahan—you know Callahan? Whose old lady works for the Metropolitan Pier Authority?—well, he had the pleasure of interrogating him, during which time this man claimed responsibility for the Lindbergh kidnapping, the Oklahoma City bombing, and 9/11. Then he laughed hysterically before vomiting on Callahan's shoes and passing out. He's in psych at Stroger if you want to see him."

"I told you this was a hunch. I didn't promise a foolproof plan."

Parseghian nodded. "And your hunches have always paid off, which is exactly what I reminded Watkins."

"I just need more time. And unless there's something else you're not telling me, Chicago PD has made less headway than us. Watkins might act like a self-righteous motherfucker, but he wouldn't know how to solve a murder if the asshole walked into his office in a pair of handcuffs."

Parseghian got up from his desk. He walked over to the nearest window and stared out. "This afternoon, Watkins is going to tell the press that there isn't enough evidence to continue to hold Mr. Oakes. He'll assure them he's pursuing all relevant leads and that we don't have a serial killer in our midst. If someone asks him about the involvement of the BJE, he'll tell them our services are no longer needed."

"Then we're done," Czarcik said. He pushed his chair away from the desk and headed toward the door.

"Sit down, Paul," Parseghian said, still gazing out the window. He rarely used Czarcik's first name, and the detective had the sinking feeling that what was coming next was a lot worse than he first expected.

Overflowing with nervous energy, Parseghian turned from the window, sat back down in his chair, fidgeted a bit, and looked across his desk at Czarcik.

"This is a bad fucking time to be a cop, Paul, and an even worse time to be part of an organization that the public doesn't really understand. There was a time when we were heroes. When *CSI* was the most popular show on TV. Didn't matter most of it was bullshit. The public thought we were magicians, protecting them from serial killers on every corner. Now we're the assholes who shoot unarmed black kids and cover it up."

Czarcik's response was immediate, almost instinctual. "If you're firing me, have the balls to do it like a man."

Parseghian held up a hand. "I'm not firing you. I'm suggesting you take your well-deserved retirement."

Czarcik seethed. At least Groucho had challenged him. Parseghian was putting him out to pasture. But as the anger mounted, he kept his composure, understanding that a violent outburst would be proven not cathartic but detrimental. Instead, he internalized. Compartmentalized. Took a deep breath and looked right at Parseghian. "What the hell is this really about?"

Parseghian threw up his hands. "Bureaucracy. Money. State debt. Defaults. The fuck do you want me to say? What it's not is some grand conspiracy." He sighed. "Or about keeping the public safe."

"Let's say I'm not ready to ride off into the sunset just yet," Czarcik said. Parseghian waited for him to continue. "I don't know what the fuck my union does, but I do know every month they wet their beak from my paycheck. And I do know that they don't take lightly to their members being let go without cause."

"Without cause." A slight smile pulled at the corner of Parseghian's mouth. "You don't want to go down that road, Detective."

But that lonely, lightless road was the very one that Czarcik was contemplating. What if he took the one less traveled—encouraged by that grade school poem he suddenly remembered—and forced Parseghian's hand? How messy could it get? He decided to rattle the cage a little longer. "And if I do?"

The boss looked tired, in no mood to engage in a battle of wills. He fixed Czarcik with his most penetrating stare. "The amount of paper I have on you for cause is longer than *War and Peace*. I just never felt the need to use it. I hope I still don't."

Czarcik had no doubt this was true. Groucho. Parseghian. They were two sides of the same fucking coin. The difference? One was an unpredictable serial killer while the other was the epitome of the company man. Equally ruthless.

"I need a month," Czarcik said somewhat sheepishly.

"This isn't a negotiation."

"I need a month," Czarcik repeated. "You won't have to pay me," he added before Parseghian could reply. This was the smart move, appealing to the boss's parsimony. "The only thing I request is continued access to the same resources I currently enjoy."

Parseghian mulled over the offer, saying nothing.

"I'd work alone," Czarcik continued. "I'd call on the other agents and detectives only when absolutely necessary. And that would be infrequently, if at all." He was slowly casting himself in the role of obsequious employee.

"What about Chicago PD? They've already invested time and manpower—"

"And gotten nowhere," Czarcik interrupted. Then, trying to appear empathic, he said, "I'll keep Watkins in the loop. Won't step on anyone's toes. Let his team lead the investigation. We won't be working at cross purposes"—he paused—"just along different lines of inquiry. I'll even share everything I find with him."

Parseghian was certain that Czarcik was being far from transparent. Such collaboration wasn't in his nature. But even if he didn't buy the reason for the detective's sudden magnanimity, he couldn't dispute the crux of his argument.

The head of the BJE had built his career on, among other things, common sense. And this made *a lot* of sense. What was the harm in getting Czarcik out of his hair for a month, and then out of the bureau for good? If luck shone upon them, maybe he really would find the killer. Plus, at the moment, the public was consumed by the gun violence in the city's gang-infested neighborhoods. They were hardly clamoring for justice for the murder of two degenerates.

"One month," Parseghian declared, holding up a single finger in case Czarcik misheard him. He tapped his thick knuckles on the desk; the sound echoed through the office.

"You'll clear it with Watkins? I don't want any bullshit from his people."

Parseghian nodded. "I'll clear it."

Czarcik stood up. "I appreciate it. But you'll understand if I don't shake your hand." He was out of the office before Parseghian could figure out how to respond.

The last thought he had before Czarcik left his office was not that the detective might get his man, but that the man might get his detective.

And this struck him as not entirely disagreeable.

"Fuckin' Czarcik," he muttered.

FIFTEEN

To astrologers, there is no earthly occurrence not foretold in the stars.

The night was clear, and many of the constellations were visible to the naked eye. To some, they held answers.

To men like Daniel Langdon and Detective Paul Czarcik, fate was determined by a single, unwavering constant: the will of man.

How ironic, then, that at the exact same time, both pragmatists should find themselves in cheap motels barely six miles apart.

Down in the South Loop, where the Orange and Green Lines passed over Congress Parkway, Daniel knelt in the bathroom of the Buford Arms Motel, introducing the calcium-caked toilet bowl to the contents of his stomach.

The headaches had been getting worse. They weren't the tension type, from which he had occasionally suffered during his years in the workforce, where it felt as if a band of hot steel was being slowly tightened around his forehead. Nor were they the excruciating, boring pain of a migraine, which had afflicted his mother all her life, sending her to a silent, darkened room to wish away the agonies of the condition. These were different. They were localized and grinding. Daniel found it hard to believe that there was not some living thing inside his skull—like in that old *Night Gallery* episode—feasting on the raw nerve endings, subsisting on the pain. He remembered those mental-hygiene films from his parents' generation, in which an anthropomorphic piece of tooth plaque jackhammered a molar. That's what it felt like.

Eventually the nausea would pass. He had already given himself a shot of Palladone. All he could do now was lie down and allow the narcotic to do its job.

If he was lucky enough to fall asleep, he prayed for a dreamless slumber. Because now he even dreamed of pain.

Daniel used to believe that there was no truer adage than that of youth being squandered on the young. Now he was convinced he'd found one more accurate: health is squandered on the healthy. He wondered if *Bartlett's* would be interested in such a profound sentiment, then realized the drug must be working.

Daniel's sole pursuer commenced his month-long assignment by meeting a freckled redhead at the El Capital, one of the city's most disreputable hourly establishments.

Sexually, Czarcik didn't have a thing for redheads, finding them more homely than exotic, but his prejudices didn't extend to conversation. This one actually had a good story. Until she was eighteen, she had been under the impression that her mother was her older sister. The revelation had affected her so profoundly that she promptly left home and hadn't been back since.

It wasn't the usual tale of small-town woe, but even as she was telling the story, he found his mind drifting back to his conversation with Groucho.

Czarcik wanted him dead more than ever.

When Czarcik arrived back at his office at BJE headquarters at a quarter past eight in the evening, he fully intended it to be the last time he ever set foot inside. From here on out, he would be on the road.

He was far from a sentimentalist in danger of being overcome by emotion at the prospect of a transition. Plus, his office held few personal items, hardly anything to clean out. There were no photos of loved ones to be swept into a cardboard box. Most detectives kept a trinket to anchor them to their civilian lives—a pocket watch passed down from a father, a mother's brooch—a necessity in their line of work. Czarcik had nothing except for a pot of black organic matter that had been given to him months ago by the department secretary. She had asked him to take care of her plant while she was away on vacation. Czarcik had taken care of it as well as he had taken care of Vanessa McDonald's fish. The secretary had never forgiven him, even refusing to take the pot back upon her return.

He had no relevant case files or paperwork to pack. These he kept under lock and key in his home office, the safest place for them. At least it had been until Groucho's unexpected visit.

The only item he took with him was an ornate hunting knife with a handle carved from a deer antler. Over the years, he had spent hours admiring the flowing curve of the blade and the way the steel seamlessly disappeared into the bone. Before security cams were ubiquitous, he had pilfered the knife from a crime scene. It wasn't relevant to the case, and its absence wasn't noticed, just the spoils of war. After all, his uncle had taken plenty of booty from dead soldiers on Iwo Jima. Back in the day, at Chicago PD, the evidence locker had been one big bazaar. In fact, it was there that Czarcik got his first taste of Colombian cocaine. In some ways, this sample had spoiled him. Finding a reliable supplier on the street whose shit was as pure was no easy feat.

He would of course miss IDA. Since access from the road was all but impossible, if he needed her, he would have to call Corrine, who just happened to be walking toward him at that moment.

"Speak of the devil," he said.

"I'll take that as a compliment," she replied.

"You need something?"

"Actually, I came to say goodbye."

Czarcik didn't respond.

Corrine continued. "The boss didn't tell me much, only that you'd be on the road for a month or so and that I was to continue to support you and address any request in a timely matter."

"There you go."

She watched him gather his things. "You're not coming back, are you?"

He stopped. Looked up at her. "What makes you say that?"

She scrunched up her nose. "I don't know, really. This just has that feel to it."

"I'll be back," Czarcik promised. "And you'll have plenty of time to think of new things to bust my balls about."

She chuckled, then said, "Paul, I know we're not really friends. Hell, I don't even know if I like you very much. But I *will* miss you. Things will be a lot less interesting without you around."

He extended his hand. Stiff. Formal.

Corrine ignored it, stepped up to him, and punched him playfully in the chest. Then she walked away, laughing.

Once Corrine was gone, Czarcik did a final dummy check, just to make sure he wasn't forgetting anything of importance.

As he turned to leave his desk for the last time, he nearly bumped into a woman. He stammered "pardon me," out of habit, but she was the one who had invaded his personal space.

He had never seen the woman before, and the first things he noticed were her deep-blue eyes. More opal than ice, as if their color wasn't quite fixed but fluctuating. The shape of her face was Eastern European, but removed by a generation or two. Raven hair offset the pools of sapphire that now held him captive. She was pretty enough to be an escort, thought Czarcik. But if she was, he would have remembered her. And he was sure he hadn't seen her before.

"Are you Detective Czarcik?" she asked, pronouncing his name correctly, which he chalked up to familiarity with a Slavic tongue.

"Czarcik, yes," he repeated.

The woman made no apology for her bold entrance, which Czarcik found both off-putting and strangely appealing. "I was told you're the person I should speak with."

"I'm sorry," he replied, unconcerned with appearances, "but as you can see, I was about to leave. Whoever directed you to me must have been misinformed."

He walked past her, and she reached out and placed a hand on his shoulder. Another audacious move. "It's about your case."

"Any information you might have about the Fernandez murders you can share with Chief Eldridge Watkins of the Chicago Police Department. The reception desk will be able to tell you where you can find—"

"No, your other case."

He swore he caught the hint of a smile, as if she knew she was about to spook him.

"A judge in Texas named Jeral Robertson."

Czarcik sat right back down, as if the color that drained from his face was physically pulling him into the chair. He tried to maintain his composure and licked his lips, afraid his voice might crack if he spoke.

For a brief moment, he wished that Groucho could be here next to him. The comedian would certainly appreciate the irony. They had each tried so hard to keep the judge their little secret. And now, this secret was being casually revealed by another stranger.

Czarcik reached over, grabbed a chair from the adjacent desk, and pulled it over. He motioned for the woman to sit down. "What about Jeral Robertson?" he asked quietly, never taking his eyes off her.

"I know who his killer is."

"The judge's killer?" He wanted to make sure there was no miscommunication.

"Yes."

"How do you know that?" Czarcik asked.

"Because he's my husband."

SIXTEEN

Twenty minutes later, Detective Czarcik found himself sitting across the table from Chloe Langdon, no closer to determining the true color of her eyes. In the restaurant's muted amber light, they appeared to oscillate even more.

They were in a booth against the back wall of Dnieper, a restaurant tucked away in a side street of the Ukrainian Village, which had been open since the neighborhood was home to actual Ukrainians, not hipsters. Although Dnieper was never crowded, it was the kind of place that somehow managed to stay in business.

Czarcik favored the eatery because it was dark and quiet. The drinks were strong, and both the staff and other patrons kept to themselves. Dnieper offered no music, only the soft white noise of a snowy television above the bar, perpetually tuned to a European soccer match. He had been coming here regularly for over twenty years. The owner, a large Ukrainian woman who always looked old but never seemed to age, had never given him a nod of recognition. Just the way he liked it.

He and Chloe had barely spoken since leaving BJE headquarters together. Just a few words about the location of the restaurant. Czarcik drove them. Chloe had no car, as she had taken the L and then walked over to his office.

Now, in lieu of a formal introduction, Chloe thrust a stack of glossy folders at him. He opened the top one. Inside were articles about the

Judge Robertson case. In the left inside pocket were photos from a color printer; screen grabs from the infamous video. They were poor quality, but Czarcik could still make out the terrified expression on the face of Judge Robertson's daughter as her head snapped back in pain. In the right pocket were printed maps of what looked like the judge's property, with various spots circled in black marker.

Czarcik closed the folder and placed it at the bottom of the stack. He opened the next one. More articles. He scanned them quickly. Something about a chronic drunk driver. Maybe the clippings would prove valuable at a later date, but right now, they weren't the proof he needed to tie the two cases together.

What he needed was in the next folder. The entire sick saga of the Fernandez family, complete with court transcripts.

A waitress with coarse gray hair, wearing an apron decorated with some Eastern European flag, placed two glasses of water in front of them. In a thick accent, she asked if they wanted anything else to drink.

"I hope you don't have anywhere else to be tonight, Mrs. Langdon. We could be here awhile," Czarcik warned. She shook her head. He turned to the waitress. "A double Cutty on the rocks."

"For you, miss?" the waitress asked.

"A glass of wine. White, please. Whatever kind you have." The waitress nodded, seeing no need to furnish Chloe with the name of the wine she would be bringing.

Czarcik watched the woman walk back to the bar. When she was out of earshot, he turned to Chloe. "OK, Mrs. Langdon, I guess the first—"

"Chloe," she interrupted. "If we're going to be seeing a lot of each other, and I'm afraid we are, it's Chloe."

"Chloe . . ." He liked the way her name sounded as the syllables rolled off his tongue. "I guess we should start with the obvious. But first, I need to let you know, I'll be your only contact with both the Bureau of Judicial Enforcement and the Chicago Police Department. I don't want you talking to anyone, no matter who they are or who they say they are. If you have any questions about that, you check with me first. This might sound irregular to you, but it's necessary. Is that clear?"

If she found it odd, she didn't show it. She nodded.

"I'm assuming you saw me on TV, or on the internet, identified as the detective working the Fernandez murders?"

"That's correct. I googled the case after I found these folders. My husband's folders."

"Well, if you watched the entire press conference, you would know that we have a suspect in custody. What makes you think we have the wrong man?"

"Because unless my husband is psychic and in the habit of collecting newspaper articles about people who are about to be murdered, he's responsible."

"Where is your husband now?"

"I don't know." She paused. "But unless we find him quickly, a lot more people will die."

The waitress returned with their drinks. "Can I bring you some food?" she asked.

Czarcik motioned to Chloe. "If you're hungry, it's obviously on me."

She shook her head. "Just the wine, thank you."

"Nothing for me either," he told the waitress. Again waiting until she was gone, he gulped down the Cutty, feeling as revitalized as a Bedouin drawing from a desert well. "Why don't you start at the beginning? Tell me everything."

Chloe took a sip of wine. Her red lipstick left a ghostly print on the glass, a permanent reminder of her presence. She closed her eyes and furrowed her brow.

She took a deep breath and began. "I'm not exactly sure what's relevant in your line of police work, Detective. So if there's something I'm not explaining correctly, or something extraneous, please don't hesitate to interrupt me."

Extraneous. She was educated. Even if most people knew the word and understood its definition, they didn't use it in casual conversation. Instead, they said *useless,* or maybe *unnecessary.*

Still, she wasn't trying to impress him. Putting on airs. Her speech was natural, slightly eloquent. It didn't have the forced cadence of someone trying to sound intelligent.

"Let me worry about that. The more you can tell me, the better," Czarcik assured her, trying to appear as sympathetic as his nature would allow. "But I may interject sometimes with additional questions."

She nodded and took another sip of wine. He could tell she was an infrequent drinker. "I'll start with the cancer."

Czarcik surprised himself by feeling a pang of compassion for this woman whom he barely knew. "I'm sorry."

She waved him off. "Not me. My husband. Daniel."

"I'm still sorry."

She nodded and continued. "About six months ago, Daniel was diagnosed with Grade IV glioblastoma. Do you have any background in medicine, Detective? They call it the Terminator for a reason. It's a virtual death sentence." She held the stem of her glass and made circles, generating tiny whirlpools in the wine, seeming to lose herself momentarily in the miniature funnels. "I know I sound cold," she said finally. "Clinical. But I assure you, it's taken me a long time to get to this point. You should have seen me the first month."

"We all deal with grief in different ways. I've seen people erupt in hysterical laughter at the funeral of a loved one."

He wondered if his given example was inappropriate, but it didn't seem to bother Chloe.

"The doctor gave him about a year. Optimistically. Realistically, after one particularly brutal appointment, he admitted that it would probably be a lot less."

"There was nothing they could do? No treatment? Not even experimental?"

Chloe shook her head. "It was far too advanced for chemo or radiation, and surgery would have killed him on the spot. The tumors were wrapped completely around the brain stem and metastasizing quickly. It's the kind of situation where they sit you down in a room and tell you to make sure you have all your affairs in order. The prescription? Enjoy the time you have left."

"This came on quickly, this cancer? Out of nowhere? No signs, no warnings?"

"Looking back, you know, you always remember things. Hindsight is what it is. Maybe he was forgetting things more than usual. A couple of headaches. But nothing catastrophic that you couldn't chalk up to stress or simply getting older. Those silly little things we joke about being senior moments."

Czarcik held up his empty glass and motioned to the waitress. "More wine?" he asked Chloe. She shook her head.

"Naturally, once we got the news, Daniel quit his job immediately."

"What line of work was he in?"

"He was an engineer at CellCom out in Naperville. Been there over ten years. He had a pretty senior position. Well-liked by all his coworkers. You know, you always hear these horror stories about how cold and callous large corporations can be, but CellCom couldn't have been more accommodating. When he explained to his boss the reason he was leaving, the company offered to keep him on salary until . . . well, you know."

"You're right, usually you hear the opposite. Corporations aren't generally known for their benevolence."

"We were very lucky in that regard. We were also fortunate that I never had to work. Full time that is. Daniel was compensated well for the majority of his employment." She sighed. "So . . . we did exactly what the doctors ordered. What most people would dream of doing. Took one big trip to Italy. But that kind of travel wore Daniel out quickly. So instead we did a lot of driving. He liked that. Taking country roads through small towns, venturing off the beaten path to go antiquing. Saw a lot of plays. A lot of movies." She laughed. "If I never hear the phrase 'farm to table' again, it will be too soon."

The waitress brought Czarcik another drink. She glanced at Chloe's glass and didn't even bother asking.

"Other than the illness, sounds like the perfect life."

Chloe stared across the bar, lost in memories of a world far different from the one represented in the photos of prewar Kiev that lined the walls. "It was," she said quietly, giving herself a few seconds to compose herself before taking a sip of wine. Czarcik didn't press. She would continue when she was ready.

"Then, about a month ago, something changed." She chewed on her lip. "It sounds so clichéd. Like I rehearsed it, but other than saying a dark cloud came over him, I don't know how else to describe it."

"His mood changed. His personality," Czarcik offered.

"Drastically."

"Precipitated by the cancer, I presume?"

Chloe smiled. "I like to think so. Personality changes, even drastic ones, are common at this stage in the disease's progression." There was something about the way she said this. Czarcik thought she desperately wanted to believe it.

"I know it's personal, but I'd like to hear the specifics about these personality changes."

"That's fine, but I should probably start with what Daniel was like before. Before he got sick. You know, we'll have been married twenty years this coming January." She snorted bitterly. "Some anniversary."

Czarcik forced out a small compassionate smile.

"Anyway," Chloe continued, "we met at the University of Wisconsin. Up in Madison. I was finishing up my degree in comp lit, and he was a graduate student in engineering. I was working part time at the university bookstore. That was when bookstores still sold books, instead of stuffed animals and god-awful vinyl releases of albums that had never been released on vinyl in the first place." She blushed. "I'm sorry, that's Daniel talking. He was a bit of an audiophile."

"The good old days," Czarcik corroborated.

"I keep getting off track. Where were we?"

"You met in the bookstore."

"Right. He needed a book. I showed him where it was, we got to talking, and he asked me out for coffee." She fiddled with her drink. "It's funny; I'll never forget the name. *Fluid Mechanics and Circuit Analysis.* Can you possibly think of anything more boring?"

Smiling. "I can't."

"For our one-year anniversary, he gave me a wrapped copy." She began to cry.

Chloe continued with her story. Her demeanor changed. She became more serious, less wistful. But there was something else, thought Czarcik. He could tell she was now *working.*

The memories that came easily, the life snapshots that may as well have been recalled from a favorite movie or beloved book, were replaced by careful deliberation. She was trying her best to build a profile of the man she loved with pieces that had not yet crystallized in her consciousness.

Or pieces that needed to be invented. Czarcik wasn't about to swallow the grieving-widow routine just yet, even if nothing Chloe had told him thus far raised suspicion.

"Daniel was one of those people you would describe, superficially, by saying 'everybody loved him.' But if you knew him well, that wasn't entirely true. Everybody *liked* him." She realized how this came out and clarified her statement. "I don't mean this as a judgment. He was as good a man as there was."

It wasn't lost on Czarcik that Chloe had started referring to her husband in the past tense.

"What I mean is that although he had a ton of acquaintances, he didn't have a lot of close friends. I think some of it was the result of him being an only child with hardly any family. But he wasn't socially awkward or anything. In fact, he could be extremely charming. But at heart, I think he preferred to be alone."

"Nothing wrong with valuing one's privacy. Reminds me of myself." Czarcik surprised himself by revealing this much unprompted. He chalked it up to the liquor, even though he was only on his second double Cutty.

Or those eyes. Those eyes were doing something to him.

"No, nothing at all," Chloe agreed. He prompted her to continue. "Well, to make a long story short, after Madison we moved to Chicago. Daniel received an offer from ClearTel that was too good to pass up. Remember them? They had those goofy commercials with the animated wire that was constantly looking for something to connect to. But it can't, because the world has gone wireless."

"I do remember those commercials," Czarcik recalled, "and they *were* goofy."

"Phallic too." She paused to gauge his reaction. "Daniel would tell me the marketing folks would have knock-down, drag-out fights about how large and rounded the pins in the cartoon plugs could be."

"Now I know why my cell phone bill was so high. Research and development."

"Cell phones were really taking off during this time. They'd gone from a convenience to a necessity, literally overnight, and the company couldn't build out its network fast enough. Workers with Daniel's skills were in high demand."

"Did you work as well?"

Chloe looked down into her wineglass. "I worked at our local branch of the Chicago Public Library. Wasn't brain surgery, but it suited me."

"Most jobs aren't brain surgery . . . besides brain surgery."

"There you go," she said, smiling. "I meant that it wasn't the most challenging job. But I was surrounded by books, which were my passion. And the truth is, because of Daniel's job, we didn't really need the money. I forget if the term *yuppie* was still used at the time, but it described us perfectly."

Try as he might, Czarcik couldn't picture Chloe working in a library. While the literary part fit, the drudgery of the job—filing, stacking, refiling, restacking—seemed a bit stifling. Unlike most people who instinctively tried to sound smarter than they were, Chloe seemed to be the rare type to downplay her pretensions. At that moment he realized why she wasn't drinking. It wasn't because she wasn't a drinker, but because she didn't enjoy a ten-dollar bottle of shitty chardonnay and didn't feel the need to pretend to.

Czarcik swirled the ice in his glass, listening to the familiar clink, clink, clink. "Again, my aim isn't to make you uncomfortable, but I'm sure you can guess my next question."

She smiled without looking up. "Kids." His silence was an affirmation. A long pause. "We both wanted them, of course," she admitted. "Me probably more than him, but nevertheless, it was in our plans. We tried the natural way . . ." She blushed, or was simply flushed from the few sips of wine. Czarcik couldn't tell which. "When that didn't work, we saw doctors. Endless doctors. The problem was with me. A congenital defect of the fallopian tube. No need to go into the details, but pregnancy wasn't unlikely, it was impossible."

"Adoption?"

"I wanted to, Daniel didn't." She looked him right in the eye. "I know what you're thinking, Detective. You're a cynic, and a cynic would think this was a convenient out for a man who never wanted to have children in the first place."

It's not what Czarcik was thinking, but he didn't deny the accusation. Her intuition revealed more about herself than it did him. So he just let her continue.

"But that wasn't it at all." She took a deep breath. "He didn't want to adopt a child because he admitted that he could never love it as much as he would love his own. I tried to convince him otherwise. Because for me, I knew it *would* feel like my own. I explained that adoptive parents were just as devoted as biological ones, often more so." A tear didn't fall but took shape in the corner of her eye. "He told me there was a difference between devotion and love and couldn't live with himself pretending there wasn't." She blinked, and the tear was gone. "I wanted kids so badly . . . but I knew he was right."

"As much as you wanted children, you never considered leaving him? For some couples, that's a deal breaker."

Chloe looked at him hard, her blue eyes darkening to near black. She reached across the table affectionately. The contact was electric, and Czarcik pulled back in surprise. "You've never been married, Detective. Or even in love."

It wasn't a question.

She leaned close to him, almost whispering. "Otherwise, you'd know that you'd do *anything* for the one you loved."

Suddenly, those eyes were no longer a window, but a mirror. He didn't want to look into them anymore. In fact, he didn't want to be here at all. But since they were far from finished, he drank the remainder of his drink, caught the waitress's attention, and raised his empty glass.

Neither spoke until the waitress returned with his drink. Czarcik eagerly downed half of it. And just as the burn of the liquor abated, so did the cloud that had momentarily obscured their conversation.

"Where were we?" he asked with renewed focus and interest.

"I mentioned the changes I began to see in Daniel. The . . . *darkness*. One night, after a particularly bad day, we were lying in bed. He looked up at the ceiling and just said, 'I can't take it anymore.' And you know what I said to him? I said, 'I know.'"

Czarcik finished his drink.

Chloe continued. "The next week—our final one together—was pure bliss. Daniel was a changed man. Full of energy and passion. I didn't know what was real, what he was faking, and what might be a placebo effect at having embraced the inevitable. And to be honest, I didn't really care. I just gave in to it. Allowed myself to live in the moment. We made love every day, sometimes for hours. After, we'd read Dickinson, Whitman, and Frost to each other, and not ironically. Especially Frost. He was Daniel's favorite. He loved the profound simplicity of his poems.

"We bought the most indulgent foods at Moveable Feast—pâté, caviar, foie gras—and made picnics in Lincoln Park near the Peace Garden. We spent lazy afternoons at the Museum of Contemporary Art and the Art Institute, as well as these weird little galleries in Old Town.

"So at the end of the week, we're lying in bed. I'm absolutely exhausted. He sees my eyes closing. He takes my face in his hands, kisses my lips softly, and says, 'I will always love you.'" Chloe allowed the moment to sink in. "When I woke up, he was gone. I knew I'd never see him again."

She was finished. But for Czarcik, this was the critical part of the story. He couldn't afford for her to get lost in a tangled memory vortex. "You didn't contact the police?" he asked.

"It was his choice. What he wanted. I owed him that much."

"Did you have any idea where he was going?"

Chloe looked at Czarcik as if dumbfounded. He saw the question in her eyes: Could he really have missed the implication of what she had left unspoken? Just as she opened her mouth to add something more, he spoke. "He was going to kill himself."

Now she *did* clarify. "He was going to die . . . on his terms."

"I understand," Czarcik said quietly. And although he did understand, he pressed on. "You had no idea where he went? Where he was going to end it? What he was going to do with his time left?"

Chloe shook her head. "All I knew was that he withdrew two hundred and fifty thousand dollars from our savings account."

The amount startled Czarcik. "And that was fine with you? You weren't afraid? I don't want to be crass, but all that money going up in smoke had to make you nervous."

She smiled. "Like I told you, Detective, Daniel did *very* well. We didn't live ostentatiously, and we had no children or dependents. Trust me, he wasn't leaving me destitute."

"Still . . . you weren't curious about what he needed that much money for?"

Chloe shook her head. "If he needed it, he needed it."

Czarcik finished his drink and motioned to the waitress. "Haven't you had enough?" Her tone was more curious than judgmental or accusatory.

"Is it making you uncomfortable?"

She rolled her eyes. "I just didn't know cops typically drank this much on duty."

"Cops don't." Paused. "At least not openly."

The waitress arrived. "Another drink?"

Czarcik glanced playfully at Chloe. "No, thank you. That will be all."

The waitress gave him a confused look and took his empty glass back to the bar. "Please, go on," Czarcik encouraged.

Her body visibly relaxed. The hard part was over. The rest was just details, as important as they were. "And then I found the folders," Chloe said, referencing the pivotal event that led her to this point. "The ones right in front of you."

Czarcik leafed through them, not really looking at anything inside. "Tell me about that."

"There's an unfinished part of our basement. It's where the washer and dryer used to be. But we moved those upstairs for convenience. We never redid it. No point. Daniel built some wooden shelves that I used for my canning." Czarcik shook his head, not understanding. "I make preserves in my spare time. Usually just strawberries and blueberries, but I've made raspberry and peach in the past. One summer we spent some time up in Michigan, and I brought back some rhubarb to try. But that's really more of a spring fruit."

He wanted to tell her that he didn't give a shit about spring fruit, summer fruit, winter fruit, or any fruit for that matter. He wanted to hear about the folders, but he allowed her to continue at her own pace.

"The other side of the basement Daniel used for a workspace. Not really an office, but a place where he could fool around with his gadgets. He liked to tinker with electronics and things like that. He had dozens of plastic containers filled with microchips, transistors, wires, tiny screws—all those hobbyist things. I knew I was going to have to clean it out eventually. Otherwise they would have been a constant reminder of him. And that wouldn't be healthy. But at the time, it was just comforting for me to wander around the space. Feeling his presence everywhere. That's when I saw the folders sticking out of an old cardboard box. At first, I just assumed they were warranties or other papers that should have been filed away in his upstairs office, where he kept the important documents. Or maybe some old issues of *Popular Mechanics* . . ."

Chloe finally took a sip of wine.

"When I opened the folders, my heart sank. I'm embarrassed to tell you what my first thought was."

There was no need to tell him. Czarcik was well acquainted with what kinds of unspeakable things were usually recovered from criminals' private lairs.

"But then I chastised myself," Chloe continued. "I knew Daniel as well as you can know a person. He wasn't some pervert. Some sadist. Then I read the articles. They were all stories of horrific abuse or suffering, printed out rather recently. I couldn't imagine why someone as sensitive as him would want to read them, much less collect them."

The reason was all too obvious to Czarcik.

"Naturally, my curiosity got the best of me. So I googled all the stories, wanting to see if there were any updates, because some of them were years old. Out of the six cases, the perpetrators in two of them had been violently murdered." She took another sip of wine, struggling with giving voice to the truth. "Even though one of the cases had a suspect—the Fernandez murders, which is how I knew to contact you—I understood immediately what Daniel had done."

On the surface, it all made sense. No gaping holes, no flaws in her logic. And if there was one truism more true than even *the spouse did it*, it was Occam's razor: the simplest explanation is usually the right one.

Yet something about this story, this confession, bothered him.

He wasn't sure whether it was the story or Chloe herself. Each was eminently believable. But there was also something about being *too* perfect. And in many ways, that's what this was. The story was the perfect tragedy, Chloe the perfect martyr. But real life didn't usually work like that. It was messy. Messy and confusing.

"Let me play devil's advocate, Chloe. These were all bad people. Some of them outright criminals with long rap sheets. Surely it isn't inconceivable that a few of them would meet a violent end?"

"Then why would he have printed the articles? And saved them?"

He nodded. She had a point.

She picked up her purse and placed it on the table. She reached inside, pulled out a receipt, and handed it to Czarcik. "It's for Thiopental. Do you know what that is?"

"I don't, but I have no doubt you're going to tell me."

"It's a very fast-acting animal barbiturate. Sometimes given to pets before they're put down. Well, we didn't have any pets."

She waited for Czarcik to fill in the blanks.

"But none of the victims had Thib—whatever it's called, or anything like that in their systems. I've seen the autopsy reports myself."

"Did you see the one on the chicken?" she asked. "The one that I read was tied around that woman's neck?"

"We're not in the habit of doing autopsies on animals," Czarcik said a little defensively. This wasn't actually true, and he was slightly embarrassed he hadn't authorized it.

"Well, if you had, I'm certain you would have found it in the animal's system. Daniel was so gentle. He wouldn't have wanted to hurt an animal. But if he had to, he would have made sure to cause it the least amount of discomfort."

While not exactly a smoking gun, the Thiopental did bolster Chloe's case. But what she didn't realize was that Czarcik was already convinced. After all, what was more likely? That this ordinary man just happened to print out articles of random crimes, then grew obsessed with the cases and gathered personal information on the perpetrators, only to have these perpetrators suddenly die in especially grisly ways? Or Occam's razor?

"You wouldn't happen to have any pictures of your husband on you, would you?" Czarcik asked.

Chloe looked at him like he had lost his mind. "Of course I do. Hundreds." She handed him her iPhone. "Just flip through them," she instructed.

Czarcik studied the first photo on the screen: Daniel reclining on a puffy chair, his feet up on the ottoman. In one hand, he held a beverage. His other was draped across Chloe's body as she slept contentedly with her head on his chest.

Chloe had obviously chosen her favorite photos to store on her phone. But Czarcik wasn't interested in an impromptu slideshow. He cared about one thing—whether the man with the kind eyes and easy smile could conceivably be Groucho. He flicked his finger right to left a few more times across the screen: the happy couple on the slopes of Vail; hiking in the forests of Appalachia; Daniel behind the wheel of a Chris-Craft motorboat, his glasses spotted with mist, his thick dirty-blond hair damp, looking positively Kennedyesque.

There was no reason that the man in these photos could not have been Groucho.

Nor was there any way for Czarcik to reconcile the happy husband with the masked lunatic who had broken into his home. "Thank you," he said as he handed the phone back to Chloe.

"Did you recognize him?" she asked, her eyes narrowing.

Czarcik shook his head. She gave him some time to reconsider. "But the two of you look very happy," he quickly added.

Usually, Czarcik could have polished off a few more double Cuttys with little effect. But exhaustion lowered his tolerance. The adrenaline rush he felt after learning new information about a case had long since dissipated. Chloe, too, had to be growing weary. Her psychic burden was much larger. "Chloe, just one more question."

She waited, expectant.

"When you found the articles, after your suspicions were confirmed, why did you contact the police?"

She looked at him with a combination of incredulity and pity, as if he were nothing more than a child, forever unable to grasp the simplest of concepts.

"Because it was the right thing to do," she replied.

And lied.

Chloe was a fine actress, thought Czarcik. Eminently believable. She had no tell, the kind that damns a poker player or nervous criminal. But the moment the words left her mouth, Czarcik could not have been more certain. He knew beyond a shadow of a doubt that she was lying. He wasn't sure how he knew. That would come later when he had time to play their conversation over and over again in his mind. But he was equally certain that if he pushed, if he probed for any weakness or inconsistency, she would pick up on it—if only unconsciously—and become much harder to read.

For now, he had to play along. "Of course" was the safest response.

"So . . . what do we do now?" Chloe asked.

Czarcik shifted in the booth, stretching his aching muscles, suddenly reminded of how long they had been sitting there. "Well, I'd like some time to review those files of yours. I assume that's OK?" She nodded. "And then, well, I'll attempt to do what we both want done."

"And what's that?"

"Find your husband."

As if it were a sign that it was time, for now, to conclude their meeting, the door to the restaurant swung open. Two large and very drunk Eastern Europeans made a beeline for the bar, conducting that inebriated dance where one lost his balance only to be rescued at the last minute by the other, after which the roles would reverse.

"I'd like to be involved as much as possible, Detective. After all, if it weren't for me, the trail would be cold."

Such presumption would normally have bothered Czarcik, as would Chloe's use of colloquialisms she had probably gleaned from too many Dick Wolf procedurals. He could have easily told her that allowing a civilian too much access to an active investigation was completely against department protocol, which, of course, it was.

But there was something not entirely unappealing about having to see Chloe Langdon again.

It's because of the lie, he told himself. *Why did she lie about contacting me?*

"I'll keep you apprised," Czarcik assured her. "After all, nobody knows him as well as you do."

They exchanged contact information, and she thanked him for the wine. After a few more awkward goodbye formalities, Chloe took his arm firmly.

"There's one more thing you should know about my husband, Detective Czarcik. When he begins something, he always finishes it."

"Glad to hear that. Because so do I."

SEVENTEEN

Driving home from Dnieper, he called Corrine Fumagalli at home. She answered on the third ring.

"Corrine. It's Paul Czarcik."

"When I said I'd miss you, I didn't mean so soon."

"Very funny." He could hear her chewing. "Were you eating dinner?"

"Nah, Slim Jim. And playing *Punic Wars: Hannibal's Revenge.*"

"What's that?"

"MMOG. Massively multiplayer—ah, forget it. You're too old." Chomp, chomp. "Why you calling me at home?"

"I need a favor."

"That much I figured."

"I need any information you have on a Daniel Langdon." He spelled it.

"Got it. Call you in the morning." He could hear soft music and the sounds of electronic warfare in the background. She had gone back to playing.

"No chance you're going back to the office tonight?"

She laughed. "No chance." He was about to hang up. "Especially since I'm not even sure you still work for the bureau."

"Then call it a personal favor."

"Tomorrow morning."

Czarcik hung up, searched through the contacts on his phone, and dialed another number.

"This is Detective Paul Czarcik of the Illinois Bureau of Judicial Enforcement . . . Yes, that's right . . . I need to see you right away. Where are you? . . . Ten minutes."

King Kong and Godzilla—Kong on his left, 'Zilla on his right—ushered him through the back door of the Italian restaurant.

The restaurant was closed, but Sal Cicci sat alone at a table in the back, dressed in an expensive suit and drinking a glass of red wine. If he had been roused from bed, he certainly didn't show it.

Czarcik's escorts walked him halfway through the restaurant. Cicci motioned to the empty chair across from him and poured Czarcik a glass of wine.

"Want some friendly business advice?" Czarcik asked, slipping into the chair. "You want to look like a legitimate real estate player"—he jerked his thumb at Cicci's muscle—"lose Tweedledum and Tweedledee. Potential investors don't like to feel like they're walking into a scene from *The Godfather*."

Cicci wasn't pleased. "You ask me here, when I should be at home, spending time with my family, and then you give me a hard time about my employees?"

"Take it easy, Sal. I'm just kidding."

"Well, I'm not in the mood for it. You guys are getting a hell of a lot of mileage out of me for nothing."

"Nothing? I wouldn't call it nothing that the state's attorney hasn't had the time to take a closer look at your business practices."

Cicci took a long swig and poured himself some more wine. "You motherfuckers keep taking your pound of flesh. So tell me, what the hell do you want?"

Czarcik looked over at the two bodyguards, then back to Cicci, who dismissed them with a flick of his hand. Once they were gone, he asked, "Does the name Daniel Langdon ring a bell?"

"Don't think so. Should it?"

"Probably not." He took another sip of wine. "This is excellent, Sal. I'm usually not much of a wine drinker. What is it?"

"A 2008 Brunello di Montalcino," Cicci said impatiently. "Look, can we finish up here? I want to get home."

"If somebody was moving nearly a quarter million in cash through the city—in what, I don't know. Guns, drugs, whatever. Would you know about it?"

"Cicci Industries is a diversified portfolio of—"

"Cut the shit, Sal," Czarcik yelled, pounding his fist on the table. Cicci grabbed the stem of his glass before it could topple over. His two employees returned to the room but Cicci held up a hand, stopping them in their tracks.

To Czarcik, he said, "I would know about it."

"This Daniel Langdon. I don't think he's anybody you should or will know. But I want you to remember the name. You hear it, among any of your . . . businesses, you give me a call."

Cicci nodded, and Czarcik stood up. He finished his wine, then reached across and polished off Cicci's glass. "Oh, what the hell." He grabbed the wine bottle from the table and took it with him to the door. "Damn fine wine," he said before leaving the restaurant.

He could feel Cicci's eyes on the back of his head, and knew that the mobster would have loved to put a bullet there.

His BlackBerry vibrated the moment he got back into the Crown Vic.

"Czarcik."

It was Corrine. "I forgot to ask. How official do you want this?"

"Meaning what?"

"Meaning, I can get you background from the IRS, DMV, IAFIS, sex offender registry, department of corrections, or do you want me to go . . . deeper."

"What I'd really like is a snapshot of their financial health."

"Whose? You told me the name of one guy, Langdon."

"He and his wife. Her name is Chloe Langdon."

"How's bank statements and a comprehensive list of all their accounts?"

"You can do that?"

Corrine laughed. "Please. Banks—the big ones, with FDIC insurance—are as easy to hack as the utilities."

"Good girl."

"Don't call me that, prick."

He sat motionless. A subject in a lab experiment. Or a newfangled yoga pose.

Czarcik was at his desk, in his home office, hands in front of him, palms down.

Spread out in a semicircle—like large hands of blackjack—were the six folders given to him by Chloe Langdon, the contents of each removed and piled haphazardly on top. To his left, an ashtray. In one of the notches on the rim sat a cigarette, its ash nearly the length of the cigarette itself.

His eyes moved across the surface of his desk. Back and forth. He was seeing the folders, but he was *thinking* about Chloe. She had been forthcoming with him. Sincere. At least for the most part. And yet she remained inscrutable.

He had spent hours interviewing her, looking into those eyes, and yet he felt it was her husband on whom he had a better handle. A husband whom he had only met in the dead of night behind a dime-store mask.

Chloe had given him the folders in no discernible order. And there was no way to tell whether her husband, Daniel, had organized them by any criteria other than sheer randomness.

So Czarcik was forced to bring some structure to the proceedings. He knew that Daniel was responsible for the murders in at least two of the cases. And he knew that the Judge Robertson murder was first. There was no question about this. So he placed a paper tent, with a #1 written in permanent black marker, on top of this folder.

Number two was the Fernandez murders.

The next four were in no particular order—at least not yet. Number three, at the moment, was a pedophile priest in Tennessee accused of raping more than fifty boys, making him one of the country's most prolific serial rapists.

Number four was Miriam Manor. Number five was a trucker from Minnesota with a little drinking problem. And number six was a private reform school that sounded more like a North Korean reeducation camp.

Czarcik then printed out a map of the United States. He took a Sharpie and drew circles around the locations of all the crimes detailed in the folders: Dallas; Chicago; Duluth, Minnesota; Tennessee; rural Indiana; and the Everglades.

From Dallas, the scene of Judge Robertson's murder, he drew a line directly to Chicago, mostly following I-35, where the Fernandezes had been killed.

He leaned back in his chair and allowed his eyes to roam over the map. If Daniel was being logical, if time was of the essence, and if he was not actively trying to evade the authorities—all of which Czarcik assumed to be true—from Chicago he would have either gone to Minnesota or Indiana.

By going to Indiana first, he would have then had to backtrack to reach Minnesota, and then double back through Indiana in order to reach Tennessee and finally Florida.

But if he first went to Minnesota from Chicago, he basically had a straight shot through Indiana, Tennessee, and then Florida.

Of course, he could do something completely illogical, like traveling from Chicago down to Florida, then back up through Tennessee, over to Indiana, and across the Upper Midwest to Minnesota. But that route seemed the longest and least likely.

He made an educated guess that Daniel's third stop was Duluth. He put a #3 on the folder of the drunk driver. Then he reordered the other folders. So #4 went on Miriam Manor in Indiana, #5 on Tennessee, and #6 on the warm, wet Everglades in Florida.

Occam's razor . . .

On the map, beginning in Dallas, Czarcik drew one continuous line that connected all the cities in numerical order. Upon close inspection, it looked like a misshapen, upside-down V.

Pleased with his progress, Czarcik lit another cigarette and poured himself a couple of fingers of Cutty, neat.

He was far too wired to even think about sleep and still baffled by some aspects of his theory. If Daniel had in fact followed the assumed route, why hadn't he yet reached Minnesota? And if he had, why was he waiting to claim another victim?

A quick Google search revealed that the trucker named in the accident had not yet been killed, at least not in a way violent enough to warrant inclusion in the local papers. All the entries with the trucker's name that the search engine pulled up were articles from the accident and subsequent trial.

After accessing the Minnesota secretary of state's database—perfectly legal for all BJE employees—Czarcik quickly found the address for Edgar Barnes. With a little luck, and a little nose candy to help him power through, he could be there by morning.

By midnight, Czarcik had the Crown Vic stocked with all the necessary supplies: a carton of cigarettes, a few expensive cigars, and a small baggie of the good stuff.

The Chicago expressways were uncharacteristically deserted, and Czarcik pushed the Crown Vic into Wisconsin in less than an hour. The rolling pastures of the Dairy State soon gave way to towering limestone cliffs, which, on the night of this full moon, threw long, irregular shadows across the road. Czarcik savored the taste of his twenty-dollar Romeo y Julieta and watched as the tendrils of smoke danced around the car's interior before slipping out the cracked window. He passed silo after silo, giants in the night, guarding barren fields from cosmic invasion. It wasn't until he crossed over the Black River that he felt the need for a little chemical pick-me-up.

Dawn greeted him at the border of the Gopher State, a sad, purplish morning.

He gassed up at the next rest stop, stretched his legs, took a leak, and bought a bag of salted peanuts, which he finished before returning to the car.

Czarcik was hoping to reach the home of Edgar Barnes before the trucker left for work. He wasn't confident that he could obtain the information he wanted with a phone call. Without looking the man in the eye, Czarcik feared he would be dismissed as an overanxious cop or, worse, a crank.

Barnes lived in a small development called River Run on the outskirts of Duluth. Zoning regulations seemed to require the body of a rusty automobile to be prominently displayed on cinder blocks on the front lawn of every home. The houses were all built on solid ground, but their cheap siding and plastic outdoor furniture recalled late-century trailer park.

The welcoming committee was an old man with a single gray tooth, sitting in a lawn chair on the side of the dirt road leading into the development. A dog, his elder in canine years, slept at his feet, opening one eye as cars passed by. The animal was waiting for its owner to die. Czarcik remembered a story he once heard about a hospital cat who could predict imminent death and would sit on the edge of patients' beds when the grim reaper was near. He thought this dog might have the same ability.

Barnes's house was indistinct from that of his neighbors. It was surrounded by a metal fence with a "Beware of Dog" sign hanging from a screw. The gate was open, swinging in the breeze, with no sign of the animal.

Czarcik parked in front of the house, on the street, leaving the driveway unoccupied in case Barnes just happened to be returning from a long haul. He flicked his cigarette into the damp grass from the car's open window, slipped his gun into the back of his jeans, and got out of the car.

The steps leading up to the house were fairly well maintained for the area, meaning they only squeaked loudly instead of collapsing into a pile of termite-infested wood. Behind a filthy screen door was the main door to the house with equally filthy windows. Decals from various unions going back decades were affixed to the panes. Czarcik pulled the screen door open; the well-rusted hinges screeched. He rapped on one of the windows, not too hard, afraid he might dislodge the glass.

When no one answered after a few seconds, Czarcik moved his face close to the glass, making sure not to touch it, lest he contract some communicable disease. He squinted into the gloom. The living room—or what he presumed was the living room from the presence of a dilapidated couch and TV—was empty. He knocked again, fully anticipating the same result.

Still no one came to the door, so Czarcik descended the steps and walked around to the back of the house. He saw a concrete patio with jagged fault lines, the result of endless Minnesota winters, from which an abundance of weeds had sprouted. A cobweb-covered Weber grill, its ash catch overflowing, recalled barbeques long forgotten. Children's toys from the seventies were strewn across what was left of the backyard's brown grass. The Barnes family didn't seem to be much for entertaining.

Czarcik took in the white-trash ambiance before returning to the front door, knocking a little harder this time. He thought he heard a slight rustling from within, but it very well could have been his imagination or simply the wind blowing through the cracked glass of the outdoor porch light. Inside the metal housing, piled to the top, was a mound of moth parts. The beacon that precipitated their demise had burned out long ago.

The screen door was cracked open far enough for Czarcik to touch the main door without causing any undue noise. He grasped the doorknob with both hands to minimize the sound and turned it, hardly surprised to find it open. The savory stench of human odor comingled with rotten food slapped him in the face as he stepped inside and quietly closed the door behind him.

Rods of diffused sunlight sliced through the moth-eaten curtains. Weirdly illuminated dust hung in the air as if suspended in a solution. Czarcik's stomach rolled at the thought of breathing in this mixture of insect parts and dandruff. The smell of stale cigarette smoke, which hung over the room, was a welcome relief.

A day-old TV dinner lay on the coffee table in front of the couch. The now-shriveled chicken hung over the aluminum partition, resting on the adjacent congealed gravy. The final item, the mashed potatoes, looked as hard as concrete.

The living room was separated from the kitchen by a chest-high wall that went halfway across the room. From his position by the door, Czarcik could see through the kitchen window into the backyard, where a few mangy squirrels now played tag atop the Weber.

A pile of magazines lay at the foot of the couch, as if the reader was too lazy to simply place them on the table. Czarcik made a bet with himself. Among the periodicals, he would find at least one tabloid newspaper, one lowbrow home and garden magazine, and one devoted to outdoor pursuits. He bent down and leafed through the stack. *Guns & Ammo*, *Field & Stream*, *National Enquirer*, *US Weekly*, and an issue of *Redbook* from last year. People, like crimes, were so predictable. It was amazing how the different strata of society hewed so closely to their stereotypes. Did the Barneses actually enjoy these pursuits, he wondered. Or did they think this was what they were supposed to read, what they were supposed to have, how they were expected to live. *Like fucking animals.*

As he stood back up, a familiar click from behind jostled him out of his musings. Then a double-barreled shotgun was jammed into his kidney.

"Hands up, mister. Real slow." She pronounced the *o* as if she were having an orgasm. Pure Minnesotan.

Czarcik complied. She was big and hardy, capable with a firearm but still clinging to the last vestiges of her country femininity.

"Take it easy," Czarcik said in his most reassuring voice, the one he used to use on the streets when he had to talk down a dealer with the shakes and a gun. "I'm a police officer from Chicago."

"And I'm a citizen of the United States of America," she countered. "And I know my rights. You're trespassing on private property—so I have the right to shoot you dead."

She was partially correct, although Czarcik didn't think he was in a position to educate her on the vagaries of the law, which would undoubtedly be used as precedent were she to make good on her threat and subsequently face trial. Instead, he thought it best to appeal to the less analytical side of her brain.

"You're right, ma'am, but I came to help you."

"You got a warrant?"

"I said I'm here to help you, not arrest you."

She pulled the muzzle back and jabbed him in the rib cage again. "That's a laugh. Cops coming to help. What's one all the way from Chicago want with me?"

"May I turn around?" When he didn't receive another poke, he turned slowly to face her, hands up in a gesture of surrender. She raised the gun and moved it toward his neck, too close for his liking. But he could tell by the tension in her finger that she wasn't ready to shoot. Looking directly into her eyes, he began speaking in a slow and steady tone, feigning gravitas with every word. The effect was almost hypnotic, as he'd hoped.

Then, in one swift motion, he slapped the barrel to the side, wrapped his fingers around the warm steel, and yanked it from her hands as she cried out in surprise.

In less than a split second, their roles were reversed.

She fell right on her ass and scurried backward until she hit the wall. "If you're going to kill me, make it quick," she pleaded, genuinely frightened.

"I told you; I'm a cop."

She laughed. People like her, who lived in River Run and considered flypaper an acceptable form of pest control, had little faith in the benevolence of the police.

Czarcik placed the stock of the gun on the ground and rested the weapon against his leg. He reached into his pocket for his wallet and showed her his badge. She squinted for what she no doubt considered an appropriate amount of time and nodded officially; for all she knew, it could have been a badge for mall security.

He grasped the double barrel and extended his arm, handing her back the weapon. A peace offering. "Here. Can we talk now?"

She staggered to her feet, took the gun back, and motioned to the couch. There were a million places he would have rather sat—including the edge of a septic tank—but he didn't want to insult her. They took their places on opposite sides of the couch, and he felt something beneath the cushions crunch under his weight. He didn't even want to think about what it could be. *The bones of dead vermin are brittle.*

"I'm looking for Edgar Barnes," he told her.

"I'm his wife, Mona Travers. He's given me enough shit; I didn't want his name too." Czarcik couldn't tell if she was trying to be funny. "He in trouble?" she asked.

"I'm not sure yet."

Mona shook her head, more annoyed than frightened. Obviously, Edgar and trouble went together like Velveeta and Hamburger Helper.

"Christ, this isn't about that bitch in a wheelchair again, is it?" she asked, now full of piss and vinegar.

"What do you mean?"

"I mean, how long are some people going to live in the past for? Edgar paid his dues to society. Too long for just an accident if you ask me. But she sued, like all of them do. We've paid her all we can already, so no matter how many of you she sends out to collect, you're not squeezing another penny out of us."

His fantasy was brief but powerful—splitting the woman's head open with the butt of the shotgun. The image disturbed him. Not because of its violence; he was more than at peace with his own basest instincts. But because she had managed to elicit this emotion. He was no stranger to vile individuals so deluded with self-pity they believed themselves the victims of the crimes they committed. This had never made him angry before. If he had allowed himself to care for the real victims—in this case, wheelchair-bound Carlee Ames—his career would have ended long ago.

But then he realized it wasn't anger he felt. It was envy. Envy of Daniel. Czarcik had read the *Reader's Digest* story too, which Daniel had so kindly left in what was now folder number three. Had he been free from societal constraints and ramifications, as Daniel was, he would have killed Ms. Mona Travers on the spot just to restore a sense of cosmic justice to the universe.

Czarcik shook his head, trying to clear his thoughts. He was getting too close to Hollywood territory. All those stupid movies where the detective begins to empathize with the killer. These films would usually begin with a poorly translated quote from Nietzsche. The one about looking into the abyss. And the abyss looking back.

When he realized he had been silent for too long, he said, "That's not the issue," barely remembering what the issue was. "I'm here because we have reason to believe that your husband might be in danger."

"It's that ass Cletus," she blurted out with absolute certainty. A situation like this was in her purview. The fact that a cop might stop by to warn her about her husband's safety from a man named Cletus didn't surprise or disturb her. "I told Eddie not to lend him that two hundred. I tell him all the time, he's got too good a heart. But don't you think three months is enough time to expect it back?"

Everything about Mona Travers annoyed Czarcik. He was so tired of traveling to places where the perceived theft of the equivalent of one month's cable bill could lead to murder. He had come to accept this in the city, where you could be killed for anything. But even in the hinterlands, where the faces and the speech were different, it was the same. No one valued life anymore, except their own.

Czarcik had no reason to disabuse her of the notion that his visit had something to do with this Cletus character. "What I'm more interested in, ma'am, is your husband's schedule. Is he employed by a single company? Does he have a consistent route?"

"Been working for Stampft the past two years. Before that, he did a decade or so with Fulbright. Last few months he's been running potash from the mines in Hastings all the way across the Rockies and into San Diego."

"Any idea if he uses the same route each time?"

"The *fastest* route each time," she clarified. "Sooner he gets there, sooner he gets back, sooner he can go out again to make a living."

"I assume he can't make it on a straight shot?"

"Probably *could*," she said defensively, as if he was questioning her husband's work ethic. "But I don't let him. Seen too many truckers get highway hypnosis and end up in a gully. He usually picks up his haul around quitting time. Drives a few hours and then gets some shut-eye at a rest stop near Rochester. Sleeps there for a few hours and then, depending on the weather, calls it a night again somewhere around Denver."

"This truck stop in Rochester. He always stops there?"

"They got the nicest showers. Plus, he's got some buddies out that way. They play some cards and get a bite to eat at that diner over there."

Czarcik nodded. "When was the last time you spoke to your husband?"

She hesitated for a moment. "Just last night. He was making good time somewhere in Utah."

"That's good to hear," he assured her. As he stood up to leave, his foot slipped on one of the magazines, forcing him to grab the couch to steady himself.

Mona misread his look of disgust as one of concern. "My husband . . . you think it's serious?" she asked, as if contemplating the possibility for the first time. "I always tell him to keep that Buck knife right by his side when he's on the road."

Czarcik smiled, imagining what Daniel would do if he got ahold of that Buck knife. "I'd rest easy, ma'am. That Cletus seems like he's all talk, don't you think?"

As Czarcik walked out the door, he hoped that Mona Travers would chew on that question for a long time.

EIGHTEEN

Czarcik sat in his car, drawing slowly on a cigarette. Breathing deeply. Feeling the smoke fill his lungs, the nicotine course through his veins.

From the moment he pulled up to *Casa de Barnes y Travers*, he knew that Daniel would never have killed Edgar in his home. In some ways, that was unfortunate; Mona would have made for lovely collateral damage.

But Daniel was too smart.

River Run was the kind of place where neighbors pretended to keep to themselves but were, in reality, acutely aware of outsiders. A visitor would raise suspicions, and if a cop came around later asking questions, they would remember it. Nor could he have relied on the cover of night. These residents were no nine-to-fivers, whose circadian rhythms were in sync with most of the civilized world. They were just as likely to be found outside at three in the morning as they were to be fast asleep in their prefab homes.

Czarcik tossed his still-lit butt onto the front lawn, confident that the ratio of dirt to grass would prevent an accidental flare-up.

If Minnesota, not Indiana, was Daniel's third port of call—and Czarcik was still firmly convinced it was—he would have chosen somewhere completely secluded to carry out his business. Or busy enough to ensure anonymity. Like a truck stop. And if Daniel put as much planning into every kill as he did Judge Robertson and the Fernandezes, he would certainly have been aware of Barnes's regular route and schedule.

Remaining in such close proximity to the house made him feel dirty by association, so Czarcik drove away from River Run and pulled into the nearest gas station, parking off to the side of the main building, where customers left their cars overnight to be serviced.

He lit up a cigar and googled Rochester, Minnesota, truck stops. Although there were numerous options, it was fairly obvious that Mona had been referring to the Walter Mondale Rest Area, whose website looked more appropriate for an amusement park than a place that made 90 percent of its sales from gasoline, beef jerky, and CDs of REO Speedwagon's greatest hits. The color photos of the amenities made it look like a place you almost wanted to visit.

He was about to dial the main number for the establishment when he realized he had missed a call while interviewing Mona Travers. He looked at the number. A BJE extension: Corrine. He called her right back, and she answered on the first ring.

"What did you find for me?"

"Good morning to you too," she said.

"Good morning, Corrine. Now what the fuck did you find for me?"

"Well, this couple certainly wasn't hurting for cash if that's what you were wondering."

"Lay it on me."

"They had about a million liquid. Another million tied up in short-term investments—CDs, annuities, bonds, things like that. Two mil in retirement accounts, growing slowly but steadily. And another two invested in the market. Oh, and five hundred K in company stock for a company called CellCom. Basically, these two are the poster couple for responsible fiscal planning. And filthy fucking rich. Assholes."

"Can you tell me if Daniel recently withdrew a quarter million dollars in cash?"

"I can, and he did. How'd you know that?"

"Don't worry about it. Can you tell me from where?"

"Did it in person. The Chase branch on Franklin and Madison. You know, the one right by the river."

"Thank you, Corrine."

Czarcik hung up. Even if he didn't believe Chloe's entire story, he had never really thought this was about money. Now he was certain it wasn't.

Back in the car after grabbing a coffee and taking a leak, Czarcik dialed the main number for the Walter Mondale Rest Area.

After explaining who he was, he was put on a brief hold before being transferred to a cordial young man who introduced himself as Riley Coates, vice president of regional operations. Expecting absolutely nothing, Czarcik was floored when Riley replied that his request—the archived video feed from the entrance to the rest stop—would be fairly easy to obtain. *This kid could give those dimwits back in Chicago a lesson in efficiency,* he thought. After a few more questions, Czarcik thanked the man and promised he'd be in touch.

Next, he placed a call to Chloe Langdon. Before she answered, he felt a flutter in his stomach and dismissed it as acid indigestion.

She picked up on the second ring. "Hello."

"Chloe, it's Paul Czarcik."

She waited a moment before happily exclaiming, "Detective, hello."

There was no time for pleasantries. "When Daniel left, you don't have any reason to believe he didn't use his own car, do you?"

After a few seconds, she said, "Only if he thought someone had discovered who he was. Identified him. And as far as we know, that isn't the case. I guess it's possible he could have ditched his car right away and bought another one. I mean, it's certainly not here or at his office."

"Then can you give me the make and model? And the license plate too?"

"It's a midnight-blue Lexus GS 350. And the license plate . . . can you give me a minute?"

Czarcik chewed on the cigar, which had burned itself out about halfway down, as Chloe went to locate the paperwork for her husband's automobile.

Nothing suspicious about this. In today's world of smartphones, voice recognition, and single-touch calling, nobody remembered numbers anymore. Still, in missing persons cases, where a loved one vanished, a license plate was a lifeline and would usually be memorized by anyone with a vested interest. As long as that person wanted the missing found.

"Paul?" She startled him, partly because she used his first name instead of "Detective," which she had favored. He liked the way his name sounded coming from her lips. "It's DAM, like Delta Alpha . . . Meatballs, and then the numbers three-four-seven."

"D-A-M three-four-seven," he repeated back to himself. "OK."

She gave him some time and then giggled nervously. "I guess you're not going to fill me in?"

"Honestly, Chloe, there's not much to say. I reviewed the files you gave me, and I'm trying to ascertain where your husband might go next."

"And . . ."

"And I'm not sure yet."

More awkward silence. "But you'll let me know?"

"I promise."

The rhythm of their call bothered him. It was too intimate. Too easy. Too unlike the conversations he had with strangers whom he viewed with barely concealed contempt.

"Where are you?" she asked quietly, lending further credence to his thoughts about their interaction.

"Minnesota. But I'll be home in a day or two."

"OK, let me know. Safe travels." Unnerving. And if he was really being honest with himself, everything about Chloe Langdon unnerved him.

He wasn't sure why. But like the dogged detective he was, he would find out.

And there was an added benefit. He would get to see her again.

A few hours later, Czarcik rolled into the Walter Mondale Rest Area.

After taking another leak and grabbing another black coffee, he found the management office, where he was immediately met by one Riley Coates, who arrived bearing a gift: a terabyte hard drive containing all the footage from the security camera between the dates that Czarcik had given him.

The kid would make a great partner, thought Czarcik, if only he didn't have such stupid fucking hair. It was bright red and styled—or whatever the opposite of styled was—in a miniature afro. With his freckles and bad teeth, he reminded Czarcik of Alfred E. Neuman.

"Here it is, Detective," Riley said, "just like you asked."

"It's all on here?" Czarcik was amazed at just how much media could fit on such a small device.

Riley reached out and tapped the drive that Czarcik now held. "Everything. The camera is mounted right by the entrance, angled to get a shot of the license plate of every car that enters, for situations like this, I guess. Although to be honest, nobody has ever requested it before. Least not as long as I've been here, which is a good three years."

Czarcik made sure to appear satisfied. "I don't owe you anything for the trouble?"

"For the trouble, no. The only thing that cost anything was the drive, and I cleared that with corporate. Said they were more than happy to help out in an investigation." Riley paused for a moment. "You know, one of the things we have to overcome here is people's preconceived notions of truck stops. Lot of people think we're just gas pumps and restrooms, maybe some maps back in the day, but we actually provide a lot more services—"

Czarcik touched his imaginary hat and pointed to the kid—a gesture of gratitude—and began to walk back to his car.

"Hey!" Riley called out to him. "Any way you can tell me what this is all about? We just don't get much excitement around here."

Czarcik considered his request. After all, the kid *had* gone out of his way to help. Then images of that horrible *Mad* magazine mascot filled his head.

"No," he said, and continued to his car.

The holy trinity of nicotine, caffeine, and cocaine allowed Czarcik to make excellent time on his trip back to Chicago. The only traffic he hit was just outside Milwaukee. A Brewers game had just let out, and ten thousand drunken fans were attempting to inch their way onto the highway. It was too late to take the bypass, so Czarcik found himself packed in with the other vehicles, stopping and starting, lurching forward by the inch, trying to find a break in the traffic to jump lanes.

In the car next to him, a fan wearing a plastic construction hat, emblazoned with the Brewers' retro ball-and-mitt logo, rolled down his window, screamed, and shook his fist at Czarcik in solidarity.

Czarcik gave him the finger.

The fan recoiled, shocked, as the driver of his automobile sped off, unaware of the exchange.

Czarcik pulled up in front of his apartment building after night had fallen. Storm clouds had marshaled over the lake, debating whether to advance on the city or disperse over the horizon.

Although the evening was cool and Czarcik had driven most of the way with the windows open, his back was still a sheet of water, as he had been in the same position for the better part of six hours.

His body cracked at every flexion point as he stretched, standing on his tiptoes, reaching for the full moon overhead. He needed a good long workout. Getting older was a son of a bitch. He reached into the back seat, grabbed the hard drive that Riley had given him, and shut and locked the door.

His apartment smelled stale, as if he had been gone for a week or even longer.

Worse, he couldn't shake the uncanny but irrational feeling that since Groucho's visit, his house was no longer truly his own.

Ridiculous. He was just exhausted. But as desperately as he needed sleep, he also knew he had to work quickly. If he could determine that Daniel had never been to the rest stop, and therefore never targeted Edgar Barnes, then the entire time line would be useless. On the other hand, if Daniel had sought out the trucker, as the security camera would confirm, then Czarcik's hunch was still accurate. But if it was, the question remained: Why had Daniel not finished the job?

Czarcik was getting ahead of himself.

He powered up his laptop, which was loaded with an image-stripping program. The concept was simple. The user fed various data—words, pictures, numbers, coordinates—into a modified search engine. The software would then match this input with similar data from a video feed. It was how investigators were able to so quickly identify how many times suspected bank robbers staked out a branch. Just upload mug shots of the assholes, and let the computer cull through thousands of hours of video at the speed of light.

Before connecting the terabyte drive to his laptop with a USB 3.0 cord, Czarcik poured himself a drink. Cutty, neat. Just like a glass of warm milk. He allowed his lids to rest as the images from the truck stop flew by on his screen. The program ran silently in the background, its millions of virtual eyes on high alert.

Just as Czarcik was about to slip into that fleeting state of consciousness—not sleep, but not wakefulness either, when thoughts became confused and reality malleable—he was jostled by a loud beeping.

The software had a hit.

There on the screen, the image paused, was good old DAM 347. Czarcik moved his cursor over the image and clicked the mouse. The footage played in real time. On the screen, Daniel's Lexus pulled into the truck stop and drove out of the camera's field of view.

Sure enough, Daniel had been there.

Czarcik let his head drop onto the desk. It hit the wood hard, though not hard enough to draw blood, but he was too tired to care.

So he allowed himself to sleep, queuing up the lingering mystery with the hope that his subconscious might gift him the answer by the time he awakened.

Why hadn't Daniel finished the job?

NINETEEN

Czarcik woke four hours later, inexplicably and completely refreshed.

It was a phenomenon he first noticed in high school, when he would stay out all night drinking beer with his friends. He had no idea whether this phenomenon occurred with everyone or it was a biological quirk specific to him, but without fail, the more exhausted he was, the less sleep he needed to recover.

The process seemed counterintuitive. People were always babbling on about how they were so tired they managed to sleep for ten or twelve hours straight. Not Czarcik. When he reached the point of complete and utter exhaustion, when sleep wasn't a desire but a physiological imperative, he only needed a few hours to recharge.

And recharged he was. He rubbed his face where the wood from his table had made a deep indentation, stood up, and stretched.

In the kitchen, he powered up the coffee maker and began to brew a pot without changing the filter. Drank it black and hot. Walked to the bathroom to freshen up, and estimated how long it would take him to reach rural Indiana.

It was still early in the morning, before rush hour. If he could make it out of the city and over the Skyway before the daily madness began, he could probably be there in three hours.

Now was not the time to second-guess himself.

Czarcik was certain that Indiana was the next stop on Daniel Langdon's 2018 Cross-Country Slaughter Tour. But why was it taking him so long? Over a week had passed since his car had pulled in to the Walter Mondale Rest Area.

And again, the niggling question: Why had Daniel allowed Edgar Barnes to escape? Could he still be in Minnesota, waiting? Revenge being a dish best served cold?

That didn't make sense. According to Mona Travers, Barnes had been home recently. And even if Daniel didn't want to kill the trucker in his own home, the time frame provided him plenty of opportunities to follow him to another locale. But would he take the time to follow Barnes all the way across the country? To Denver or even San Diego? As Czarcik had learned from Chloe, time was one thing that Daniel Langdon didn't have.

So many unanswered questions.

He did a bump of coke and lit up a cigarette.

Czarcik contemplated calling Miriam Manor and telling Reverend Seamus Bradley—or whomever answered the phone—to be alert for any suspicious activity.

He wasn't worried about them fleeing in panic. From what he had read, the cult—and that's what it was, a cult, not a religious boarding school—seldom left their compound. Once in a blue moon the girls would be taken to a fine establishment like Shoney's or Golden Corral, just so the reverend could tell the parents of any future residents that their daughter's stay would be filled with similar recreational outings.

What he *was* worried about was the safety of the girls. But then he recalled Chloe's story about her husband's unwillingness to adopt. Someone so concerned about his ability to properly love a child not biologically his would take every precaution to ensure no harm would come to the girls of Miriam Manor.

And although it was Czarcik's job to protect the reverend and his family, too, he didn't think a couple of hours would make a difference. He wanted the element of surprise, which was far more important for his ultimate goal—stopping Daniel.

He didn't need any additional cocaine for the drive. He was now well rested enough that coffee alone would get him through. Just to be safe, however, he stashed a gram in a hollowed-out mini shaving cream canister that he kept in his Dopp kit.

The road was slick with dew, and Czarcik was careful not to spill his coffee as he walked over to the Crown Vic. He placed the mug on the roof of the vehicle and opened the door.

As if he were in a sitcom, the coffee slid across the roof, down the windshield, and all over the hood. The mug bounced off the tire, onto the ground, and somehow didn't shatter. "Motherfucker!" Czarcik kicked the mug in anger against the curb. This time it did shatter. Across the street, a woman walking her dog glared at him. He glared back and bared his teeth. She hurried along.

Fuck the coffee. Just get on the highway and go, he said to himself.

Coffee. No coffee. None of it mattered.

What Detective Paul Czarcik could never have known was that by the time he had been asleep for two hours the night before, into his second cycle of REM sleep, it was already too late.

Across the Chicago Skyway, past the belching factories of Gary, into God's—or the Devil's, depending on your predilection—country, and finally into the sleepy and sleeping hamlet of Bridgeport, Daniel Langdon had arrived.

Daniel sat in his car, parked in the deserted lot of a long-ago-abandoned asbestos factory.

The car was as dark as the windows of the factory. They looked like the dead eyes of prisoners, rows and rows of them, peering out from inside their cells. A few of the windows were broken, and the moonlight glinted off the glass shards, giving the appearance of life.

From his vantage point, Daniel could see the entire south side of Miriam Manor. He didn't need to use the military binoculars that rested on his thigh.

The compound occupied about five acres of land. The main building, a low-slung concrete structure, held the girls. According to the stories he had printed from the internet, there were probably thirty to forty of them at any given time.

As a private facility, not operating under the guidelines established by the Indiana Board of Education, Miriam Manor was under no obligation to disclose to anyone just how many "students" were currently enrolled. Or being held prisoner. As long as the building met the fire code and was up to health department standards, the school could operate with impunity.

A newer addition connected to the main building was home to Reverend Bradley and his family. Constructed badly, out of cheap materials, the structure had been built a few years after Miriam Manor was founded.

The staff ladies stayed in the main building with the girls, although they had their own shared room.

On the south side, where Daniel waited, the property line was defined by a narrow brook that curved along the eastern flank until it petered out into a large sewer pipe. The western edge butted up against the backyards of modern homes, complete with decks, swing sets, tree houses, and barbeque pits. Daniel wondered what these seemingly normal residents thought upon gazing over their back fence and seeing a squadron of young girls, wearing long dresses no matter the weather, working the land like indentured servants.

The front of Miriam Manor was colonial, if only by default, as secular concerns such as design and architecture had no place in the cult's belief system. A long dirt road—really just a county highway—wound its way from the front porch to the main road.

There was no need for gates or fences. These broken girls would never attempt to escape. The threat of eternal damnation, beaten into them daily, was stronger than their thirst for freedom.

The entire compound was dark. Lights out for the girls was ten o'clock, no exceptions, and the reverend, his family, and the staff ladies usually turned in soon after. Not even a single bulb remained lit. Should a frightened girl awake in the middle of the night and need to relieve herself, she would have to wait until morning. And if by chance she wet the bed, as many of the young ladies were prone to do as a result of nerves, malnourishment, and sexual abuse, she could look forward to a morning beating followed by laundry duty where she had to handwash the soiled undergarments of the other residents.

The saga of Miriam Manor, mostly firsthand accounts from former students and staff, was voluminous. Daniel had needed days to read through them all.

What he was most concerned about was the presence of so many innocent women, children really. He had to be even more thorough than usual with his preparations so none of them would get hurt or, God forbid, killed.

For days he had scoured the property from every angle and perspective imaginable. He knew its rhythms better than he knew his own.

As companionship during these interminably long stakeouts, Daniel had downloaded some of the reverend's sermons. Most of it was the usual religious drivel preached from pulpits all across the country—part inspiring, part chastising, all of it contradictory and hypocritical.

Then he came across one called "A Harlot's Repentance." The gist of the sermon was that any woman who had been abused, especially sexually, should look into her heart to better understand the reasons for her assault and to ask forgiveness in the eyes of the Lord. The reverend related a particular story about a female parishioner of his, when he was still active in quasi-mainstream churches, who was accosted by a pickup truck full of local boys while walking home from a school dance. They dragged her into the woods and took her innocence unnaturally—as he put it—with both their bodies and nearby tree branches. The girl had nearly bled to death before her mother, worried because she hadn't returned, went out to look for her daughter and found her crawling along the side of the road.

The distraught girl had of course blamed the boys for her ordeal. She wanted to go to the police to press charges until she met with the reverend, who convinced her that walking alone at night dressed in a short skirt was all the permission the boys needed. Who did she think she was to deny the urges put into the hearts of men by the hand of God?

Although the girl could never regain her innocence, she was saved, according to the reverend, after accepting Jesus and begging forgiveness of the boys. So sayeth He. The reverend had paused there, allowing his congregants to bask in His grace.

Later in the sermon, there was a bizarre interlude in which the reverend spoke about siblings laying down with siblings. At that moment, Daniel knew that the reverend fucked his own daughters. He had again felt the bile rising in his throat, burning his esophagus. He rolled down the window and spit the acidic sputum onto the dirt.

Unless the residents of Miriam Manor played musical chairs, or beds, every night—highly unlikely considering how regimented everything was—Daniel knew exactly where everyone was. He had been in the compound the night before, a benign dry run, to make sure everything would go down as planned. Risky but necessary.

He had gained entry into the main building through an unlocked storm door that led down into the basement. There was no alarm. Most homes, especially ones that catered to children, were designed to keep danger *out*. Miriam Manor was built explicitly to keep people *in*. The absence of an alarm reinforced just how completely the wills of the girls had been broken.

One of the few newspaper articles that had been written about Miriam Manor told a story about one girl who mustered the courage to escape. She managed to make it to the county sheriff. Bloody and beaten, weak from exposure and dehydration, she pleaded with the sheriff for assistance. A few hours later, she was delivered back to Reverend Bradley—her current legal guardian—who had immediately contacted the sheriff upon her escape, completely devastated that one of his wayward girls might be lost and confused. The following week, the girl's parents received a phone call. Their daughter had been killed in a freak farming accident. There was no autopsy. The reverend had counseled against it. Such desecration of the body, created in His image, would be an affront to the Lord.

So as not to arouse any undue suspicion, Daniel hadn't cut the telephone line on his reconnaissance mission. He planned to wait for the next night. It would only take a few seconds, and he had already identified where the single wire ran into the compound from the wooden telephone pole in the street.

From the dank basement, Daniel had ascended the steps—making sure they could support his weight—to the first floor, which housed the girls and the staff ladies.

The sleeping quarters were as expected. The girls were packed like sardines into a combination of bunk beds and single mattresses on the floor with no frames or box springs. Although he knew it was an inappropriate comparison, Daniel's mind had flashed to the blueprints of slave ships he remembered from history books, where men considered mere chattel were crammed into the belly of a vessel for a transatlantic trip to hell.

In the adjacent room, through a doorless arch, slept the three staff ladies. Here Daniel had decided to diverge from his original plan. He had always planned to kill them. Painlessly, most likely with a single gunshot, but kill them nonetheless. But he increasingly had second thoughts. Although these women were adults, they were also stuck in some strange, perpetual adolescence. All had been raised in extremely religious and undoubtedly abusive households, where they had been inundated with the same poisonous rhetoric preached by the reverend. To them, being plucked from obscurity and given a purpose under the exalted auspices of Reverend Bradley would have been like being handed the ball in the ninth inning of the World Series. An opportunity you didn't squander. An opportunity you embraced with every fiber of your being. They would no sooner question his authority than spit in the face of God.

So while blind devotion didn't necessarily absolve them of their sins, Daniel decided to consider the extenuating circumstances and show mercy. Their real penance would be their joyless, loveless lives.

Right off the main room was a locked wooden door that provided access to the addition where Reverend Bradley and his family lived. From what Daniel could tell, the family now consisted of just three children: thirty-year-old Roger, twenty-eight-year-old Sarah, and twenty-six-year-old Clarice. He recognized them from their photos in the Miriam Manor recruitment pamphlets he had studied. Each slept in their own room. Each was old enough to know better. Although they were under the absolute control of their father, and on occasion even incurred his wrath, they also took their own personal pleasure in meting out abuse. The girls had told countless stories of being alone with a Bradley child, far from the prying eyes of the reverend, only to be subjected to the same merciless torment.

Tiptoeing down to the far end of the hallway, Daniel had silently turned the knob on the door that led to the marriage bed of Reverend and Mrs. Seamus Bradley. The reverend was sleeping on his back, his white hair still perfectly coiffed, wearing some kind of old-school pajama getup, the kind people wore in silent, black-and-white movies whenever there was a scene of someone getting woken up in the middle of the night. In fact, Daniel was certain the only reason he wasn't wearing a goofy sleeping cap was because it might mess up his hair, of which he was obviously very proud. The reverend's hands were folded across his chest, and his snores were punctuated with an annoying whistle.

On her stomach, her long, unkempt hair spilling around her like some sinuous squid, was his morbidly obese wife, Dorothy. She also snored, although hers were of the more traditional, slovenly variety. The snort of a pig combined with the hacking cough of a longtime smoker.

Daniel had watched them sleep so peacefully, lost in dreams of God, Jesus, paradise, or whatever the fuck these people fantasized about, worlds away from the nightmares of their charges. Nightmares that came fast and furious with every night spent under their roof. Nightmares of humiliations and degradations. Endless loneliness. And pain. Always pain. Constant and unrelenting.

The anger had coursed through his veins. His temples had throbbed, and he had feared it would trigger a massive headache or worse. Part of him had wanted to slit their throats right then and be done. But he knew that would be impetuous.

He would return the next night, as planned.

TWENTY

The moment was now at hand.

Daniel stood on the edge of the property, Miriam Manor in his crosshairs. In one hand, he held his trusty medical bag; in the other, a Beretta with a suppressor that he had purchased illegally at a sketchy pawnshop in Dallas.

Afraid that the light from the full moon might give away his approach on the off chance that somebody in the compound was awake and looking out the window, he hunched over, making himself as small as possible, lupine, and scurried across the grass until he reached the doors of the storm cellar.

His black leather gloves were secured tightly to his wrists with duct tape. The rest of his neoprene suit was designed to retain any organic material that might fall, seep, or ooze from his body.

He opened the bag and took out the mask. There was no reason he couldn't revisit Groucho. Only that cop, Czarcik, had seen his disguise. Still, he hated being predictable.

This mask was even creepier—Raggedy Andy.

He slipped the mask over his head, already covered by a latex bathing cap, and pulled the handle of the storm doors. He had brought a crowbar, just in case, but the doors were unlocked, as he expected.

Once inside, Daniel allowed his eyes to adjust to the dark. Although nothing in the cellar had changed since the previous night, something about it felt different, as if it could sense the impending slaughter and was emitting an aura of its own.

Daniel's senses were primed. He was more focused; everything was sharper.

He was surrounded by boxes of donated food, stacked in columns around him, stamped with the logo of the donating entity, usually churches or religious charities. Most of the donations were staples—canned fruit, ramen noodles, powdered milk—but there were also perishables years past their expiration date, leaching out of the cardboard boxes and staining the stone floor.

Even though the basement was muggy, Daniel shivered.

He stood at the bottom of the wooden stairs that led up to the first floor. As he had done the previous night, he placed one foot on the first step, feeling the tension, anticipating how much it would creak. Just to be safe, he ascended the stairs with his back hugging the basement's stone wall. He didn't know how much this really helped, but he had seen the technique used in countless movies, and either way, he made it to the top without making much noise.

Daniel stepped into the hallway of the main floor. It wasn't as dark as he remembered. At first he thought it was a result of his heightened senses, until he located the source of the illumination. There was a single bathroom across from the girls' room. A thin sliver of soft light glowed from underneath the door. Just then, the door opened, and out stepped a small girl with tired eyes and hair mussed from sleep.

For this he wasn't prepared, since nighttime visits to the toilet were expressly forbidden and would result in a beating the following morning.

Daniel anticipated the inevitable scream of surprise. She had to be just as shocked, even more so, to see him. But instead, the girl tilted her head and examined him quizzically.

He almost laughed out loud, realizing how he must look to her. In this child's world of actual demons and tangible evil, a large Raggedy

Andy prowler might not be sheer madness, but the result of divine providence. That was one of the few benefits of true faith—*anything* could be explained away as the power of God.

The prudent thing for Daniel to do, of course, was to leave the compound immediately. But he had already granted a stay of execution to Edgar Barnes; a second one was unthinkable. Plus, even with the bathroom light, it was still fairly dark in the hallway. Compounded by the fact that recollections, especially from children, were notoriously unhelpful to authorities, Daniel didn't foresee having too much to worry about.

He kneeled down in front of her and flipped up his mask so it rested on top of his head.

"Hi, sweetheart. I didn't mean to scare you." She stared at him stoically. "I know I look a little silly in this costume, but I'm dressed up this way as a surprise for Reverend Bradley." She remained expressionless. "Can I ask you a favor?" She nodded. "I need you to go quietly back to your room and try to fall back asleep, but make sure not to wake up any of your friends."

He casually took her hand in a small gesture of gratitude and noticed the faded bruises on her forearms, as if she had recently been restrained. He fought back a tear and looked directly into her eyes, making sure she could understand him. "But sweetheart, this is a promise. Those bad people who say they're taking care of you . . . they're never going to hurt you ever again."

What happened next was so unexpected that Daniel momentarily forgot the purpose of his visit. She threw her arms around his neck and buried her face in his chest. But she didn't cry.

When her grip wavered, he gently pushed her back and held her face in his hands. "Go ahead," he said, smiling. "You think of the sweetest dream you've ever had. You'll be asleep in no time. And then in a minute or two, I'm going to go in and talk to the staff ladies."

He touched her arm, releasing her, and she turned and walked quietly back to her room.

As Daniel watched her disappear into the inky blackness, he was struck by a powerful childhood memory. His mother had read to him from a classic children's book. He never cared for the book, and one particular section terrified him. A woman awakens, sure something horrible has happened to the children in her home, and sprints down the hallway to the room that houses the girls. Drawn abstractly, with slanted black lines and forced perspective, she appears more specter from hell than human—at least she did to Daniel. And as he found himself staring into the black portal of the doorway, he thought of that scene. *She ran faster and faster,* he said to himself, remembering the urgency with which she arrived to comfort the children.

A few minutes later, when Daniel entered the room, the young girl was back in bed as promised. He half-expected to find her peering over the covers, clutching them tightly, with only her head visible. But she was on her stomach instead, head turned to the side, sleeping deeply with a smile on her lips.

With so many of them packed into so small a space, the girls had grown accustomed to ambient noise during the night. None of them stirred as Daniel made his way through to the staff ladies' room.

He went inside.

On the cot closest to the doorway slept the oldest and most obese of the three women. She wore a dirty nightgown that looked as if it hadn't been washed in weeks. A meaty slab of arm was folded over her head, revealing a sloppily shaved armpit. Her breathing displayed the telltale signs of sleep apnea.

It was beyond ironic that a facility so obsessed with withholding food to near starvation levels would allow its staff ladies to be such gluttons. Or maybe it wasn't ironic at all. Maybe it was just another way to show the girls that those in power were allowed to flout one of the seven deadly sins while the girls wasted away.

Daniel reached out and covered the sleeping woman's mouth with one hand while brandishing the gun directly in front of her face. Normally he would have pressed it up against her temple, but she would be groggy and confused upon waking, and he needed her to quickly grasp the situation at hand.

"Shh . . ." he cautioned as her eyes shot open. "Be very, very quiet." Her eyes stayed wide with terror. "I don't mean to scare you, but I need to make sure you understand me. Now, I'm going to remove my hand from your mouth. If you make a sound, I'm going to have to shoot you in the face. If you understand exactly what I've told you, please nod your head."

She complied, nodding vigorously. "Good." He removed his hand from her mouth. "You OK?" She nodded again. "It's OK, you can speak, but just whisper."

Daniel jerked his head toward the two other staff ladies who were still sleeping. "Can you wake them up quietly? And if either of them scream, it's lights out for all of you."

"I'll wake them." She spoke so quietly, so meekly, that Daniel had trouble reconciling that this was the very same woman who, if all the reports were accurate, took perverse pleasure in torturing her charges.

He motioned to the other ladies with the gun. "Do it. Do it now."

The beastly woman carried out her job with aplomb. In less than a minute, Daniel had all three staff ladies sitting on a cot in front of him. They were disheveled and sad, beyond pathetic, and it was impossible to look at them without acknowledging the insidious cycle of victimization.

"Do all of you believe in God?" Three heads bobbed up and down simultaneously and without hesitation. "Fine, that's fine. So when I swear to God on what I'm going to tell you next, I want you to believe me unconditionally." He paused, allowing his words to sink in. "If you do exactly as I say, all of you will live. If you don't, I will kill all of you. But first, I'll defile you."

Daniel wasn't sure what that even meant, but he was certain that whatever indignities the women could conjure up were a powerful-enough deterrent.

"When I tell you to, the three of you are going to go into the girls' room and guard the door. Under no circumstances will you let a single one of them out. It will be scary. You're going to hear gunshots, screaming, and other loud noises. But I promise, none of you will be hurt. I imagine the girls will be terrified. It's your duty to calm them down. I don't care how loud—or how quiet—it gets. You're not going to open the door or leave the room. I know the window in the room faces east. The moment you see the first light of dawn, one, and only one of you, will leave. Don't look around, don't delay, just run out of the house and head to the nearest neighbor. From there, call the police and tell them that there have been shots fired at Miriam Manor. Tell them people are hurt. Probably dead. Do I make myself clear?"

Again the three heads nodded in unison.

"Oh, one more thing, ladies. I contemplated killing you. I've heard what you've done to these girls. The scars you left on them will last a lifetime. But you've been given a second chance. Change your ways. Devote yourself not to Jesus, but to your fellow man. Because if I hear differently, I'm going to return and drag your souls to hell."

As ridiculous as he looked, standing there in his Raggedy Andy disguise, Daniel could tell they believed him implicitly.

"Go!" With one word he released them. They scurried into the girls' room. For a few seconds, Daniel listened to the muffled sounds within. They seemed to be following his instructions.

Daniel took off the Raggedy Andy mask. It was no longer necessary.

A single wooden door separated the Bradley family from the undesirables under their care.

From his reconnaissance the night before, he knew it had a simple lock, and could be jimmied open easily with a common lock-picking tool. There was no need for the epoxy he had used to gain access to Czarcik's apartment.

The first room he entered was that of the youngest Bradley, twenty-six-year-old Clarice. She slept on her mattress, her pillow thrown off to the side. In one motion, Daniel picked up the pillow, pushed it into her face, stuck the suppressor deep into the fabric, and pulled the trigger. The sound was further muffled by the goose down. He tossed the pillow off to the side and examined his handiwork. Clarice Bradley was almost unrecognizable. He thought he could even see her spine through the gaping wound.

There was no question she was dead from the single shot.

Next was twenty-eight-year-old Sarah. The shooting of her sister hadn't roused her, and she slept facedown in her pillow. The path of least resistance would be to place the gun against the back of her skull and simply pull the trigger.

But why not test the efficacy of the knife that he had bought in the same pawnshop where he had picked up the Beretta? It reminded him of Stallone's knife from *Cobra*, with a devilishly curved blade attached to a pair of brass knuckles. In addition to its frightening appearance, Daniel liked the knife's functionality; it allowed him a firm grip for maximum leverage and mitigated the danger of slicing off his own fingers.

He walked over to Sarah and gazed upon her body, watching it rise and fall to the rhythm of her breathing. A single slice nearly severed her head. The second one did the trick.

Daniel had the presence of mind to grab Sarah's nightgown, easing her body onto the floor before it slid off and crashed onto the wood.

Roger Bradley's room was next to that of his parents, so Daniel had to use an abundance of caution. He turned the doorknob slowly, expecting to find the thirty-year-old in a position similar to his sisters. Instead, he found Roger very much awake. And very much occupied with himself. Daniel was so surprised he allowed a quiet laugh to escape. Caught off guard and completely humiliated, Roger screeched like a girl, threw the pictures he had been holding with his free hand up in the air, and dived under the covers like a frightened child.

Daniel moved quickly. He walked over and was about to rip the covers off Roger when he glanced at the photos, now strewn all across the bed. He could immediately tell what the images were.

Until now, Daniel had been fairly restrained. But witnessing the blatant and graphic violation of children, something snapped. He tore the blanket from the blubbering man, who instinctively threw up his arms in front of his face for protection. "Please, please don't hurt me," he wailed.

"Open your fucking eyes, you pervert."

Roger closed them tighter, as if trying in vain to escape a supernatural horror.

"I said open them." Daniel's voice was strangely calm even as his pulse was racing. *Easy, Old Hoss,* he thought to himself. The last thing he needed was to throw a clot at this critical juncture.

Reassured by the steadiness of Daniel's voice, Roger opened his eyes. The moment he did so, Daniel thrust the muzzle with all his might right into Roger's left eye socket and squeezed the trigger repeatedly.

Daniel quickly fled the scene. He sprinted across the hall and kicked open the door to the reverend and his wife's room without even bothering to check whether it was unlocked. The door was made of cheap wood and flew off its hinges.

They were already awake, fighting back sleep and trying to get their bearings. Daniel stood in the doorway.

Reverend Bradley instinctively reached for the landline phone on his nightstand. He grabbed the handset and furiously punched 9-1-1. He tried a few more times—Daniel watching, smiling—before realizing that the line had been cut.

Daniel knew that the reverend kept his guns locked in his den. To reach them, to escape, Bradley or his wife would have to go through Daniel. And that wasn't happening.

With all the Bradley children dead and the staff ladies taking care of the children, Daniel could finally take his time.

To Reverend Bradley, he said, "I'll give you a moment to get your wits about you. But try anything funny . . ." He held up the gun, making sure they saw it.

Dorothy Bradley looked at her husband, completely terrified. "Seamus, what's happening?" Daniel almost felt bad for her. Thinking this frail old man could protect her.

Reverend Bradley studied Daniel, then turned to his wife. "It will be all right, Dorothy. Just do as the gentleman says." Daniel could tell the reverend was racking his brain, trying to think of a way out of this predicament. Trying to place him. Figure out who he was. What he wanted.

Daniel allowed his face to go slack, to become an expressionless mask, no more revealing than the one he had worn when he entered Miriam Manor. "No, no, it most certainly will not, Reverend."

He could tell that Dorothy believed him. Her husband, however, was still confident in his powers of negotiation. "Just tell me who you are, my son. How you're hurting. Together, we can work through this."

Daniel had to admit, he was a powerful and persuasive speaker, and he could easily see how an unsophisticated congregation could be enraptured by his oratory.

"You haven't guessed?" mocked Daniel. "I go by many names. Belial. Beelzebub. Ba'al."

"Impossible."

Daniel tried to suppress a small smile. "Come now, Reverend. Of course it's possible. After all, isn't that what you've built your whole sick little empire on? The existence of evil. You hold these girls hostage, offering them protection. Salvation. You must believe in the Devil and all his minions. Or what would you be? A worthless pederast? Just a regular old hypocrite?"

"You filthy heathen!" the reverend spat with white-hot anger. Daniel didn't think this was an act. A hypocrite he may have been, but Reverend Bradley was also really pissed off.

"Let me ask you something," Daniel said, turning his attention to Dorothy. "Did it ever give you pause? All the injustices you visited upon these poor innocent young women. Did you ever step back and wonder what perverted version of religion could endorse such evil?"

"It was . . . the word of God," she stammered, hardly convincing.

"And your love of God is absolute?"

"Of course," she answered quickly, seemingly aware of her previous hesitation.

Daniel began to pace around the room, considering his options while always keeping one eye on the couple. "Then renounce him."

"Excuse me?"

"Renounce Jesus Christ."

"Don't you dare, Dorothy," the reverend chimed in.

Daniel trained his gun on him and ran his thumb over the rear sight. "I'll get to you, Reverend. But right now, I'm having a conversation with your wife. Interrupt us again, and I'll shove a crucifix right up your ass. And that's not a euphemism."

Reverend Bradley hung his head. Daniel turned his attention back to Dorothy. "Listen to me," he said, as if talking to a child. "I want you to renounce Christ. And if you don't, I'm going to insert the barrel of my gun—"

"I renounce him," she said as quickly as the words would come.

Daniel chuckled at the speed of her abnegation. "Now repeat after me. I embrace Satan and all his disciples."

She began to cry.

"Say it!"

"I embrace Satan . . ."

"And all his disciples . . ."

"And all his disciples . . ." she repeated.

"And I'm the Devil's whore."

"And I'm the Devil's . . ." She managed to force out the word "whore" through choked sobs.

Daniel nodded. Satisfied. Amused, but not surprised, at how fleeting her faith truly was. Although he wasn't raised religiously by any measure, he had attended Sunday school as a boy and remembered the stories of the Christian martyrs who endured unspeakable tortures rather than renounce their faith. Boiled to death. Skinned alive. Fed to wild beasts.

Despite Dorothy's self-proclaimed piety, all it took was a little arm wringing to usher her into the camp of the nonbelievers.

With a dull throb just beginning to thrum in the outer reaches of his brain, Daniel was losing patience at her contrived innocence. Her faux propriety. All her fucking bullshit.

He walked over to Dorothy and grabbed a handful of her hair. She yelled out in both pain and surprise and grabbed his wrists. He yanked her forward, and pushed her toward her husband, as if shifting an uncooperative manual transmission. As she struggled, Daniel squeezed the back of her neck, surprised at how fragile it felt, and forced her head into her husband's crotch.

He placed the gun against the side of her head.

Through all the commotion, Reverend Bradley still had the bedsheets covering the lower half of his body. It was hard not to laugh. They seemed embarrassed of each other and of each other's bodies.

"What's the matter, Reverend? Picturing your own wife, instead of little girls, doesn't get the juices flowing?"

As Dorothy stared at her husband's crotch, Daniel withdrew his knife. His fingers slipped through the brass knuckles. Curved around the handle. The weapon fit like a glove.

And in one swift motion, he castrated the reverend.

Reverend Bradley spasmed. A reflex. No pain yet.

Dorothy immediately began gagging at the sight of her bloodied husband. Daniel grabbed a pillow and thrust it into her face, preventing her from screaming or helping. She couldn't breathe and struggled against him, panicked.

Her husband stumbled off the bed and collapsed onto the floor.

Daniel held the pillow tight as Dorothy gasped for breath. She clawed at his arms with her sausage fingers, weakened from a lack of oxygen. Time moved slowly as she died. The seconds turned to minutes. And then Dorothy Bradley was no more.

Reverend Bradley sat on the floor, propped up against the wall like a puppet thrown from the bed. He was covered in blood, and he was in shock, his eyes glassy and unfocused, operating independently of each other, creeping Daniel out.

His body was still trying to process the loss of one of its most vital organs. He still didn't appear in pain, which pissed Daniel off.

Inside Daniel's bag was a small plastic jug containing the jet fuel.

Stupid.

Fire would pose far too great a risk to the girls. Set aflame, Reverend Bradley would tear through the house in agony before he was consumed.

There was no way to tell what else might catch fire. The ancient floorboards, the drapes, the peeling wallpaper—most of it was flammable. The girls were so used to heeding authority, even caught in an actual inferno—as opposed to the metaphoric one they were threatened with daily—they might not immediately head to safety.

He knew his conscience couldn't handle injuring a single child, much less engulfing an entire house of them in a raging conflagration.

Daniel cursed himself silently. Upset that he hadn't considered this before.

It was the tumor—definitely the tumor. That goddamned tumor. It had to be, wreaking havoc on his cognition.

Reverend Bradley remained in position, his back against the wall, looking like a football player trying to recover after a particularly fearsome collision.

With fire no longer an option, Daniel needed another way to dispose of him.

Daniel kneeled down and held the knife right in front of Reverend Bradley's face. The man was far too weak to even protest, much less defend himself, and could only watch helplessly, his eyes rolling skyward, following the trajectory of the knife, as Daniel drew it across his forehead from temple to temple.

And in that moment, Daniel was sated.

But there was still work to be done.

Daniel reached over and grabbed the corner of the bedsheet. He soaked it in the pool of blood that was forming on the floor, then smeared his note just above the headboard. In big baroque letters— Romans 12:19.

The numbers corresponded to an often-misquoted Bible verse: "'Vengeance is mine; I will repay,' saith the Lord."

The verse was thematically appropriate and would keep the police busy. They'd waste precious time visiting local churches and mental institutions, searching for former congregants or patients who displayed signs of aberrant religiosity.

Dawn was approaching.

Per his instructions, a single staff lady would soon take off to the neighbor's like a banshee. Cutting a dark figure across the barren farmland. And help would come, once the neighbors quieted down this young woman babbling incoherently about a demon in the night.

Daniel would be long gone. He was prudent above all else. Even if part of him wanted to wait for Czarcik, to see how smart the detective really was.

And miles to go before I sleep . . .

That felt right.

183

TWENTY-ONE

Seventy miles outside Bridgeport, Indiana, Paul Czarcik turned on a local radio station.

An overly excited meteorologist was informing listeners that they could look forward to an unseasonably warm weekend. The Colts were heading into spring training with an uncharacteristic number of questions about the offensive. The Dow was up, the S&P flat, and the NASDAQ down slightly. There was a protest at Valparaiso, something about transgender-friendly libraries.

And then came the news that mattered.

The rest of the bodies were discovered by authorities when one of the women who worked at the facility, a Ms. Diane—

"Fuck!" he yelled, and pounded on the dashboard. The vibrations sent the ash from his cigarette all over his shirt. Two of his knuckles bled.

Furious with himself for wasting a single moment, Czarcik only managed to pick up bits and pieces of the report.

Initial reports are that all of the dead are members of the Bradley family . . .

The property houses approximately thirty children, ranging in ages from . . .

Families have been notified . . .

Police are saying it's much too early to speculate about a motive . . .

Reverend Seamus Bradley has been the subject of considerable contro-versy over the years . . .

Found among the belongings in thirty-year-old Roger Bradley's room were about a dozen pairs of girls' underwear . . .

Czarcik clenched his jaw, and his teeth bit clear through the filter of his cigarette. He jammed his foot on the accelerator.

He was an hour away from Miriam Manor; he would make it there in half that time.

The relative isolation of the compound kept the casual onlookers to a minimum. The residents whose homes bordered the property were milling around, having been awakened by the sirens and then drawn outside to the flashing red and blue lights.

Two local stations were on the scene. Reporters were interviewing the neighbors, since they had been given a "no comment" by the cops.

The police had cordoned off the area around the entire compound, not just the buildings. A single strip of yellow police tape blocked the driveway leading up to the main house, replacing the metal chain that usually discouraged trespassers. An enterprising journalist could have found a way inside; it wasn't heavily guarded. But out here, in the country, when the authorities said to stay away, even the most intrepid reporter listened.

Czarcik parked on the main county road that ran in front of the property, right between a cop car and one of the vans from the television station. The black-and-whites—which were really a shade of dark blue—all bore the insignia of the county sheriff.

Miriam Manor was located within an unincorporated area of Bridgeport. It was one of the reasons Reverend Bradley had been able to avoid prosecution. Operating in a nebulous municipality made it harder to convince anyone to claim jurisdiction, which was why the county sheriff was now taking charge instead of the town's police force.

Czarcik ducked under the police tape. The sight of him, a man in civilian clothes, walking into the area with such confidence, sent a blond female reporter scurrying in his direction. She charged at him, her microphone leading like a lance. "Sir? Sir, are you with the FBI?" she inquired.

"Go fuck yourself."

She gasped.

Czarcik smiled, pleased with himself. He knew that where she came from, the authorities, even the most surly, treated the press with at least a modicum of respect. At worst, they were dismissive and curt. Never vulgar.

Welcome to the big city, bitch, Czarcik thought as he continued on his way.

Large firs, chosen to provide privacy rather than promote any aesthetic, lined the dirt driveway that led up to the main building.

Halfway up the driveway, Czarcik was approached by an officer holding up his hand. The cop was young and visibly angry, pissed that something like this had happened in his county, or at least pretending to be, so his superiors would think he took his job seriously. "May I help you, sir?" he asked, trying to sound as authoritative as possible.

Czarcik reached into his back pocket and pulled out his wallet. God, the kid was green. A stranger at a crime scene. At a mass murder. Reaching into his pocket. Czarcik should have been tackled and cuffed.

The kid deserved to have a gun pulled on him, but it was only a badge that Czarcik shoved in his face.

The kid inspected the shield, as if he could tell how to identify a convincing fake. He pronounced the name on the badge incorrectly and then asked, "What's the Illinois Bureau of Judicial Enforcement doing here?"

Czarcik ignored his question. "Can you tell me who's in charge?"

There were two types of county cops. Those impressed by a big-city police officer and those resentful. They were both equally useless, but only the latter might pose a problem. Fortunately, the kid was among the former.

"Yes, sir," he replied, looking away from the badge, seemingly satisfied. "That would be Sheriff Lundin. Want me to call in for you?"

Czarcik nodded. "Please."

The cop smiled, proud he was able to assist. He pressed the button on his walkie-talkie and spoke into his shoulder where the microphone was attached. "Sheriff . . . it's Barksdale. I'm out on the driveway. We got a Detective . . ." He looked at Czarcik for help with his name.

"Czarcik."

Barksdale repeated it, butchering the pronunciation again. "He's come from outta state."

Silence. Czarcik thought that maybe the kid, in all his eagerness, had forgotten to turn on the walkie. Then the radio crackled to life. A female voice, which threw Czarcik for a loop, said, "Bring him to me."

Officer Barksdale accompanied Czarcik up the remainder of the driveway, past cops of different ranks, most of them with little idea of what to do in such a situation. Massacres were not in the training manual.

The day was muggy. A soft mist hung in the air, ready to be burned off by the sun at any moment. But for now, the sun remained behind the clouds. In the distance, back on the road, the lights of the squad cars flashed silently through the fog. Eerie.

Barksdale led him into the house.

As soon as Czarcik entered, he was overcome by the smell.

It wasn't death, which he expected. That he was familiar with, a smell you never forgot. This was something more earthy, though no less revolting.

Then he realized. It was the smell of teenagers, teenagers who had been brainwashed to believe their bodies and all their natural functions were foul and dirty. Puberty was never discussed. Sanitary habits never taught or learned. He remembered the opening shower scene of *Carrie* and shuddered.

"This way," Barksdale said. Czarcik followed him through the main building.

Young girls of various ages, some with adults whom Czarcik assumed were their parents or guardians, were talking with officers scribbling furiously on notepads. Some of the girls were crying, some looked shell shocked, and some, exhilarated.

Barksdale pointed down the central hallway. "There," he said, identifying a dour woman with a silver crew cut. "That's Sheriff Lundin."

Lundin looked up as Czarcik approached her. "Sheriff, my name is Detective Paul Czarcik. I'm with the Illinois Bureau of Judicial Enforcement." He went for his badge. Lundin waved him off with none of the forced importance her position might dictate, a woman more than comfortable in her own skin.

"Bureau of Judicial Enforcement? That's out of Chicago, isn't it?"

"That's correct."

"Well, you boys don't waste any time." Her tone was friendly, oddly relaxed even if every other word out of her mouth was a swear. "How the hell you hear about this so fast, and what the hell you doing out here anyway?"

Once Czarcik had gotten over the frustration of being late to the party, he'd had some time to think about his cover story. "I was working a case near the state line. Cult murders. Shit you don't want to imagine. The bureau heard about this situation of yours. Thought it might be our man, so I headed out this way." Czarcik paused, feigning deference. "Hope I'm not stepping on anybody's toes."

"Shit," the sheriff said smiling. "First call I made was to the FBI. Those federal bastards told me there was nothing they could do, on account of it not being interstate and all. Wouldn't even help with forensics. So we're flying partly blind here, Mr. . . . the hell did you say your name was again?"

"Czarcik."

"Whatever. If you're offering some help, we'll take it."

Czarcik nodded. "Well, I don't know how much help I can be, but I'd love to have a look. See if it fits our man's MO."

"Let me show you what we got." Sheriff Lundin draped her arm collegially around Czarcik and led him into the belly of the beast.

Since Czarcik already knew this was Daniel's handiwork, part of him thought he would be better served heading straight to Tennessee. But he was already here, and Daniel had a habit of taking his time between murders.

The previous crime scenes had been clean, but not perfect. If there was even the smallest chance that Daniel might have left something behind, something that might confirm where he was going next and what he planned to do, then Czarcik wanted to hang around and see what he could find.

Then there was protocol. Czarcik now had an ID on the murderer, as well as a theory about his motivation. Surely he had a responsibility to relay this information to Parseghian, who could decide how best to act on it.

But the source of this information was a single person: Chloe, whom he didn't entirely trust. Wasn't it just as dangerous to provide potentially false information as none at all?

At least that's what he told himself.

"Give me the big picture, Sheriff. Then we can take a look at the individual crime scenes."

Sheriff Lundin ran her fingers through her short-cropped hair. Scratched her head. "Seems the suspect knew where he was going. Otherwise he would have woken the kids. But he headed straight to the room where the teachers, or supervisors, or whatever the hell they call them around here, slept. Makes me think it might have been a parent, or relative, of one of the girls. Maybe even a former student. Somebody who had been here before."

"Makes sense."

"He tells one of the women to make sure she keeps all the kids quiet. Makes them stay in the room as he goes around the house butchering the family. What kind of madman does that?"

Czarcik knew exactly what kind but kept his mouth shut. "You've already interviewed or are in the process of interviewing all the kids?" he asked.

"We started interviewing them," Lundin confirmed. "But after the first ten or so all had the same story, we didn't think it made much difference to continue."

"Some of their parents are here, I see." Czarcik motioned to a few of the adults. "I assume the others are on their way?"

"Can I be honest with you, Detective?" Sheriff Lundin began, in a tone that said she was going to be regardless of Czarcik's response. "I know how we're looked at out here, as a kind of backward rural community. But we're as embarrassed by these people and their primitive ideas as you are. We call some of these parents, explain there's been a terrible tragedy. You know what their first question is? Not, 'Is my daughter OK?' But, 'What has she done to make God so angry?'" Sheriff Lundin shook her head. "Guess that's the kind of mentality you're dealing with in people who would send their daughters away to this goddamned shithole."

"Why didn't you shut it down, then?" Czarcik asked. "There must have been a million reasons you could have used as just cause."

"You'd think so, wouldn't you?" Lundin replied with genuine anger. "But these are minors who were sent here voluntarily by their parents. Legally, it's a church, not a school, so the Department of Education has no authority. Only thing we can get them on are health and fire safety statutes, but every time there's been an investigation, they've been found to be up to code. The good old Constitution, freedom of religion, protects them from everything else," she said bitterly.

"What about the women who worked here? Did you interview them yet?"

Sheriff Lundin nodded. "A mixed bag. One is practically mute. I'd say retarded, but you can't say that nowadays. One was hysterical. Just continued screaming, 'They killed them, they killed them all!' Then babbled incoherently. And the last one told us what we needed to know. Said a man pulled a gun on her, then gave her instructions to watch the kids and contact the authorities at the first light of day. You want to question her yourself?"

Czarcik shook his head. Sheriff Lundin looked at him peculiarly. *What kind of detective are you?* she seemed to be thinking.

"But I would like to see the bodies now," Czarcik said.

Sheriff Lundin escorted Czarcik into the Bradleys' quarters. The bodies were already bagged and tagged.

"We weren't expecting visitors," Lundin said apologetically. "Want me to speak to the coroner? See if you can sit in for the autopsies?"

"No need," Czarcik said, distracted. He walked into the master bedroom with Sheriff Lundin following close behind.

"Now in here, there's some details we left out of our statements to the press," Lundin explained.

"I'm listening."

The sheriff scratched her face. "It's the way Reverend Bradley was murdered."

Czarcik was getting annoyed. "Well, what is it?"

"I'm trying to think of how to say it . . . clinically."

"OK . . ."

Finally, Sheriff Lundin made a slicing motion across her body. "He was castrated."

Czarcik clenched instinctively. "Ouch."

Sheriff Lundin nodded. "Sometimes it's good to be a lady."

Once he had time to process the latest revelation, Czarcik surveyed the scene in the master bedroom. A fucking mess. A bloodbath.

"What do you think, Detective?" Sheriff Lundin asked. "This your guy?"

Czarcik gave her a noncommittal look and pointed to the wall where "Romans 12:19" was now dry. "I assume your men cross-referenced the appropriate verse?"

"Didn't need to. Most of the people in this area are good church-going folks. They can cite scripture like you and I might know Beatles lyrics. Handful of them could recite the verse from memory."

"And . . ."

Sheriff Lundin took her time replying. "'Vengeance is mine,' says the Lord. Or something like that."

Czarcik wasn't remotely surprised. It was just like Daniel. Mysterious enough to keep the locals busy looking for erroneous Satanic links, and playful enough to keep him engaged. Unlike the other murders, Czarcik had a sneaking suspicion that this one was meant specifically for him. Not the targets, of course. They had been chosen well ahead of his involvement. But the theatrics. As if Daniel knew Czarcik would appreciate them.

That didn't make sense. Daniel wanted him out of the way. In his mind, Czarcik was an impediment, not a toy. And Daniel was a lone wolf, not a puppet master.

Besides, Daniel would have absolutely no way of knowing that Czarcik was on his tail. He was confident in his belief that his threats, as Groucho, had gotten through to the detective.

"Detective?" Lundin was staring at Czarcik, waiting for a reply.

"I'm sorry, what was that?"

She offered a wry smile. "I just said, 'I don't know what's going to happen to this place, but I sure would hate to be the insurance adjuster.'"

The Rush came just as Sheriff Lundin let out a chuckle. Czarcik's synapses were electric. The world before his eyes was a black pool of blinding colors.

Insurance adjuster.

That's what had triggered it. Unlike his usual bouts of inspired mania, he didn't think this one would go away until he grabbed the clue. He couldn't afford to let the answer come to him organically. He felt the need to grasp the phrase, wrap his burning brain around it, and force the answer to reveal itself.

He wanted a cigarette. A drink. Blow. Anything to jump-start the process, to cause the random impulses to coalesce into something cogent. He said the words quietly but aloud.

Insurance adjuster.

He forced himself to ride along the stream of consciousness, from the headwaters of the words.

Insurance adjuster.

A common job. And what was it at its essence? A determiner of damages. Damages for the client. The victim. The customer. Reverend Bradley had a policy, no doubt. Who would it revert to? His wife? Dead. His children? Dead. Relatives? Unlikely. Then who? What could this chain of policy ownership reveal? Some secret? Whose . . . *secret?*

With that final word, Czarcik had the key. He wanted to let out a victory cry. *Secret.* That's what it was. A secret. Only whose?

Sheriff Lundin was already staring at him as if he was out of his mind, so Czarcik quickly excused himself and walked hastily from the house.

It wasn't until the warm Indiana sunshine, finally breaking through the clouds, hit him square in the face, and the smell of freshly cut grass mixed with manure filled his nostrils, that he realized just how stifling the atmosphere inside the charnel house had been.

He lit up a cigarette and sucked the thick smoke deeply into his lungs. Then he took out his phone and placed a call.

"There's been another murder, hasn't there?" the voice on the other end asked.

"You've seen it on the news?"

"No. I just woke up," Chloe said. She sounded as though she was still half-asleep. "But I figured that's why you were calling."

His call waiting beeped. Czarcik ignored it. "I'm in Indiana. And I think you should meet me here."

"Do they want to question me?" she asked.

"They have no idea who you are and no idea who was responsible for the murders."

There was a brief silence. "Thank you for your discretion."

"But I think that *we* should have a chat."

Chloe hesitated before saying, "Where should I meet you?"

A soft breeze blew through the firs. Czarcik could smell the evergreen.

More parents were headed into the compound, their faces a combination of relief and stoicism. They passed by fellow parents leaving with their daughters, huddled like refugees from some third world war zone.

"Just get in the car and drive. I'll call you soon and tell you where to meet me."

"I need to shower. I can be there in a few hours."

Czarcik ended the call and walked back to his car. He leaned up against it, watched the police working, the families leaving, and lit another cigarette.

Whoever had called while he was on the phone with Chloe had left a voicemail.

"Detective Czarcik, this is Salvatore Cicci. Of Cicci Industries. Call me back at your convenience, please. I have some information I think you'll be very interested in hearing."

Czarcik got in the car, away from prying eyes and listening ears. He called Sal back, got his secretary, and waited too long for the man to pick up the phone.

Sal was chipper when he answered. "Detective. Apologies for the delay, but I was on the phone with Adelman Jones. Naturally, I couldn't just get off." Adelman Jones was one of the biggest real estate management companies in Chicago. Czarcik doubted this was whom Sal was talking to. Didn't want to give him the satisfaction of admitting he knew of the company.

"What do you have for me?"

"A friend of mine heard about a deal going down in Chinatown. Shark fins and black bear bladders coming in from the Pacific Coast. Apparently, some Chinamen will pay a pretty penny for this shit. Supposed to have medicinal properties or something. Entire shipment is supposed to be worth three hundred grand. This the kind of stuff you were talking about?"

"No."

Czarcik pulled away from Miriam Manor. No reason for him to go back; his work there was finished.

Even if one of the investigators managed to stumble upon something of significance—an accidental forensic hit—it would be of limited help in foretelling Daniel's future plans. The folders told him as much as he could learn from the crime scene.

Czarcik's thoughts at the moment weren't even on Daniel. They were on Chloe, and what he had realized just before he called her.

From the beginning, he hadn't trusted her. Not completely. She may have played the role of the guileless grieving widow, but she had lied to him before. And now he knew why.

What was worse, however, was that he'd underestimated her. *This* was a mistake he swore he wouldn't make again.

TWENTY-TWO

1990

Fucking regulations. Fucking codes, ordinances, rules, and regulations.

The politicians were on some kind of crazy health kick. If the madness continued, soon smoking would be completely banned in restaurants. This wouldn't do for Officer Paul Czarcik, currently in the second year of a pack-a-day habit.

Thankfully, Rosalita's Café catered to smokers, with a large plastic ashtray as the centerpiece of every table.

Czarcik sat alone in the back of the restaurant, reading the *Sun-Times*. He had just gotten off his shift and was tired and sore. There was a Bulls game on tonight, which he was looking forward to watching. Michael Jordan impressed him. The kid from North Carolina had become a bona fide hero in the city. Some of the cops, mainly the young black ones, proclaimed him the greatest of all time. This was lunacy to Czarcik. The Bulls hadn't even won a single championship. And the way the Pistons and Celtics were built, an NBA title didn't seem likely any time soon.

A waitress who was probably born at Rosalita's and who was likely to die there approached Czarcik, her pad and pencil in hand. "What can I get you?"

"Coffee. Black, please."

She scribbled something on her pad, even though it was less than ten steps to the counter.

Czarcik turned to the obituaries, as he did every day after reading the sports section. A morbid and semi-obsessive habit. Although he wasn't yet thirty, he had a perverse fascination with those who died younger than him.

And there she was, halfway down, the second obit on the page. The name meant nothing. Didn't clear away the cobwebs. But her picture. Those eyes. Those eyes burned his soul.

"Nothing else I can get you?" His coffee was in front of him, the waitress waiting patiently. He opened his mouth to speak, but no sound came out. He returned to the paper, and the waitress eventually walked away.

Her name was Genevieve Kuzma. She was a freshman at the University of Chicago, where her father, Dr. Wilson Kuzma, taught philosophy. There was no mention of an illness. Or an accident. No cause of death was listed.

Czarcik knew what this meant. Genevieve Kuzma had killed herself.

Jillian Eig was only eighteen years old but, as she explained to Czarcik, had been smoking since she was twelve. She was a brilliant hyperactive child, born to two brilliant and completely unequipped parents who considered cigarettes a safer alternative to mood stabilizers.

She sat on her dorm room bed, legs crossed underneath her, wearing a two-toned, long-sleeved Poison T-shirt. Czarcik sat mere feet away from her, on Genevieve's bed, his feet on the floor.

The roommates had known each other for only a single semester—Jillian was from Saint Paul—but they had bonded immediately, like long-lost sisters.

Czarcik made Jillian rehash the discovery of the body. She had found Genevieve hanging from a curtain rod in the communal bathroom. The investigators were thorough. Foul play wasn't suspected. It was a perfectly ordinary, if tragic, suicide.

"And she didn't leave a note? Nothing?" he asked. Jillian shook her head, the tears welling up in the corners of her eyes. "But you know why she killed herself." Jillian nodded.

"Because of him," Czarcik said quietly. He didn't need a response.

Czarcik lit up a cigarette and leaned back on Genevieve's pillow. His eyes drifted to the painted concrete wall next to her bed, which acted as a bulletin board. Flyers for local bands. A mini U of C pennant. Camel Cash. Normal teenage stuff. There were no photographs of her parents anywhere in the room.

"Why didn't she tell anyone?" Czarcik asked.

For the first time in their conversation, Jillian seemed unsure of herself. "You really a cop?" Czarcik reached into his pocket, took out his badge, and handed it to her. She inspected it, seemingly satisfied.

"Who was she going to tell?"

Czarcik shrugged. "A counselor? The university? The police?"

"Man . . ." Jillian shook her head and snuffed out her cigarette in an ashtray next to her bed. "He told her if she spoke a word of it to anyone, she was going right back to the hospital. She said that was worse than home. And besides, who's someone going to believe, a kid with a history of mental and emotional problems, or the esteemed professor?"

"I would have believed her."

"Well then, I guess you're a day late and a dollar short, aren't you?"

The funeral was held at St. Boniface Catholic Cemetery. The priest went through the usual liturgy. Dr. Kuzma spoke eloquently about his daughter. He quoted Descartes, Kant, and some other assholes nobody in attendance had ever heard of.

Mrs. Kuzma was completely out of it, pumped so full of tranquilizers she couldn't even sit up without the support of her husband.

The funeral was well attended. Most of the mourners were colleagues of Wilson Kuzma from the university.

Czarcik stood in the back, then left before anyone could notice him.

It was after midnight when Czarcik pounded on the Kuzmas' apartment door.

The professor opened it, his hair askew, as if he had been sleeping. Czarcik was in street clothes. Dr. Kuzma looked him up and down. "I'm sorry, but we're not having visitors until tomorrow."

"I'm not a visitor." His speech was slow, softened by alcohol.

Dr. Kuzma tried to place Czarcik. Then a flicker of recognition passed across his face. He pointed to Czarcik. "You're that cop. The one who quoted Virgil to me." He was pleased with himself.

"I know," Czarcik said. Dr. Kuzma cocked his head, curious. "I know why."

The smile melted from the professor's face. "Then you better come in."

Dr. Kuzma led Czarcik down the apartment's short hallway to his study. He looked over his shoulder and held a finger to his lips. "My wife is asleep. She had a long day."

They entered the study, and Dr. Kuzma closed the door behind them. The two stood in the lair of a serious academic, or at least one who took himself seriously. Every wall was dominated by a bookshelf, and every bookshelf was filled with books. There was a large dark wooden desk centered in the back of the room. Two well-worn leather chairs sat in front of it. To the left, flush against the bookshelf, was a leather couch. On the right wall, just off the corner of the desk, a wet bar.

An intimidating space for people intimidated by such things—children and first-year grad students.

The professor walked over to the bar. "I'm sorry, I don't believe I recall your name."

"My name is Paul Czarcik."

"Well, I'd offer you a drink, Paul, but if you'll excuse me for saying so, it seems you've had a bit already."

Czarcik smiled—more of a snarl—and joined the professor at the bar. He grabbed a bottle of Four Roses and brought it over to the couch. He unscrewed the top, plopped down, and took four big swigs.

Dr. Kuzma studied him. "Rather rude."

Czarcik wiped his mouth with his shirtsleeve and leaned back on the couch. "You buried your daughter today."

The professor sat down in the chair behind his desk. He stared across the room at Czarcik. "My daughter was a very sick young woman. While I dreaded it, I feared this day was inevitable."

"I spoke to her roommate. I know what you did."

"Impressionable women can have such rich imaginations . . ."

Czarcik choked down the rising bile. "I could arrest you, you know," he threatened.

"If you could have, you would have."

Czarcik took a final sip of bourbon. He screwed the cap back on and placed the bottle on the floor, where it fell to its side. He rubbed his face. "Help me understand."

Dr. Kuzma morphed into professor mode easily. "You know, according to Nietzsche, good and evil are simply man-made constructs designed to keep the masses in check."

"We both know that's a gross oversimplification of his argument. Is that the kind of crap you teach your Philosophy 101 students?"

The professor shook his finger at Czarcik. "I knew you were no ordinary cop. So tell me, what is it you want to know?"

Czarcik focused, his eyes pleading. "Why?"

"Because I could," Dr. Kuzma replied without an ounce of regret or contrition. Czarcik felt as if the wind had been knocked out of him. The professor bared his teeth. "What did you expect?"

Paul Czarcik believed in evil. Not in any metaphysical sense, but in the sense that the world was filled with very bad people who did very bad things. He was faced with it every day. He saw it in the streets. He saw it in the ghettos and in the crack dens. He saw it in the half-way houses and the battered women shelters. In the free clinics and emergency rooms. He saw the brutality, the pain, the hopelessness. The assaults, rapes, murders. This was Chicago, not Kansas; he had seen the worst that humanity had to offer.

And right now, he saw all of that in the face of Dr. Wilson Kuzma, professor of philosophy at the University of Chicago.

Czarcik got to his feet, unsteady. He grabbed the cushy arm of the sofa.

Somehow he made it out of the apartment and down to the street before he vomited all over the base of a parking meter.

He thought back to Genevieve's funeral. To the Lord's Prayer. For something, no matter how ephemeral, to hold on to.

And then he vomited again.

TWENTY-THREE

The Middlesex Diner was located about three miles from Miriam Manor in the town of Little Stockholm, thus named because of the large number of Swedish immigrants who settled the area in the mid-1800s.

The diner was founded in the 1950s and hadn't changed much since. But what appeared to outsiders as quaintness was in reality smartly packaged frugality. Only cash was accepted and nobody complained—which said as much about the clientele as one needed to know. The countertop was Formica, the mugs thick porcelain, and the slowly rotating pie display fully stocked with a dozen different flavors.

Czarcik sat alone. The mini jukebox in each booth played songs for a quarter. At the time of their actual release, they would have cost a nickel. Tommy James and the Shondells' "Crimson and Clover," Looking Glass's "Brandy," and Louis Armstrong's "What a Wonderful World," which, as far as Czarcik was concerned, was timeless.

A wise-cracking, gum-snapping waitress in her midforties approached. "Can I start you off with some coffee, sugar?"

"Please."

"How you take it?"

"Black—"

"—Black."

She answered for him, at the same time. He wasn't remotely amused. "One of my many talents. I can tell what someone is going to order before they even open their mouth. You're a black-coffee man if I ever saw one."

"That's pretty good," he admitted, friendly enough to placate her but with a hint of aloofness. If she could read people as well as she claimed, she would know he wanted to be left alone. She went off to fetch the coffeepot as he lit up a cigarette.

As she walked away, Czarcik's gaze traveled from her polyester-clad posterior to the handful of other patrons in the diner. A grizzled regular at the counter, nails and teeth yellow as fresh honey, was reading a newspaper. A middle-aged man, gaunt and tired, with jet-black hair poking out from under a trucker's cap, sat at the other end of the counter, opposite the old-timer. He wore a shirt covered in a coat of grease that didn't look as if it was coming off with a single wash. A few booths behind Czarcik, two long-haul truckers were arguing about politics.

The bell above the door to the diner jingled. In walked Chloe. Sunglasses on, her hair done up, she looked like the lead in some old film noir. All eyes momentarily turned to her, then turned back to their food. Their papers. Their problems.

The waitress was about to tell Chloe to sit wherever she wanted. Then she caught her looking at Czarcik.

Chloe slipped into the booth. Czarcik didn't rise to greet her. She took off her sunglasses. He was surprised to see how tired she looked.

"I heard about it on the radio. Absolutely awful." Czarcik nodded and studied the contours of her face, like a cartographer who'd just come into possession of an old map. "But that's not why you called me out here. You could have told me it was Daniel over the phone."

He slid his pack of cigarettes out of his shirt pocket and tapped one into his palm.

"I didn't realize you smoked," she said. He offered her the pack by way of a response. She seemed to consider it before declining.

"You lied to me," he said as he fiddled with the unlit cigarette, rolling it between his fingers.

She hesitated slightly. "That may be true, but unless you tell me what you're talking about, what I'm supposed to have lied about, I can't give you an explanation."

He believed her. She didn't know what he was talking about. In fact, he was absolutely certain that she assumed her plan had worked to perfection. And with a lesser man, it might have. "When we first met, toward the end of the conversation, I asked you why you had come to me. Do you remember what you said?"

"I said, 'Because it was the right thing to do.' Or something along those lines. And I still believe that."

"Only a liar would remember that. You know why? Because only a liar would take the time to conceive it."

Chloe picked up her sunglasses, threw her purse over her shoulder angrily, and stood up. "I don't need to stay here and listen to this."

He reached out and grabbed her wrist. "Sit down."

She complied.

Finally, he spoke. "You don't want your husband to commit suicide."

"Of course I don't. But that was his choice. If he wanted to go out on his own terms, I wasn't about to stand in his way. I owed him that. And if you're trying to make me regret it, I came to terms with my guilt a long time ago."

"But that's not *why* you came here."

"Enlighten me," she said angrily.

He was curious to see how long she would continue to deny it, how long she would continue the charade.

"The one constant of almost every life insurance policy is a clause that voids it if the policyholder commits suicide. It's drafted not so much to prevent suicide—insurance companies are soulless beasts—but to discourage fraud. So, as you well know, if the medical examiner rules

Daniel's death a suicide, you get nothing." He studied her reaction. She sat sphinxlike, neither confirming nor denying his claim. "Now, as crazy as it seems," he continued, "if Daniel is killed—even if it's in the middle of a homicidal spree, the insurance company is compelled to pay out. And if he's captured alive, we both know he'd never live long enough to ever make it to prison. But even if he dies while incarcerated, you *still* get the money. This is why you need him stopped. You need him"—he searched for the right word—". . . preserved."

Czarcik thought he knew Chloe well enough to gauge her response. He expected her to protest or obfuscate.

Instead, she looked away like a petulant child. When she turned back to him, her eyes were rolling storm clouds. "Fuck you, Paul," she spat. The third word cut him the deepest.

Chloe stormed out of the diner. This time, Czarcik didn't attempt to grab her wrist. The bell jingled in her wake, punctuating her departure. The waitress looked over at Czarcik. He held up a single finger, as if to say, "I'll be right back."

Chloe was standing next to her Jeep as he stepped out into the blinding late-morning sunshine. He approached her, uncertain whether she would respond with anger, diffidence, a heartfelt apology—Slap!

Her wedding ring caught his bottom lip, and a metallic taste filled his mouth. Concurrently, something in his trousers stirred. He touched the back of his fingers to his lip and came away with blood. Chloe lit into him.

"Who the fuck do you think you are to question my motives? I come to you, by my own volition, as a private citizen trying to do the right thing. If it wasn't for me, you and your idiot colleagues would be standing around with your dicks in your hands."

Czarcik was taken aback by her vehemence. He had clearly touched a nerve.

"And what if I *do* want the money? Whose business is that? Certainly not yours. And why shouldn't I? Isn't that why people take out insurance in the first place? For the unthinkable. Would you rather he leave me destitute? I sacrificed my entire life for him. Went happily wherever his work took us. Put my own dreams on hold. You're goddamned right I want my money."

Czarcik had been moving closer and closer, almost gliding, as her righteous indignation reached a fevered pitch.

"The sheer nerve of you—"

He kissed her. Or she kissed him. Either way, their lips met. It was brief. The blood from his lip that transferred to hers was the only evidence it occurred.

Chloe pulled away. She looked afraid, conflicted. He stared at her, defiant.

She shook her head and then got into her car. A few seconds later, Czarcik was left standing in a cloud of dust.

As he watched her Jeep disappear over a ridge, he realized two things. One, he was falling for her, as inappropriate as that might be. And two, she was still lying to him.

Almost as soon as the insurance explanation had come to him, once he had a moment to think it over, he realized it was faulty.

If Corrine's information was accurate, and Corrine's information was *always* accurate, then Chloe Langdon didn't need the money from a life insurance policy. She had more than enough to get her comfortably through life, provided of course she didn't suddenly begin living like the Rockefellers.

But he had wanted to see what happened when he accused her of having a financial interest in locating her husband. Why had she allowed him to go on thinking she was a money-grubbing soon-to-be widow? Why hadn't she told him she had plenty of money?

What was she hiding?

The bells over the door jingled as he walked back into the diner. He approached the waitress who was standing behind the counter, organizing the pies on the plastic turntable. "I'll take my check now."

She cracked her gum, an especially annoying habit. "She took a piece out of you, huh?" Czarcik was confused. She pointed to his lip, which he had forgotten was bleeding.

"Just the check." The waitress nodded. Before she could go retrieve it from a stack of other checks next to the cash register, the gaunt man in the trucker's hat caught her attention and handed her his check with some cash. "Keep it. Thanks."

The waitress fixed him with a smile and walked over to the register, taking a brief detour to leave menus in front of a couple who had just sat down at the counter.

The man tipped his trucker's hat to Czarcik on his way out and pointed to his lip. "I feel for you, friend. I had a woman like that once."

"Get the hell away from me," Czarcik replied without looking up. The man just snorted and walked away. A few seconds later the bells jingled as he left the diner.

A moment later, a scream ripped through the diner, a scream of unbridled excitement.

The waitress stood in front of the register, looking at the bills in her hand as if they had just materialized out of thin air. She was joined by another waitress and one of the cooks, both of whom looked stunned as well, as she babbled incoherently through tears of joy.

Czarcik could glean the main points: before he left the diner, the gaunt man in the trucker's hat had given her a thousand-dollar tip.

For a man who had seen so much wanton cruelty, Czarcik had also witnessed his share of random acts of kindness. The widow leaving her fortune to the mailman. An anonymous gift to keep the soup kitchen stocked through the holidays. Nice for the people affected, but small acts of charity didn't leave him with that warm and fuzzy feeling about humanity. This poor sap was probably just some guy trying to impress—

I had a woman like that once . . .

Czarcik spun toward the door so quickly that the wind he generated blew the menus off the countertop. He raced toward the exit. No one paid him any attention.

The bells didn't jingle and jangle, but whipped up one hundred and eighty degrees, smashing into the top of the door.

Czarcik exploded into the bright sunshine. He sprinted over to the road that ran in front of the diner, looking frantically both ways as his eyes adjusted to the brightness. There wasn't a single vehicle in sight. No trace of the man in the trucker's hat. The highway was a straight line for miles in each direction, giving Czarcik a 50 percent chance of catching him if he was to get in the Crown Vic and burn rubber.

Those were fool's odds. And Czarcik was no fool.

But he knew who else was on the highway, and he knew which way she was heading.

Czarcik jumped into the Crown Vic, threw it into reverse, and fishtailed onto the blacktop. He jammed his foot on the gas as soon as the car straightened out and shot forward, hugging the double yellow line down the middle of the highway.

A truck coming from the opposite direction thought he cut it a little too close and laid on the horn. Czarcik was too focused to even give him the finger.

He gripped the steering wheel, his knuckles white, as the speedometer's red needle rose past one hundred. Three minutes later he saw the familiar square body of the Jeep Cherokee as the highway curled around a bend. After making sure there was no oncoming traffic, Czarcik swerved across the solid yellow lines, going the wrong way on the two-lane highway, and pulled up next to Chloe.

She was staring straight ahead, lips tight, still angry, concentrating on the road, oblivious to the man next to her frantically gesturing for her to pull over. She finally caught movement out of the corner of her eye, motioned for him to pass, then realized who it was.

She saw the look on his face. She rolled down the window.

"Pull over, now!" he screamed at her.

She did immediately. Once she was safely on the shoulder, she craned her neck out and looked behind her. He was already out of his car and charging over. "What the hell is wrong with you?" she asked. He was pale, breathing fast. "You look like you've seen a ghost."

"Close enough," he replied, his elbow resting on the open window. As he tried to catch his breath, he looked up and down the highway, on the off chance that a gaunt man in a trucker's hat might whiz by. But all he could see were the dark outlines of enormous wind turbines, their arms flailing in the distance like spastic giants.

TWENTY-FOUR

The Holiday Inn Lockport looked like every other midwestern Holiday Inn. And every other Clarion Inn, Comfort Inn, Quality Inn, and Sleep Inn.

The folks in the respective marketing departments were the only ones who could spot the differences, and only because it justified their jobs. For everyone else, besides the different complimentary breakfasts—watery eggs and turkey sausage instead of Canadian bacon and stale muffins—there was nothing to distinguish one mid-scale hotel chain from the next.

This was exactly what Czarcik wanted. Conformity and anonymity.

It was sweltering inside the domed room that housed the indoor pool and looked down upon the atrium. The curved-glass windows appeared to be sweating.

But the hotel was busy, and this was the only area where they had any privacy. The only person in the pool was an old man in a bathing cap—his loose flesh riddled with malignant-looking moles—swimming so slowly it was amazing he remained afloat. Plus, the noise from the Jacuzzi drowned out their conversation.

The two sat on uncomfortable metal pool chairs with no cushions, around a small matching metal table. Chloe's back was to the windows. Czarcik wanted it this way. Through the condensation, he could make sure they weren't being watched.

"I still don't understand how you can be so sure it was him." She thrust her phone at Czarcik, a picture of Daniel showing. "Is this what he looked like?"

He shook his head and waved off the phone without even glancing at the picture. "I told you, I didn't get a good look at him. Other than his hair. Jet black. At least from what I could see under his cap."

"Daniel has light hair. Dirty blond."

He didn't find it necessary to point out the possibility of hair dye. Or a wig. "He hasn't attempted to contact you?" he asked.

"Don't you think I would have told you that?" He raised his eyebrows. "What the hell is that supposed to mean?"

"I just want to make sure you're being completely honest with me. If you're not, and I find out, it's not Daniel who's going to be in trouble."

She averted her eyes, pretending to be insulted. Or maybe she was insulted. "Well, I am."

"I hope so." He watched as the old man climbed up the ladder and out of the pool, went over to his reclining beach chair, and began to dry off, using the towel between his legs like a lumberjack sawing wood.

The old man called out to them. "You get in now while the water's warm. Have it all to yourselves."

Czarcik raised a hand, thanking him, but also letting him know they were in no mood for small talk. The man stuck his fingers in his ears a few times, forcing out the water, then left the pool area.

Czarcik turned back to Chloe. "Are you sure that Daniel didn't take his phone with him?"

"It's still at home. I'm positive. I can get it for you if you want. But I've already looked through his call log, and there's nothing out of the ordinary. Not even any numbers I don't recognize."

"Maybe . . ." Czarcik pondered.

"Plus, if Daniel really wanted to disappear, why would he bring it with him? With his background, he knew how easily you could trace a call. There'd be no reason to take the risk. If he needed a phone for anything, I'm guessing he just picked up one of those disposable ones they sell at 7-Eleven."

"Hmm . . . I don't know."

"You know what else I can't figure out," she said, suddenly chatty. "The one thing Daniel wants is to be left alone. To be allowed to complete his . . ." She struggled for the word before choosing "destiny." "It's the one unspoken thing he's asked of me. If what you say is true, and you really did see him, why would he risk that?"

Czarcik thought for a moment, watching the tiny ripples throw abstract shadows onto the tiled walls just below the glass. He remembered Daniel sitting on the edge of the bed, taunting him, still their own little secret. How he could have used any disguise. A balaclava. A woman's stocking. But he chose Groucho Marx. Ho, ho, ho.

"Because he's fucking with me," he finally admitted.

Chloe looked at him, bemused. She knew Czarcik was a selfish, self-centered man—that much was obvious from their first meeting—but it was the height of narcissism for him to believe he was anything but an unwitting pawn in Daniel's grand plan. She knew her husband, she knew his faults. They were grandiose in nature. He hadn't left his death-bed, left the love of his life, only to play an existential game of chicken with some nothing cop—excuse me, *detective*—from the city. "I really don't think he'd bother with that. You're . . . incidental."

She waited to see whether the detective was offended. And while she waited, she thought of something else.

"If he knows about you, then he knows about me." Quietly she said, "He knows I've gone to the police. Betrayed him."

"Then you're not safe," Czarcik told her.

The color rose in her cheeks. "He would never hurt me. Not in a million years."

Czarcik didn't really disagree, despite what he had just told her. Even if Daniel knew that Chloe had gone to the police—and since he had seen them together, he certainly did—he would have understood her reasoning.

Still, Czarcik had made a career out of refuting assumptions. And not being a neurosurgeon, he had little idea about the effects of a rapidly advancing brain tumor. That old gray mush was fickle, he knew that much, and any disruption could make a person's behavior highly irregular. It would be safer to keep Chloe close by, for both professional and other less noble reasons.

"I'm sure you're right. Still, I'd feel better if we stayed together."

"You don't think I should go back to Chicago?"

He believed she really didn't want to go. "It's ultimately your decision. But I wouldn't suggest it."

"And you? What are you going to do?"

Czarcik looked out over the water. A family—a mother, father, and two small children—had just come down with their towels and water wings. Their prosaic concerns of water safety were worlds away from his own worries.

"He beat me to Indiana," Czarcik admitted, the closest he would come to a mea culpa. "He won't beat me to Tennessee."

Chloe pushed back from the table and stood up. "We're not leaving right now, are we?"

"No."

"Then I'll get two rooms for us."

Czarcik shook his head. "Why don't you grab something to eat in the hotel restaurant. You're probably starving. I'll handle the rooms, then I'll meet you." He offered up a smile.

The bed in room 405 was fine. That wasn't the problem.

It was two in the morning, and Czarcik had been lying in bed for hours. He was now intimately familiar with the Picasso-like pattern of water stains on the ceiling above him.

He had walked Chloe to her room hours ago, made sure she locked the door—both the deadbolt and the chain—made her promise to call him immediately if she noticed anything suspicious, and then left her to her own devices. Probably to sleep.

He had already watched a movie rented for $7.95 through the hotel's entertainment service, polished off two mini bottles of gin and one of Canadian Club, and burned through half a pack of smokes. A documentary about Australia's most dangerous animals was on the Discovery Channel, and he was trying to keep his eyes open until he could learn what could possibly be more dangerous than the Irukandji jellyfish, the most venomous of the box jellies, whose sting could bring on a cerebral hemorrhage in less than twenty minutes.

Just as his eyes flickered shut, his phone rang. The mobile was next to him on the bed, and he glanced down at the screen. The number was unavailable. He let it ring again and then hit Accept to answer the call; he pressed the speaker icon immediately after. "Hello?"

Silence.

He was already angry at himself for playing into the caller's game. Again he said, "Hello?" More silence. He could feel the open line. Dead air. A greeting. A warning. A cold kiss.

He hung up the phone and sat up in bed. It didn't ring again. But he was now wide awake with no chance of falling asleep.

After learning that the most dangerous animal down under was in fact a taipan, a harmless-looking snake that could fell a hundred grown men with the venom from a single bite, Czarcik lit up a cigar and went for a walk around the property.

The call could have come from anywhere. From back home in Chicago, Tennessee, or even the British Virgin Islands, but Czarcik could sense that the caller—why be coy, he knew who it was—was close by.

He puffed on the cigar and did a few laps around the parking lot. Just the usual traffic—or lack thereof—for this time of night. A handful of road trippers checking in for a hot shower and a few hours of sleep. Some good ol' boys drinking out of the back of a pickup, trying to appear inconspicuous in case Czarcik was a cop. They all looked under-age, and Czarcik considered stopping by—to ask for a beer. In the distance, just over the on-ramp, the lights from the twenty-four-hour gas station and fast-food restaurants glowed like a low-rent aurora borealis.

There was nothing extraordinary, or even interesting, about the night.

Czarcik tossed his cigar into a storm drain, swiped his key card through the reader on the side entrance of the hotel, and headed back to his room. Dawn would arrive in a few hours, and a pot of black coffee would be his lone companion for the remainder of the night.

He unlocked the door to his room, stepped inside, and threw the deadbolt and chain behind him. As he walked into the room proper, what he saw on his pillow made his blood run cold.

There, sitting right on top, like some kind of mocking mint, was a pair of glasses and a large, fake mustache.

The kind that Groucho Marx would wear.

In his long and sometimes distinguished career, Czarcik had been threatened countless times. Angry spouses, incensed parents, gang-bangers assuring him they knew where he lived—nothing in a very long time had scared him as much as this bushy bundle of faux whiskers, felt paper, and cheap glue. Angry at himself for being so unsettled, he rushed to his holster, thrown over the back of the room's single chair. He was certain the firearm would be gone, and a second later, he would feel the cold muzzle on the back of his neck. But there it was, his Glock, sleeping in its leather pouch, just where he had left it.

He unsnapped the holster and slipped the gun into the back of his jeans.

He kneeled down on the floor and threw the hanging top sheet onto the bed in order to get an unimpeded view underneath. Just dust, crumbs, and a condom wrapper.

Leading with his gun, Czarcik walked the perimeter around the bed, hesitating briefly before the closet doors. He threw them open. An extra set of bedding, a few wooden hangers, the hotel safe—

Something smashed down on his wrist.

He dropped the gun and cried out in pain . . .

. . . then pushed the ironing board back against the wall of the closet.

He rubbed his throbbing joint and picked up the gun. Although he wasn't above pumping a few rounds into the ironing board, he thought it might reflect poorly on his state of mind should the hotel have to be evacuated.

The bathroom was the only other possible hiding spot. He moved slowly but with purpose. Pushed the shower curtain back with the muzzle of his gun. Empty. He spun around and pointed the gun behind the door. No one there.

Back in the main room, he checked the windows. All locked. Before leaving the room, he checked the doorknob. The lock hadn't been jimmied. The strike plate was flush.

The room was just as Czarcik had left it, aside from the little gift that had been placed on his pillow.

Behind the front desk, dressed in a cheap but still immaculately pressed suit, even at this ungodly hour, was a dark-skinned black man. From the islands, Czarcik assumed. Or Somalia. He flashed his guest a broad grin, showing no outward surprise at seeing him wandering the lobby so late at night.

"Good evening, sir. How can I assist you?"

"I'm in room four-oh-five."

The manager punched in a few numbers. "Mr. Czarcik, yes," he confirmed, pronouncing the name better, albeit in a thick accent, than most native English speakers, even ones of Balkan descent.

"You wouldn't have happened to give anyone else the key to my room?" Czarcik inquired.

The manager furrowed his brow, half-offended, half-concerned. He was the kind of man accustomed to being accused of things for which he was not responsible. "Certainly not, sir," he replied, doing his best to remain polite. "We require all guests to show identification when requesting additional room cards."

"And nobody inquired about my room? Asked for the room number?"

The manager shook his head. "We wouldn't give out that information even if they did." Then, trying to be helpful, he said, "But I've only been on since midnight. I can call the manager who was here before me. I'm sure he's asleep, but I have his cell number."

Czarcik held up one hand. "No, thank you. That won't be necessary."

Then he wandered off.

Instead of returning to his room, Czarcik took the elevator up to the second floor, turned right at the ice maker, and continued past the vending machines to the end of the hallway. He stood outside room 235, Chloe's room.

About to knock, he caught himself. What the hell was he doing? What would be the purpose of waking her up in the middle of the night just to tell her that her homicidal husband had left a present on his pillow? It would only frighten her. Plus, he would have to explain the relevance of the mustache.

He leaned against the door and slid to the floor. An exhausted guard dog.

The irregular position was strangely relaxing, and he found himself drifting in and out of consciousness while speculating about Daniel's next move. But just as soon as his eyes were about to close for an extended stay, the door opened, sending him crashing backward into room 235. His head hit the carpet, and he shot up, fully awake, to find a confused Chloe staring down at him.

"Paul . . . what are you doing?"

"What are *you* doing?" he countered.

Taken aback, she answered. "I'm a light sleeper. I heard scratching on my door, went to see what it was, and . . ." She motioned to him. He was still sitting on the floor with his legs splayed out in front of him, looking and feeling ridiculous. "So . . . what are you doing here?"

He answered as honestly as circumstances would allow. "After the diner, it made me nervous to leave you alone. I know you think he would never hurt you, and you're probably right. But I've made a career out of being suspicious. And the truth is, with the tumor, we're not entirely sure how your husband might react."

Then, trying to mitigate his concern, he added, "I don't sleep much anyway."

Her faced softened. She held out her hand. "Come."

They made love in the quiet hours of the morning.

There was something oddly familiar about it for both of them. Neither was self-conscious. They took their time exploring the tastes and textures of each other's bodies. But it was the sex of immediacy, of convenience, not white-hot passion.

When they were finished, Chloe fell asleep in his arms. Czarcik couldn't remember the last time that had happened.

In fact, he couldn't remember the last time he had made love to a woman at all. It wasn't that the urge had deserted him. He wasn't *that* old. Nor had the drugs and liquor left him unable to perform. When he wanted to, he still could.

And with Chloe, he had *really* wanted to.

With the escorts, he didn't. He wanted their companionship. Their stories. Their hopes and dreams. But their bodies, that was left for the ordinary customer.

The irony wasn't lost on Czarcik. Most men paid for sex to experience the superficial, the physical sensation, divorced from any emotional attachment. He wanted the opposite. He was paying for the chance to glimpse into their souls.

With Chloe, it was far more complicated. He was torn between trusting her implicitly as the person who had given him nearly all his information about Daniel and trusting his own instincts—namely, that there was still something she wasn't telling him.

She was an enigma, for sure, one which he sought to decipher. But she was also a woman of flesh and blood, one who stoked in him those desires that, try as he might, he couldn't intellectually explain away.

He pondered this conundrum as he fell asleep, his hand resting on the swell of her form.

Chloe lay awake, her mind racing. But it was racing around a void, searching for something she couldn't quite grasp.

She wasn't besieged by any of the normal emotions she expected to experience. Guilt. Regret. Even cautious optimism. They were all there, of course. But they were more like items in a storefront. Nothing that she could feel in her core.

What she did feel was a strange sense of déjà vu. But that was ridiculous. She had just met Czarcik. Certainly, she had never been with him before. And, of course, this rogue cop was nothing like her husband.

Nothing, she told herself again.

Czarcik awoke to the sound of the shower. Just to be sure he wasn't actually in the middle of a torrential rainstorm, he blindly felt the bed next to him. Empty. He stole a few more minutes of sleep before opening a single bloodshot eye. According to the angry red digital numbers beside the bed, it was just after nine in the morning.

Even though he had been up most of the night, it was still rare for Czarcik to sleep this late. His first thought, which he laughed off as mere paranoia, was that he had been drugged. But a cursory glance around the room found no more unwanted calling cards, and his holstered gun was right next to the bed, on top of his clothes, which had been thrown off hastily the night before.

The shower sounds were almost hypnotic. But the more Czarcik allowed himself to be lulled by the falling water, the more he convinced himself that something was amiss. He imagined a dream—walking through the steam-filled bathroom, ripping back the shower curtain, only to have a naked Groucho Marx spin toward him and bury a knife in his chest. It was so vivid he actually bit the inside of his mouth just to prove to himself that he was awake.

"Good morning." He flinched, but the figure wasn't Groucho; it was Chloe. She came out of the bathroom, through the parting steam, one large hotel towel wrapped around her torso—showing just the right amount of cleavage and leg—and the other wrapped around her head.

Czarcik contemplated his options. This was uncharted territory. The women he was used to left long before he fell asleep and certainly never stayed the night.

He supposed he could pull her back down onto the bed. Or join her in the shower for a quickie up against the mildewed wall. He could even go against his nature and play Casanova, whispering soft nothings in her ear.

Instead, he said good morning in return.

Chloe sat down on the bed and began drying her hair.

"I could justify it a million ways," she began, an answer to his unspoken question. "Just in the shower, I came up with half-a-dozen reasons: I needed to feel protected. I was subconsciously furious at Daniel for leaving me and wanted to punish him. I wanted to have something to hold over you. Most of these even have some truth to them. But if I'm being honest, which I always am, the *only* reason last night happened was because, at the time, I wanted it to." She looked at him for the first time since he had been inside her. "You OK with that?"

Czarcik didn't know if he was OK with it. But he couldn't figure out why he wouldn't be. So he just nodded and gave her a wink. She smiled and tipped her head toward the bathroom. "I'm going to finish up."

The bathroom fan rumbled to life, dispersing the last of the warm vapor still hanging in the air.

Czarcik rolled over onto his side and grabbed his BlackBerry with its rudimentary browser. He pulled up a map of the United States and estimated that it would take them about half a day to reach their destination in Tennessee.

Daniel could already be there. Of course, if history was any guide, he needed time—days, at the very least—to prepare for the kill. Only now, Czarcik no longer had the benefit of surprise. He could no longer travel unfettered. Daniel knew the detective was following him. Although now that Czarcik thought about it, who was actually following whom?

Even after Chloe had brought him the Rosetta stone of the folders, Daniel had *still* been a step ahead. How long would he allow Czarcik to nip at his heels like some overeager pit bull? Or would the knowledge that Czarcik was so close force him to alter his plans?

There were a panoply of options that Czarcik had to consider. Daniel could continue to Tennessee on schedule, simply avoiding—or toying with—the detective, as he had done thus far. Or he could make a beeline for Florida, then double back to the Volunteer State. Of course, if he felt his plans were compromised, he could ignore Tennessee altogether, just as he had done with Edgar Barnes in Minnesota.

And one final possibility also loomed. The nuclear option. Daniel could blow up his plan altogether. He could trade vengeance for sport and zero in on a far more formidable target—Czarcik.

The thought intrigued the detective more than it alarmed him. In a battle of equals, he had little doubt he would prevail. Daniel was smart and resourceful, and certainly inspired, but in many ways he was still an amateur. He had been successful thus far because his victims had absolutely no idea they had been marked for death, certainly not by a complete stranger who had no more of an emotional attachment to them than the hundreds of other people they passed on the street each day. The element of surprise had been absolute.

Such an extreme pivot didn't seem particularly likely, but Czarcik thought to himself, Daniel had proved unpredictable before. Willing to deviate from his painstakingly prepared plan for seemingly unnecessary detours. His appearance at the diner and the mustache on the pillow were nice touches, if a tad theatrical, but in the grand scheme of things, they were really nothing more than diversions.

And then there was the biggest X factor of them all—the tumor. The growing mass could just as easily obliterate reason and common sense as it could gray matter.

Chloe returned from the bathroom, fully dressed, her thick hair still wet and unbrushed.

"I think you should come with me," he told her, before she could say anything.

She sat down in the chair next to the bed and picked up a brush from the nightstand. "Come with you where?" she asked.

"To Tennessee. I think you should stay with me until I catch him."

"*If* you catch him," she replied. She didn't intend for it to sound cutting, but she could tell that was the result.

"I'll catch him."

She wondered which one of them he was trying to convince.

Chloe ran the brush through her hair over and over. Killing time. Thinking about what to say next. "I . . . I can't just go with you on some kind of manhunt," she said finally. "I have a life back in Chicago." Then, as if searching for an additional reason, "Plus, you said it was dangerous."

"That's why I want you with me," he confirmed. "You're safer that way."

"Safer from whom?" she asked, her eyes narrowing. They had been through this all before. Daniel, while clearly dangerous, was not a danger to her. "Is there something you're not telling me?" She was slightly alarmed by his sudden concern.

For a nanosecond, he considered coming clean. Telling her all of it. Groucho's visit to his apartment. The late-night phone call. The mustache on his pillow. But again, he held his tongue, not exactly sure why, although if he managed to frighten her into staying, that wasn't exactly a bad thing.

When Czarcik didn't answer her, Chloe posed another question. "Is it because of last night?"

He snorted condescendingly. "Last night was because of last night." He paused, allowing her to grasp the seriousness. "This is about your safety."

She continued brushing her hair. "I need to go home to Chicago."

He wasn't in the mood to argue with her. He could tell his ploy was futile; there was nothing he was going to say to convince her.

He was surprised how badly he wanted her to stay, regardless of whether or not she was actually in danger. And this frightened him more than anything about Daniel.

TWENTY-FIVE

Daniel wasn't a religious man. He wasn't before his illness and certainly not now.

He was aware, however, that being faced with one's own mortality turned many secular men to God. But Daniel thought, like a child first discovering the inconstancies of faith, that if God was so great—or even just a little bit compassionate—he never would have allowed him to get sick in the first place.

His atheism didn't preclude spirituality. Far from it. Throughout his life, he had taken profound pleasure in higher powers. They were just of the more worldly variety. The ocean's fury. A mountain's permanence. A city's sprawling scope. He was struck by the grandiose, whether forged by nature or by the hands of man. Ayn Rand by way of Thoreau.

Was this the catalyst for his actions, even more than the tumor itself? He didn't know, which was both his curse and his saving grace.

But now, at death's door, Daniel longed for transcendence. He stood on a stone ledge, staring up into the maelstrom. Nearly fifty feet above him, Eagle Creek spilled over a ledge of granite and crashed into the Cumberland River.

Daniel was completely naked. His clothes were scattered around him on the rock. Privacy wasn't an issue. Any hikers were probably at the nearby and better known Cumberland Falls. And even if they stumbled upon him, he didn't care. Because right now, he couldn't imagine anything more sublime.

He had been on his way to Tennessee when he was forced to pull over. The pain had been so excruciating he could barely see the road ahead. He had slowly made his way off the highway at the very next exit. That was when he spotted the sign for this place. Something about it called out to him. Something all the pills, treatments, and panaceas couldn't fix.

Now, as he stood as natural as God intended, he momentarily forgot about the army of abnormal cells attacking his brain.

The water was cold and hard and almost painful. The perfect salve.

Daniel spread his arms toward the sky. Leaned backward. Inviting the cascade to wash over him. To wash away his pain.

He ran his fingers through his hair, marveling at the feeling. He wiped the droplets of water away from his eyes and looked down at his hands. The water was a sickly brown color.

He gasped in fear, then thought about the ramifications. What did it matter? The worst this could portend was death, to which he was already resigned. Part of him still recoiled at his body's deterioration.

He watched the dirty water stain his hands and then laughed out loud. Another of his body's systems wasn't failing. It was just the hair dye washing out, returning his dark locks to their natural color.

Oh, how he would have loved to be holding Chloe under that water. Embracing her body as the goose bumps warmed under the touch of his fingers. He would run his lips across her neck, then chew lightly on her earlobe. When they were younger, this had driven her wild. He thought about all the little details he cherished. The little hollow just below her throat. The way her hip bone protruded slightly when she would reach for an item on her nightstand. The soft blond hairs at the bottom of her tailbone. All of it indubitably *her*.

Daniel knew he had been a fool to believe that this detective, Czarcik, might have understood him. Understood that he was doing God's work. The work of Lady Justice. Of Travis Bickle. "Someday a real rain will come and wash all this scum off the streets." He thought they were compatriots. Maybe.

Driving through the bluegrass, before the debilitating pain had forced him off the highway, Daniel had wondered to himself whether he could really kill the detective in cold blood. Could he snuff out the life of an innocent—relatively speaking—man in order to ensure he could avenge so many others?

He stepped back, out from underneath the direct trajectory of the falls, until just the spray washed over him, and ruminated on the question. There was historical precedent, of course. On a grand scale, the obliteration of Hiroshima and Nagasaki. How many millions of lives had the vaporization of a few thousand saved?

Daniel lowered his head and watched as the water dripped down his face and fell into the pool below. It was so dark. Dark and beautiful. Timeless, eternal.

Jimson, Tennessee, was unaccustomed to such fuss. But ready or not, its close-up was now at hand.

Founded as a mill town in the second half of the nineteenth century—a *snuff* mill town to be precise—its fortunes had risen and fallen with the health of the industry on which it was built. Since the Second World War, Jimson had been in a downward spiral. The nearby city of Chattanooga had stolen most of its residents with the promise of both employment and a more exciting life. The growing suburbs had pilfered the rest.

Jimson was left to die of neglect, like so many other forgotten towns on the Hiwassee River.

Over half a century later, a curious phenomenon began to take root. The burned-out mills, once home to flying rodents and other opportunistic vermin, found new life as craft breweries. Grand old homes that had been abandoned rather than sold because there was no market for them were suddenly prime real estate. "Fixer-uppers," the local real estate agents would tell wealthy young buyers from Nashville and Memphis. An Esso gas station was transformed into a market for locally sourced meat and produce, and a foundry became a warehouse for high-end baby furniture.

According to the full-color brochure now available in every municipal building, shop, and restaurant, road trippers were encouraged to spend the day in a "charming town of yesteryear filled with all the modern flourishes of today—home to a wine bar, two antique shops, and one of the most acclaimed farm-to-table restaurants in the South."

What the brochure didn't advertise was that Jimson was also home to America's most prolific rapist.

Father Andrew Dyer was accustomed to being shipped all across the country. Since the midseventies, when he tasted his first child, a seven-year-old boy he lured into the rectory with promises of hard candy, he had been shuttled from parish to parish, from diocese to diocese, from city to city, whenever allegations of his "predilections"—which is how the Church-appointed psychologist referred to them—were brought to the attention of the local authorities.

It was a nice and easy racket, run like clockwork. There would be an accusation, the boy's parents would be told that their son must be mistaken and warned against bearing false witness, and Dyer would be moved to another place to carry out the will of God.

The only problem was that Dyer didn't believe in God and had become a priest because it gave him access to young boys. It wasn't until Milwaukee in the early aughts that the wheels really came off.

A documentary filmmaker rounded up a bunch of Dyer's accusers. All had similar stories, all passed a polygraph, and all, now in their forties, were no longer content to remain silent. After the film aired, premiering on HBO and then running weekly for nearly six months on MSNBC, dozens of other victims came forward.

At first, the Church obfuscated, equivocated, and stonewalled. Then when the breadth of Dyer's crimes became impossible to deny, officials blamed a single fallen priest, not an institutional failing endemic to their chosen calling. They also tried to paint the accusers as either bitter lapsed Catholics with a grudge against the Church or as mentally unstable apostates. The Catholic League predictably rallied around the Church, arguing that no other religion would have been so erroneously persecuted in modern-day America.

In the end, the Church's insurance company paid out nearly $80 million to the survivors. Some were thrilled at the settlement; others called it hush money. The only ones really punished, however, were the shareholders of Midwest Mutual.

Once it became clear that Father Dyer was going to escape any form of prosecution for reasons as capricious as an embarrassingly short statute of limitations, one of his victims, a former altar boy named Jimmy O'Bannon, tracked him down to a cushy retirement community and tried to put a bullet in his brain.

Unfortunately, O'Bannon was a longtime junkie who wasn't fit to hold a conversation, much less a high-powered revolver, and he only succeeded in shooting a nurse in the leg before being subdued by the orderlies.

The retirement community, previously unaware of Dyer's history, quickly determined they didn't want an unrepentant pederast in their midst, so they released him to the authority of the Church. The Church, which by this time just wanted the whole ordeal to go away so they could continue to fill their pews and coffers, shipped him off to his current home in Jimson. The father-in-law of the organist at the local church owned the house and agreed to rent it to Father Dyer for next to nothing. To serve his fellow man was (almost) payment enough, he claimed.

On this day, Father Dyer woke up feeling so well that he thought it might be safe to detach his oxygen, at least for an hour or so. Fifty years of heavy smoking had left him with emphysema. Every time one of his victims sent him a letter—or nowadays, an email—wishing him an agonizing death, he would think, *Your prayers have been answered.*

The priest got out of bed, his old bones creaking like the floorboards under his feet, and slowly made his way to the front door. He stepped out onto the porch and bent down for the newspaper, delivered hours before by a nice dark-skinned boy with a strong work ethic. Years ago, Father Dyer might have invited him in for milk and cookies. But nowadays, he didn't mess with those boys. He wasn't prejudiced. Far from it. He loved the look of their young black bodies. But their parents weren't worth the hassle. No matter what, those parents didn't blame their own children. They'd blame him, and him only. And they would seek retribution faster than you could skin a cat.

Dyer picked up his paper, straightened up to the usual harmony of crackles and pops, and found himself staring into the eyes of a very intense gentleman.

"Don't worry, Father. No need to rack your brain," the visitor assured him, reading the priest's mind. "I'm not one of the many you've raped over the years."

Dyer knew that nothing good could ever come of projecting weakness. "What can I help you with, my son?" he asked.

The visitor laughed. "Actually, you dirty old lecher, I'm here to help *you.*"

The entire house smelled of piss. Of piss, old deli meat, and fetid water, the kind that might accumulate in the catch tray of a broken humidifier.

That was Czarcik's first thought as he sat across the cheap wooden kitchen table from Dyer, looking into his eyes.

His second thought was that he could easily snap the priest's bird-like neck before the man knew what happened.

Father Dyer was slumped in his chair, plastic tubing running into both nostrils. The pathetic spectacle didn't imbue Czarcik with sympathy. In fact, he had an urge to throw the old priest to the floor, put a boot across his neck, and finish a cigarette as the light in his eyes dimmed to nothingness.

Czarcik had long since stopped trying for justice on behalf of the victims. The futility of it was deadening. And yet, watching Father Dyer just sit there, as if he had the same right to freedom as Czarcik himself, infuriated the detective.

"Father, I have a confession," Czarcik said, trying to contain himself. The priest nodded, closed his eyes, and bowed his head. "I'm having a hard time understanding why you're not the least bit worried that I might reach across this table and choke you to death."

Father Dyer opened his yellow, cataract-clouded eyes. "Because you would have done it already. Those with true urges can't contain themselves. Trust me, I know."

"Don't you dare compare my restraint to your sickness."

"No, I wouldn't do that, Detective. But we both have compulsions, do we not? I need boys. Young boys. You need to catch demons. Yours is just socially acceptable, no matter your methods."

Czarcik tried to figure out whether there was some twisted logic to the priest's argument and realized there wasn't. He leaned across the table. The corners of his mouth turned up slightly as he removed the cigarette from his lips and poked the air as he spoke. "Father, I'm seriously considering letting him have you. And I promise, in your wildest dreams of penance, you can't imagine the hell he'll put you through."

Father Dyer sucked on his oxygen tube like a smoker savoring a final cigarette. Unfortunately, Czarcik didn't think he seemed particularly nervous. Maybe, after managing to get away with his crimes for so long, he had some sense of invincibility.

"You keep referring to this man," Dyer said. "You say I haven't wronged him, nor anyone in his family. And yet he intends to kill me. Horribly in fact. I'd like to know why."

He spoke the last sentence with such entitlement that, again, Czarcik was forced to make a concerted effort not to strike him.

"Why isn't remotely important. What's important is that he not only *intends* to kill you, he *will* kill you if you don't do exactly what I say. You're not dealing with a broken man who wants revenge for you diddling him in the confessional. You're dealing with a killing machine who will reduce you to a shivering piece of meat. Are you understanding me?"

Father Dyer looked as if he could be a part of the house itself. Not a human being inhabiting it, but a fixture, no different from the filthy rugs, peeling wallpaper, or corroded pipes. He could die here, and nobody would know; the house would simply consume him. Eventually, a cleanup crew would find his bones picked clean by various scavengers.

Finally, he spoke, the house come to life. "*Why* do you want to help me, Detective? You obviously detest me."

Czarcik knew this answer so well he wasn't even aware when it escaped his lips. "It's what I do."

The priest inhaled. His chest rattled as if he had swallowed a bag of pennies, or carpenter nails. It was a sound no living thing should make. "What would you like from me?" he asked as if he was doing Czarcik a favor.

Czarcik took out a business card and flicked it across the table. It landed under the priest's elbow. "I want you to keep the doors locked. I want you to keep your eyes and ears open. And I want you to call me if you see or hear anything out of the ordinary."

There was a faraway look in Father Dyer's eyes. He was remembering things that Czarcik didn't even want to imagine. Slowly, enunciating every syllable, he said, "Nothing about this is ordinary."

Both men knew the priest was speaking of things other than his current predicament.

Czarcik got up from the table. His head throbbed. He needed something, something chemical, to neutralize the pain. He thought about lighting up a cigar, detaching the priest's breathing tube from the oxygen canister, and blowing the smoke directly into it. But instead, he showed himself to the front door.

"Detective . . ." Czarcik stopped but didn't turn around. "We're not so different, you and I. I think that's what bothers you most."

Without acknowledging the voice behind him, Czarcik took the cigar from his breast pocket. He lit it, then blew the smoke into the air where it simply hung in an almost impossibly well-defined cloud.

"Father," Czarcik began, "I will do my best to protect you. But if I fail . . ." He paused and took another deep pull of the cigar. "I hope he kills you slow."

The night was unseasonably cool. Czarcik waited in the car, with the window open, at the end of Father Dyer's block.

From here he could see the priest's front door and the entire west side of his house. Although it was possible for Daniel to come in cold, Czarcik was convinced that he would first do some rudimentary reconnaissance. Drive up and down the street. Maybe even take a stroll with a newspaper. Get a lay of the land and really try to understand the pulse of the neighborhood. After all, that's what Czarcik would have done.

The only light in the car came from the tip of Czarcik's cigar. Killing time, he blew thick rings into the still air, savoring the taste of the burning Connecticut wrapper. Although the quiet thrill of a stakeout had long ceased to excite him, as he'd gotten older, he had begun to appreciate more and more the simplicity of inertia.

Over the next few hours, a handful of cars drove up and down the street. A few pulled into adjacent homes, the rest passed through. None stopped, slowed, or paid him any mind. He stared at his phone, alone in the passenger seat, trying to will it to ring. Finally, when the wait became unbearable, he picked it up and dialed her number.

She answered almost immediately and didn't try to hide her concern. "Where are you?"

He almost hung up. Like when he was a teenager and finally got up the nerve to call a girl, only to have her actually answer.

"In Tennessee. I'm watching the priest's house." He paused to gauge her reaction. She said nothing in return. "Where are you?" he asked.

"In bed," she answered, without a hint of subtext. "I was tired from the drive."

"Did he try to contact you?"

"You know he didn't." He believed her. Czarcik was fairly certain that Chloe was no longer part of Daniel's game. If she ever was. He had said his goodbye to her forever that fateful night. This was about a predator and his prey, and maybe one annoying fly in the ointment.

Still, Czarcik wanted to preserve the illusion that he was there to protect her, though for whose benefit, he wasn't entirely sure.

"I may have made a mistake," she admitted.

He waited, then pressed. "Something you should have told me before? It's not too late, Chloe."

"Nothing I should have told you. I meant I should have stayed with you." She sighed. "I should be there now."

"No, no, it's best that you're not," he reassured her. There was no reason to make her feel worse than she did, even if he wanted her with him.

"But I want to be," she said after a bit.

He felt something catch in his throat. "You should sleep. You've been through a lot."

"I'm too tired to sleep. Does that make sense?"

He chuckled. "Yeah. Yeah, it does."

Silence, but neither of them was ready to hang up.

"Paul, there's something I've been thinking about . . ." He liked the way his name sounded when she said it. "He only has two more stops. Let's say he completes his quest. Then what?"

"He won't. I'm getting closer. I know it doesn't seem like it, but I am."

"I believe you." She said it without a shred of doubt. The ensuing silence wasn't uncomfortable but reassuring, and Czarcik found peace in the sound of her soft breathing. "When I was a child, my grandmother lived with us for the last few years of her life. She was an immigrant. From Romania. When I couldn't sleep, she would sing me gypsy folk songs. It always worked."

"Sorry, but my Romanian is a little rusty."

Her laugh rang through the phone crystal clear. "Sing anything."

"I sound like a combination of Tom Waits and Leonard Cohen."

"That I'd like to hear."

The ash from Czarcik's cigar hung precariously, and he tapped it out the window. Chloe continued talking about her grandmother as another car, with its headlights off, turned slowly onto the street. It pulled over to the curb, on the left side of the street, so it was barely a hundred yards directly in front of the Crown Vic. The driver of the car cut its engine. From Czarcik's perspective, the vehicle was only a dark mass that had become still.

Too soon to get his hopes up. Chances were, it was just a teenager out past curfew, contemplating how to sneak back inside without waking the parents.

Czarcik flashed his brights. The other vehicle returned fire, blinding him. When Czarcik killed his headlights, the other vehicle did too. This went on for three or four volleys, an automotive riff on *Close Encounters of the Third Kind*. "Chloe . . . I have to go," he said quietly. He ended the call and put the phone down on the seat next to him.

He was still momentarily blinded, eyes shut tightly, waiting for the spots to clear from his vision. The vehicle was too far away. He couldn't tell anything about its occupant. All he could make out was the general make and model—a nondescript GMC. Maybe a Buick? Or looking again, it could have been a Ford, possibly a Mercury Sable?

Just to make sure this wasn't the craziest of coincidences—or even a dumb kid just fucking with him—Czarcik pulled the turn signal lever toward him one final time, engaging his brights. And like clockwork, he was hit with a returning flash of light.

He waited again until his vision returned to normal. They were two modern-day knights, jousting with high beams on the quiet streets of suburbia.

Czarcik turned the ignition, and the engine of the Crown Vic growled. He considered throwing his car into drive, then slamming his foot down on the gas. He could cover the distance between the two vehicles in only a few seconds. But now, the other car was idling too.

Czarcik tapped the gas. The car lurched.

But then, instead of mirroring him, as it had been doing the entire time, the other car quickly reversed, burning rubber, and went shrieking off backward into the night.

When the car reached the perpendicular street, the driver turned the wheel quickly, straightening it out, pointing it forward. He revved the engine, daring the detective to approach.

Czarcik knew that if he gave chase, his adversary would be off down the unfamiliar suburban streets and onto the highway within seconds. There was an on-ramp close by.

Even if he managed to catch up to him, what could he possibly do on the open road? He was completely out of his jurisdiction. Parseghian would flip if he knew that Czarcik was out of the state. He couldn't call for backup. He was all alone.

He had an idea. The other car was still idling. Waiting. Watching. But unless the driver had binoculars, and night vision ones at that, he couldn't see Czarcik any better than Czarcik could see him.

Czarcik reached into the back seat, found his holster, and took out the gun. He slipped it into his jeans. Then he reached up and killed the dome light so it wouldn't go on when he opened the door.

In one swift motion, he threw the brights, pushed down on the horn, and opened the driver-side door. He slipped out as inconspicuously as possible, the sound of the door hopefully masked by the horn's echo through the empty streets. Then he sprinted across the street and dived behind the safety of a small hedge.

He could see his own car, its brights still on. From where he was, it appeared as if someone were still inside. He could also see the other car at the end of the street. It remained at a ninety-degree angle to his own, poised to take off at the slightest sign of danger.

Now hidden from view, Czarcik counted six houses on the street between his own car and the T created by the street on which the other car waited. The house whose property he was on was completely dark, almost too dark for the occupants to simply be asleep. Czarcik had the feeling they were either out of town or that the domicile was deserted. Like a cat burglar, he sneaked around to the backyard.

In a stroke of luck, none of the adjacent backyards leading up to the intersecting street had fences around them. Czarcik moved as quickly and as quietly as possible. Aside from the occasional sound of his shoes on the dead grass, nothing gave away his position. The night was still, just the sounds of the suburbs.

The kitchen light in the third house was on. From the backyard, Czarcik could see inside. The countertop was granite and the appliances all new. A coffee maker that took those little pods sat on the corner of the counter.

Suddenly there was a flash of motion from underneath the back porch, only a few feet away. It was too small to be another person, but Czarcik instinctively reached for his gun anyway. *Fucking dog,* he thought to himself before he actually saw it. If there was anything that could ruin his approach, it was the incessant barking of a poorly trained canine.

The animal appeared, walking with a distinct waddling gait, just as the moonlight fell across the familiar white stripe down its back. Czarcik stepped back, trying not to encroach on its territory, but the skunk was already in position. It showed its hindquarters and released its scent.

Czarcik was far enough away that the actual spray didn't get in his eyes, but the smell was overwhelming. He pulled his shirt up over his nose and gagged. The animal beat a hasty retreat back to safety below the deck.

Quietly choking, Czarcik worried that if the smell reached the other car it might tip off the occupant that danger was afoot.

He made his way across the remaining backyards without incident, although he almost impaled his foot on a stray lawn dart, which he remembered reading were now illegal. From the last house, closest to the intersection, Czarcik had a clear view of the other car. It was still in the exact same place, engine still running.

He was fairly certain that right now, in his current position behind a wooden fence that faced the street, he was completely hidden from view. But the other car was in the middle of the road, unobstructed. There was no possible way he could approach it without being exposed for at least a few very long seconds.

And he couldn't make out the driver of the other car. If the man had a gun and was ready, Czarcik was no better than a sitting duck.

He took a few quick deep breaths, psyching himself up. It had been a while since he had physically taken down a suspect, although he enjoyed doing it. For years now his value to the bureau had been analytical, and the few times he had actually participated in a raid, he was preceded by well-armed specialists and supported by SWAT. Now was the perfect time to prove that he still belonged in the game.

A motorcycle revving up in the distance gave him the sonic cover he needed to make his move. He made a mad dash for the car. Every second he remained unimpeded was a tiny miracle. He reached the vehicle and slid under the rear bumper, just like he was back in high school on the baseball diamond, breaking up a double play. His jeans offered little protection from the asphalt. As he got into a crouched position, he noticed the blood already seeping through the fabric.

His leg throbbed, but there was no time to waste. He crept around the driver side until the door was within reach. He got to his feet—knees crackling—pulled open the door, and swung his gun around to the driver seat. "Hands on the wheel, motherfucker," he said to no one.

The car was running, the engine rumbling, as if possessed by some angry automotive spirit. Nobody was inside. Czarcik jumped back from the car, pointing his gun in every direction, in case the driver had slipped out the passenger-side door and made a break for it. But the street was as deserted as when Czarcik had first pulled up.

Then an idea arose. It was completely irrational, and yet he pictured the scenario as clear as day: turning his back on the car, walking away, hearing the distinct click of a latch being disengaged, turning around just in time to see the trunk fly open, and finally feeling the slug slam into his—

He pulled up on the trunk release and cautiously went around to look inside. It was no more occupied than the driver seat had been. Just a pair of jumper cables still in the box, a tire iron, and a box of road flares.

So much for his intuition.

Czarcik slipped the gun back into his jeans and jogged across the street, back over to the side on which his car was parked. No need for stealth. If Daniel was watching, he'd already had ample opportunities to take a pot shot.

As Czarcik headed back to his car, past Father Dyer's house, the wind picked up, kicking up dry leaves and cigarette butts, some from Czarcik himself. The car was still running, just as he had left it. Czarcik opened the door and was about to slip back inside when he saw it. Resting on the seat.

There it was, the familiar mustache. So lonely and mocking. Mischievous and yet deathly serious.

He could almost die laughing.

There was no longer any doubt that the man in the car had been Daniel, not that there really ever was. And once again, he had gotten the best of Czarcik. Especially if—

Czarcik slammed his car door shut and sprinted up to Father Dyer's house, knowing full well that in the time he had been stalking the unoccupied automobile, Daniel could have been feeding Father Dyer his own genitals.

He took the porch steps two at a time and pounded on the front door with all his might, just in case Dyer was a deep sleeper. The doorbell didn't work. Wasn't even there. A casualty of neglect. All that was left were a few sharp spikes of plastic where the buzzer had once been. After knocking hard enough to wake the dead, Czarcik put his ear against the door. Inside, it was silent. Again and again, Czarcik slammed the side of his fist into the wood, nearly separating the door's hinges from its frame.

He was too late. He could feel it. Daniel had always been one step ahead of him. This time was no different.

He just knew that Dyer would be in his living room, sitting in his easy chair, face blue and eyes bulging, his oxygen tube wrapped tightly around his neck.

Only seconds before Czarcik was about to kick in the door and come face to face with the corpse he had conjured up, he heard a feeble "Yes?" from inside.

"Father Dyer! Open the door now!" Czarcik screamed, as much from the surprise of finding the priest alive as from the urgency.

"Who is this?"

Czarcik couldn't tell whether Dyer was being obstinate, men his age really did take longer to shake off the vestiges of sleep, or he was just a complete moron. "It's Detective Paul Czarcik. From today. Now open your goddamned door!"

The priest complied, and Czarcik barged into his house, half convinced Daniel was already inside, standing behind the door and holding a gun up to Dyer's head. But again, his paranoia was unfounded. The priest was apparently alone and even seemed a little put out.

"What's the meaning of all this?" Dyer asked as Czarcik struggled to catch his breath.

Czarcik grabbed him by the shoulders. "Have you let anyone in since I left you?"

"No, nobody has come by."

"Nothing strange? Phone calls with no one there? Hang-ups? Delivery men looking for a different address? A meter reader?"

Father Dyer paused. "Just some inconsiderate detective making a ruckus in the dead of night."

Czarcik let out a deep breath. "Well, Father Pedophilia, you've got yourself a house guest."

Once Dyer realized that there was no way he was going to convince Czarcik to leave, at least not before morning, he resigned himself to the role of proper host. Fortunately for him, everything he offered—a spare bedroom, sheets, a pillow—was declined, as the detective preferred to stand guard on the living room couch. Eventually, Father Dyer returned to bed. Despite Czarcik's dire warnings, the priest seemed oblivious to the danger he was in.

The one comfort Czarcik accepted—though without the priest's knowledge—was a bottle of Gordon's gin he pilfered from a cabinet under the sink.

He took a few large swigs from the bottle and wandered around the living room, waiting for the priest to fall back asleep. As he examined the decor and absentmindedly opened and closed whatever drawers he came across, he was most struck by how normal it all seemed. Low-end American Gothic. Some shitty china. A few oil paintings of New England harbors.

In the past, when Czarcik had busted pedophiles, their homes were usually temples to their pathology. Child porn was literally *everywhere*. Falling out of kitchen cupboards, stored in the never-used oven, the icebox, the bathtub, everywhere. It wasn't like in the movies, where the investigators find a few dodgy Polaroids stored away in a shoebox in the back of a closet. In real life, the houses were overflowing with it. But in Father Dyer's case, for a man with such a long and prolific sickness, there was virtually nothing.

Czarcik brought the gin back to the couch, where he proceeded to polish off half the bottle while watching a game show in which contestants punched each other in the genitals for money and other prizes. He considered calling Chloe but then changed his mind. After all, other than hearing her voice, what was the reason for it? He had a box of Rocky Patels back in the car but told himself he couldn't afford to leave the priest alone, not even for the thirty seconds it would take him to retrieve the cigars.

When his legs began to fall asleep and the soles of his feet started to tingle, he decided to explore the rest of the house. If he was quiet, he wouldn't disturb the sleeping priest.

Other than a dirty bathroom, there really wasn't much more to see on the ground floor, so Czarcik walked over to the staircase. The gin was old but still potent, so he held the banister on his way up for support.

The wall next to the stairs was empty. Conspicuously empty. Normally, in families, it was covered with photos of the members, a time line of their lives together, which mirrored the ascent, or descent, of the staircase. In the home of a priest, it was always covered with religious items or iconography. Cheap repros of Renaissance art. A favorite psalm knitted in a frame. Dyer didn't even have a cross.

Czarcik stopped at the top of the stairs and identified Father Dyer's room by the quiet snoring from within. Again he had an urge to kill the priest on the spot, but the feeling passed as quickly as it had come.

There were three other doors in the upstairs hallway. One opened into the bathroom, the other to a narrow linen closet, and the final one greeted Czarcik with a cloud of dust. When it cleared, another flight of steps materialized in front of him, leading up to the attic.

Moonlight streamed in from the attic window, illuminating the top half of the folding staircase. Czarcik took the steps slowly, listening to the dry wood crack under his weight.

The attic was smaller than he anticipated, just a hollowed-out triangle plopped down on top of the house. Because Dyer had been forced to move so often, he hadn't accumulated much of the normal attic detritus that seems to spontaneously appear over time. There were a few boxes of old books, a few more filled with vintage clothes. And then, especially creepy considering, a bunch of post-WWII rusty toys.

At the far end of the attic was the room's lone window. Czarcik could tell by its placement that it overlooked the front yard, but it was too dirty to see out of. Its latch was rusty and broken; a person of average strength could open it fairly easily. The dust on the windowsill was smeared, but it was impossible to tell what, or whom, was responsible, or how long ago they had been in the attic. Even with the benefit of a forensics team, it would be tough to lift a viable print. And even if they could, did it really matter?

As Czarcik rapped his knuckles lightly on the window, testing the fidelity of the glass, his mind flashed back to an episode of *The Alfred*

Hitchcock Hour. In it, an unlocked window teases the audience as a probable point of entry for a serial killer. But in a wonderful twist, the killer has been in the house the entire time, dressed as a nurse. Probably subversive for its time, certainly politically incorrect today.

Satisfied that no one had entered the house through the attic, or at least unable to prove that they had, Czarcik descended the stairs and returned to his post on the living room couch.

He studied the bottle of Gordon's and contemplated polishing it off. The stale air of the attic had left him a little queasy, so instead he decided to close his eyes for just a few minutes.

A deep and unwanted sleep came quickly, and within mere seconds he was embraced in the cold fingers of a nightmare. He was one of many altar boys, walking solemnly down the church aisle, clutching the altar bell, which swung back and forth but made no sound. In the pews, the parishioners turned their faces to the procession, but when Czarcik looked at them, their eyes turned black and rolled back into their heads. Father Dyer stood naked on the altar in all his glory. Where his crotch should have been was only a black void. Whenever Czarcik stared at it, it lost shape, becoming less and less defined.

The altar boys continued down the aisles, doubled back around the pews, and then joined Dyer on the altar. Czarcik was between two boys he didn't recognize, packed in so tightly he could barely breathe. He looked out into the audience, hoping for a friendly face. In the first row, a woman dressed in Puritan garb nursed a large crow as if it were a baby. The bird pecked at her, blood mixing with milk and forming a viscous pink liquid that trickled down her engorged breast. She smiled serenely and nodded at Czarcik, trying to give him the comfort he sought.

Suddenly, swarming masses of a strange animal seemed to materialize from every conceivable space on the altar. They were smooth like eels, their movement serpentine. They had no features—their anterior and posterior were identical—but somehow made horrible hissing sounds as tiny tufts of coarse hair sprouted from their damp coat.

Frenzied children dashed up from the pews and collected them like candy before tearing them to shreds with their teeth.

The young Czarcik wanted desperately to close his eyes, but when he tried, his lids were gone. He could feel the muscles trying to work, twitching futilely. In an instant Czarcik found himself nailed to the spot no less efficiently than his Lord and Savior had been to the cross. The boy pissed his pants. The creatures slithered over, as if attracted by the smell, splashing around aimlessly in the urine.

A giant creature reached out and placed its hands on the shoulders of young Czarcik, like a coach strategizing with a star player. It opened its mouth impossibly wide, snakelike, and moved its gaping jaws toward—

Someone was tapping him on the head. Not in church. Not in dreamland. Not fifty years ago. He opened his eyes to find Father Dyer standing in front of him. The priest offered him a mug with steam coming off the top.

Czarcik realized how exhausted he must have been. Under normal circumstances, even if he had been sleeping, he wouldn't have let someone get so close. His subconscious mind would have awakened him. Some watchdog he was. Father Dyer didn't say anything. He probably assumed that Czarcik had wanted to catch a few winks.

"It's coffee. Black. I assumed that's how you like it," Father Dyer said.

Czarcik sat up. He frowned as he accepted the mug, trying to hide just how badly he wanted that first sip of the hot, bitter liquid. "What time is it?"

"A little past eight. I usually rise pretty early, and you looked . . . frankly dead. I didn't have the heart to wake you."

Czarcik felt sick being the object of Dyer's compassion. Nevertheless, he wiped the sleep from his eyes and took a sip of the coffee. He felt groggy, as if he had slept far longer than he actually had. "Has anybody come by this morning?" he asked.

Dyer held back a chuckle and shook his head. "Every time you ask me that, Detective, the answer is always the same."

Czarcik allowed himself another sip of the coffee, got up off the couch, and walked over to the living room window. The curtains almost disintegrated in his hand as he pulled them back. He looked out the window onto the porch. Empty. The front lawn and sidewalk were also deserted. Just an ordinary lazy morning. He thought about walking outside, maybe taking a stroll up and down the street, but deep down he knew it was unnecessary.

As he turned away from the window, planning to return to the couch and plot his next move, he nearly bowled over Father Dyer. The priest was only inches from his face. The proximity was vaguely threatening, and Czarcik was about to order him to move away when he noticed a thin line of drool trickling down Dyer's lower lip. His eyes were unfocused; he was looking not *at* Czarcik, but *through* him.

Before Czarcik could ask him what was wrong, Dyer collapsed forward. Czarcik didn't catch him, but his body blunted the fall, and the priest slid down the detective's body until the man's upper torso was resting against Czarcik's lower legs.

"What the hell?" Czarcik said, annoyed, and pushed the priest onto the floor.

As soon as he exerted just that small amount of energy, his head swam. Everything in front of him went blurry. He closed his eyes tightly, then opened them, but his vision wouldn't stabilize. His throat was dry, but when he tried to generate some moisture, it felt as if somebody were rubbing sandpaper up and down his esophagus.

He staggered toward the kitchen, needing to draw himself a glass of water, until he realized his legs weren't working properly. Like rubber, he thought. As he dropped to one knee, he noticed Dyer lying on the floor. But he couldn't understand, or remember, what the priest was doing there.

The floor seemed to rise up to meet his face. Then his skull smashed into the wood. He saw stars, then darkness.

Once Czarcik came to, he felt the sensation of something hard against his lips.

He lowered his eyes and could barely make out the rim of a ceramic mug. "Drink it," a familiar voice said, just out of his field of vision. "It's only water."

Czarcik didn't care whether it was strychnine, urine, or whatever liquid had recently incapacitated him; he had never felt so parched. He gulped it down greedily as the hand holding the mug tilted it without spilling a drop. "I'll get you some more," the voice promised. "It's good for you. I just don't want you to drink too much too quickly and get sick."

With the help of the water, Czarcik's body was already starting to metabolize the drug. His vision was clearing up, and he was starting to feel more alert.

He was still in Dyer's living room. Although the curtains had been drawn and the room was dark, there was enough ambient light for him to make out his surroundings.

Across the room, Father Dyer was tied to a kitchen chair. This was no rush job. His arms were lashed to the chair's wooden armrests at both his wrists and his elbows. Both his ankles were tied tightly to the chair's legs. Unless he was a superhero, and the chair his jetpack, the priest wasn't going anywhere.

As Czarcik stared at him, he didn't see Dyer but mental images of Judge Robertson's body and the chicken tied around Marisol Fernandez's neck.

It was then that Czarcik realized that he, too, was tied to a chair, but not as securely as Dyer. The rope had some give, as if the person who tied him had tried not to cause him undue discomfort.

The ropes restraining Dyer, on the other hand, cut deeply into his flesh, so deep they were hard to see with the skin folding back over them.

But that wasn't the main reason the priest was moaning in pain.

TWENTY-SIX

Father Dyer was naked from the waist down.

There was a metal, uninsulated wire between his legs. From there it snaked underneath the chair where it then was attached to some contraption that reminded Czarcik of a large fishing reel.

As a student of the more gruesome aspects of history, Czarcik was all too familiar with the favorite tortures of Middle Eastern despots and corrupt South American regimes. But since the wire didn't appear to be connected to a power source, Czarcik couldn't imagine its purpose.

Daniel returned to the living room carrying a large glass of water. He had washed out his hair dye, and Czarcik realized that this was the first time he had seen the man in person without makeup or a disguise.

He was handsome, no doubt. Classically good looking, at least more so than Czarcik himself. It was easy to see how Chloe had fallen for him.

Again he brought the water to Czarcik's lips and helped him drink. "Take it slow, Detective. Time and water. The safest way to eliminate the chloral hydrate."

Czarcik finished the entire glass without stopping to take a single breath. As he was gulping down the water, he noticed that Daniel was wearing latex gloves.

Apparently, Daniel could tell what he was thinking. "You're right, Detective. At this point, I don't really need them. But it's less about leaving prints than, well . . ." He smiled shyly. Almost embarrassed. "I'm a little bit of a germaphobe, and just being in this place, with this"—he cocked his head toward Dyer—"this thing. It gives me the willies." He took away the empty glass and placed it on the coffee table. "Besides, I think I need gloves for what I'm about to do to him."

Czarcik jerked his head toward the priest. The chair shifted. "Let that piece of shit go, Daniel. We both know you've made your point."

Daniel recoiled, feigning surprise at Czarcik's request. "Made my point? Come on, Detective. Must we continue this charade? We both know I have no point to make. That's why you find me so infuriating." He jacked his thumb at the priest. "And why I'm so dangerous to monsters like this. I'm not a product of some childhood trauma, whom you could stop if only you could get me to come to terms with my past. I don't have some psychosis that you can address with rational thought nor religious delusions to which you can appeal through the vagaries of faith. No, unfortunately for you—and *him*, and all of *them*—I just have an insatiable urge to punish those who deserve it. And because of my condition, my death sentence, all the usual barriers preventing me from doing what I know to be just have been removed."

"But who are you to decide? To play God?"

Daniel laughed long and hard, not the laugh of a crazy man but of a perfectly sane one who had just heard something extraordinarily funny. "Oh, bravo, Detective. Bravo. That was a good one."

"You can still save your soul, my son," Father Dyer blurted out, deciding this was an appropriate time to chime in.

Daniel and Czarcik turned to the priest in perfect synchronicity. "Shut up!"

Father Dyer became silent. Decades of plying his sordid trade had left him with the ability to read people, and he could tell, almost intuitively, that he was not going to be able to convince his tormentor of anything. Nor did it seem as if his self-proclaimed protector was going to be much help. And although he was clearly the focus of whatever was about to happen, he couldn't help but feel that his presence was in some way incidental. These two men were engaged in a game whose rules he didn't understand.

Czarcik spoke first. "You're right, Daniel. He deserves to die. He's not even human. So do it. Kill him. But why not include me while you're at it? Why not just kill me too? You have no compunction about murder. Why force me to take part in all this nonsense?"

Daniel considered the question, realizing Czarcik deserved a legitimate response.

"Well, I could pretend it's because of Chloe," he said finally. "No man likes to see his wife in the arms of another. But I realize she's not going to be celibate forever. Even if it happened a little faster than I thought." He considered Czarcik. "The truth is . . . I'm allowing you to be a part of this because, well, we both know you enjoy it."

"You son of a bitch."

"Don't feel compelled to protest too much. All of us are virtually powerless to change our natures. We can pretend anything we want, but in the end, we are who we are." Daniel motioned to the priest but continued talking to Czarcik. "Now what separates you and me from him, from *that*, is that our sense of right and wrong—moral and immoral—is stronger than our basest urges. We may *think*, but we don't *act*. It's the difference between madmen and, well, men."

"Look at me, Daniel," Czarcik demanded, making a show of straining against the ropes. "You call this *my* decision? I'm tied up like a pig to the slaughter."

Daniel smiled. "Let's call it a gift, Detective. My gift to you. Now you have the luxury of telling yourself that there was nothing you could do. You were incapacitated. Forced to watch. This you can convince yourself of. At the very least, when this is all over, your colleagues will buy it."

"You fucking hypocrite," Czarcik spat, visibly angry and not caring if it showed. "You may talk a good game, but I've seen your work. Seen how much painstaking care went into it. You can justify it any way you want, but I know you like it too."

Daniel took a few steps toward Czarcik until he was standing directly in front of him. "That's where you're wrong, Detective." He leaned down until he was only inches from Czarcik's face, their noses practically touching. "I fucking *love* it."

He spoke the last two words with such a dramatic flourish that he looked like an overacting silent movie star.

Czarcik wondered how much of this transformation from mild-mannered husband to serial killer was nothing more than a physiological effect of the tumor. How much of it was from the knowledge that he was in fact dying? How much was a repressed bloodlust given life by a convenient excuse? And how relevant were any of the reasons for his behavior, other than the fact that Czarcik's one job was to bring Daniel to justice?

Leaving Czarcik with spittle on his face, Daniel walked over to his current prize.

He stood in front of the priest as Dyer averted his eyes. He dropped to one knee and reached underneath the priest's chair. "How many children did you have, you son of a bitch?" Daniel asked, before turning the handle of the contraption in a clockwise rotation.

Father Dyer raised his head, like a newborn bird being fed, and screamed. Czarcik watched, too curious to take any pleasure in Dyer's torment.

Daniel let go of the reel and stood up, fresh blood splattered all over his latex gloves. Again, as if reading Czarcik's mind, he explained, "It's just a commercial-grade plumbing snake. The kind that plumbers use. The outer coat is covered in metal scales for maximum flexibility.

Almost like a snake, but razor sharp. In a ceramic bowl, through copper and PVC pipes, it doesn't cause any damage. But a human being's gastrointestinal canal is made of less sturdy stuff."

He snapped his wrist, sending drops of blood to the floor. "As you've no doubt guessed, I inserted the device into our dear father's rectum."

Czarcik had to give Daniel credit, if not some measure of respect; he was a modern-day Hammurabi.

Father Dyer's screams settled into a low moan.

Something was gnawing at Czarcik. It wasn't that the man in front of him was about to meet his end in one of the most painful ways imaginable. That actually seemed fitting. What had been bothering him, almost since the beginning, was that he still didn't know what his ultimate role was in Daniel's grand plan.

Daniel was the enigma he couldn't quite wrap his head around, like an ancient riddle that turned to sand through his fingers just as it was about to be solved. If Daniel had wanted Czarcik dead, he'd had ample opportunities to kill him already, not least of them twenty minutes ago when the detective was as helpless as a patient under heavy anesthesia.

Nor was Daniel someone who ostensibly relished the chase. He didn't send taunting notes to the police or press. He had no desire to ensure his crimes lived on in infamy, like most garden-variety lunatics who wanted to be known for *something*. He was just an unknown angel of death, cutting a swath across the belly of the country.

This made him one of the most modestly effective serial killers in recent memory. And that *is* what he was—a serial killer. Despite his self-proclaimed moral superiority, in the eyes of the law, he was no different from a Berkowitz, Dahmer, or Bundy.

Czarcik was so busy psychoanalyzing their master of ceremonies it took him a moment to realize that Dyer was screaming once again.

Although Czarcik knew he was in no immediate danger, he figured he should still mount an escape plan. His hands weren't tied particularly tightly, but they were bound in such a way that he had no leverage or range of motion. So even if he managed to get ahold of some makeshift cutting tool, there was no way he could manipulate it properly.

What he *could* do was move the chair, at least a little. While he might have been tied to the chair, the chair wasn't secured to the floor.

Unfortunately there was nothing in the immediate vicinity against which Czarcik could scrape the ropes binding his wrists. The closest piece of furniture was the couch, a few feet to his left, but that was covered in soft fabric.

Underneath Father Dyer's chair, a puddle of blood had begun to pool.

For the first time, Father Dyer emitted not only a scream, but a word. "Mercy." It was music to Daniel's ears. He flicked his fingers toward the floor, shaking off some blood, and stood up.

Daniel took Dyer by the face, his thumb pressed firmly into one cheek while his other four fingers dug into the other side of the priest's face. "How many of them begged for mercy, you fucking animal? How many of them?"

"All of them," the priest replied quietly.

With the focus momentarily off him, Czarcik looked around desperately for the closest object that could conceivably cut through the ropes. Halfway between him and Father Dyer, just off his left knee, was a heavy marble end table with chipped edges. It was a long shot even with ample time. Plus, Czarcik didn't think Daniel would allow him to shuffle his chair over, inch by inch, until he was close enough to try.

But Daniel was still busy with the priest. Getting worked up. "Then tell me, Father, why should I show you that which you refused to show others? Even the youngest and most vulnerable in your care."

Czarcik could tell that Dyer was searching for the right answer. The answer that might save him. "Because you're a righteous man. And I'm a broken old man."

"Save me your insincere self-loathing, Father. I'm obviously not righteous, just an ordinary man doing his part to bring some sense of order to the universe. You're a child rapist of the worst order. So you're going to have to do better than that."

Czarcik strained against the ropes. Daniel wasn't paying attention, his focus exclusively on Dyer.

"Tell me something, Father. And answer me honestly, or there will be consequences. Do you understand me?"

Father Dyer nodded. His face was the color of meat gone bad.

"Do you even believe in Hell?" Daniel asked.

Father Dyer took his time, then shook his head.

"Thank you for your honesty. This is something we have in common; I don't either. I believe that once I release you from your mortal coil, you're simply going to cease to exist. That's why I need to make the little time you have left hell on earth."

Underneath his chair, the pool of blood was rapidly expanding.

"Stop it, now!"

The outrage in Czarcik's voice surprised Daniel. At worst, he'd pegged the detective as being apathetic toward his methods; at best, tacitly supportive. He was even more surprised when Czarcik hurled himself—well, more like lurched—forward.

What is he thinking? Daniel wondered. Czarcik hadn't managed to free a single appendage. For all his trouble, he found himself facedown, still tied to the chair, with most of his weight borne by his knees and forehead.

Daniel looked down at the upturned man, impressed at his determination. "Jesus, Detective." Czarcik ignored him and rolled himself into the nearby coffee table. Daniel watched with a combination of curiosity and pity. When he couldn't bear to witness Czarcik's struggle any longer, he bent down and lifted up the chair. The detective was heavier than he thought, strong and muscular. He righted him next to the coffee table. "What the hell do you think you're doing?"

Czarcik was breathing deeply, trying to catch his breath. "There's no reason for you to keep me here. But if you insist on it, I'm going to do my job and try to stop you."

Daniel laughed. "You are indefatigable, my friend. But please, don't try that again. It's futile, and I don't want you knocking out a tooth. Or worse."

Czarcik nodded, but the moment Daniel turned his attention back to Father Dyer, he started vigorously rubbing the rope binding his wrists against the sharp corner of the coffee table. It was like he was back in Boy Scouts, trying to make a fire with a pair of dry sticks.

Czarcik could tell Dyer didn't have much time left. He watched as Daniel gave the handle another twist. The priest grew paler by the second.

The rope tied around Czarcik's wrist was beginning to give. He didn't know how many strands he had sliced through, or how many were left, but the tension was different. He could feel it.

Daniel grabbed hold of the snake handle like a man possessed, ready for the priest to finally meet his end.

At the very moment the priest went silent forever, his soul surely at the gates of Hell, Czarcik cut through the ropes.

He tried to time his dive perfectly with the exact moment he untied his ankles. But those ropes were tighter than he'd imagined, and he tripped forward. As he was falling, he reached for Daniel, who was transfixed by the priest, whose internal organs were now outside his body.

Czarcik reached for Daniel, his fingertips brushing him.

And then everything again went black.

It was his phone that jostled him awake. It was on the floor, right in the middle of a pool of Father Dyer's blood.

His cheek was on the ground, the wood underneath it warm. He opened his top eye, the one farthest from the floor, and saw Father Dyer staring right back at him. Pupils dilated. Coal-black soul now gone.

Czarcik groaned and reached behind his head. Felt the egg-shaped protrusion. Took his hand away, looked at it, and was surprised not to find blood. Whatever had knocked him out hadn't broken the skin. But his head hurt like hell. It felt like a bad hangover times twenty.

Again the phone rang. He knew he should answer it. Didn't want to. He was in no condition to talk. Finally, the caller gave up.

The only thing Czarcik wanted to do was go back to sleep. Slip back into that blissful state of unconsciousness.

But instead, he forced himself up into a sitting position. He swooned. The room tilted forty-five degrees, and his stomach was in his throat. He turned away from the priest before vomiting all over the floor. Mild concussion, he told himself. Nothing to do but rest. After all, as a high school tailback, he had suffered far worse and been trotted right back onto the field after a whiff of smelling salts.

The blood around his BlackBerry had begun to congeal, so he plucked it out of the hardening puddle. He looked at the screen. Thirty-seven missed calls. Fourteen texts. They were all from Chloe, the last one only minutes ago. How long had he been out? he wondered.

He was just about to call her back when the phone rang again. Chloe. He hit Accept. "Hi."

"Where the hell have you been?" She could barely conceal the panic in her voice. "I called you a hundred times. I thought you were . . . dead." She hesitated, as if speaking the word might prove prescient.

"Not yet . . . although I feel like it."

She sighed, the first breath she had taken since hearing his voice. "Where are you?" she asked.

Still suffering the effects of the concussion, he struggled to remember.

"Still in Tennessee?" she offered.

He closed his eyes tightly, allowing it to come back to him. The game of chicken with the high beams. Father Dyer. Daniel. Another murder. The pungent smell of blood and shit. Yes, he could remember, as much as he wished he could forget some of it. "Yes, still in Tennessee," he answered. "Where are *you*?"

"Florida," she replied. She was completely unaware of his head trauma, and consequently, how much it was affecting him. "When I couldn't get ahold of you, I kind of freaked out. It didn't make much sense to go to Tennessee, so I went right to the airport and bought a ticket for Miami. I landed only an hour or so ago."

"Florida," Czarcik repeated, as if the word was not one of the most well-known states, but a mysterious password he was forced to enunciate clearly. The pieces of his memory began to fall into place, like a game of Tetris. "Because that's where the reform school is."

"I knew you'd eventually end up there," she said, finishing his thought. She paused, as if something just occurred to her. "Actually, why aren't you already there?"

"Tennessee took longer than I anticipated." It was all coming back to him now.

"Did something happen?" By *something*, she meant Daniel.

"He got what he wanted, Chloe. I couldn't stop him. I was there the entire time, and I couldn't do a goddamned thing."

"Could he have killed you?" she asked.

"Many times over."

Silence. Then she asked, "You think he's here? In Florida?"

"I'm sure of it."

More silence. "How soon can you be here?"

He pictured a map—Tennessee was one big state of Georgia away from Florida—and didn't know how quickly he could get there. Especially in his condition. His head felt as if it were bouncing around a blast furnace. "I'm not sure. Let me . . . think. Get my bearings. I'll call you back in an hour."

"Leave your phone on," she admonished. She had never heard him sound so uncertain. So vulnerable. It frightened her. "What should I do in the meantime?"

"Where are you now?" he asked, forgetting whether she had already told him.

"The airport bar."

"Stay there. Have a few drinks. Once I'm on my way, I'll call you, and we'll make a plan."

"OK," she said, then waited. "Paul?"

"Yes."

"Be careful. Please."

He ended the call and realized that Father Dyer was still fixing him with his lifeless gaze.

"Burn in hell, you old bastard," he said as he tried to stand up. The blood rushed to his head, and he fought back the urge to vomit again. He took a moment to steady himself against the marble table, amazed at how much blood had been disgorged from the priest. If it wasn't a full ten pints, it was close. There were also pieces of pink flesh scattered around the body that Czarcik pretended not to see. His stomach couldn't handle it at the moment.

He walked slowly into the kitchen, aware he was probably dehydrated, and took a glass from the cabinet. But since he couldn't remember exactly how Daniel had spiked his drink, he figured the safest thing to do was drink directly from the faucet. The water tasted tinny, but at least he knew it wasn't tampered with. He drank until his stomach protested.

Czarcik had to get moving. He also needed a shower as badly as ever, so he made his way up the stairs to the second floor, glancing briefly at the door to the attic, through whose window he assumed Daniel had entered. Too bad *The Alfred Hitchcock Hour* was canceled decades ago. The last few hours would have made a particularly good episode. By the time he got to the upstairs bathroom, he was so exhausted he practically collapsed onto the toilet. He still didn't have his legs back.

He took a few minutes to gather his strength. Then he managed to undress, get into the shower, and turn on the water as hot as he could tolerate. He refused to use the priest's soap or shampoo, as if the man's moral sickness could be transferred by inanimate objects. His towels were especially verboten. Czarcik simply stood in the middle of the bathroom, letting himself drip dry, aided by the light breeze from the ceiling fan.

Before leaving the house, he thought about siphoning some gas from his car, splashing it on the curtains and flammable furniture, and setting the whole place on fire. Then watching it go up in a huge conflagration, consigning the old priest's corpse to a symbolic underworld.

But grand gestures weren't his style.

Back in his car, Czarcik was slightly amused to find the Groucho mustache still resting on the front seat. He couldn't believe it was less than twenty-four hours ago that he had been traipsing through backyards and dodging angry skunks. In the cold light of day, the mustache didn't appear threatening; it appeared laughable. Nothing more than what it was: part of a dime-store costume. Even its significance was less dire. The game was almost over. Daniel could have eliminated Czarcik but had chosen to let him go. In his mind, the detective was no longer relevant. There was one final stop. One more place to mete out justice.

Czarcik pulled the Crown Vic away from the curb, into the street, and out of Father Dyer's neighborhood. The priest would begin to rot, after which some nosey passersby would contact the police. But that could be weeks from now. There was no time for Czarcik to worry about it.

I have miles to go before I sleep, he thought to himself, wondering why that insipid poem from grammar school had popped back into his head.

TWENTY-SEVEN

1992

It was snowing lightly when Dr. Wilson Kuzma walked out of McCormick Hall, which housed his office.

The streets of Hyde Park, home to the University of Chicago, were practically deserted. Most of the students were either hunkered down in their dorms or keeping warm in the nearby coffee shops and bars.

The professor pulled his wool coat tightly shut and glanced up and down the street. The neighborhood had made strides over the past few years. That still didn't mean it was the kind of place you wanted to find yourself alone at night. But it was late, he was tired, and his car was in a parking deck only a few blocks away.

Dr. Kuzma walked underneath a crumbling concrete bridge decorated by gang graffiti and, more recently, rainbows painted by children from the local elementary school. Whenever a train crossed over, bits of colored concrete would shake loose and float down upon the passersby. An urban snowfall.

He had nearly cleared the bridge when a bum materialized from behind the last support column. The professor flinched instinctively and moved to the far side of the underpass.

"Spare a dime, mister?" The bum was well built. He didn't look as if he had spent years on the street. He wore a thick down jacket. Expensive.

If he came by it honestly, it must have been a donation. A black watch cap stopped at his eyebrows, and his face was covered in dirt.

"Not today, sorry," Dr. Kuzma apologized.

"I said, 'Spare a dime, mister?'"

"Look—"

The bum was pointing a gun at him. The professor could barely see the barrel poking out from inside the bum's jacket. But there was no mistaking his posture. Or confidence. The bum knew what he was doing. This wasn't a squirrelly meth head who had come across a weapon and hoped to make some quick cash.

"Just take my wallet, please. There's some cash and a bunch of credit cards." He reached slowly into the inside pocket of his coat.

"Keep your hands where I can see them, you fucking piece of shit."

No, this was no ordinary robbery.

The bum led Dr. Kuzma to the parking deck, right over to the professor's car. He motioned with the gun. "Give me your keys."

"How'd you know—"

"Shut up, shut the fuck up." He was angry, but it was a controlled rage. "I'm going to talk, and you're going to listen. You're going to do exactly as I say. If you don't, I'm going to kill you without thinking twice about it." The professor shut up. "Now hand me the keys to your car."

The bum took the keys and opened the passenger door of the professor's Cadillac. "Get in, and put your hands on the dash. If you move them off the dash, say goodbye." The professor slid into the seat, closed the door, and placed both hands palms down on the dashboard. The bum kept the gun trained on him the entire time, then slipped around the front of the car, opened the driver-side door, and got inside.

Dr. Kuzma glanced frantically around the parking garage, but it was empty. No help coming. The bum reached behind him and removed a pair of handcuffs from his belt. "Give me your left wrist." The professor hesitated. "It makes no difference to me if I kill you right now and toss you off the side of this garage."

The professor took his hand off the dash and held it up. The bum snapped on the cuff. He then took the other cuff, pulled it toward the floor, and secured it to the metal bar that controlled the movement of the passenger seat. The chain on the handcuffs was short, and the professor was forced to remain hunched over.

"I can't move."

The bum punched him in the mouth. Even with leather gloves and little room to wind up, he managed to draw blood. The professor groaned, checked his teeth with his tongue, and went silent.

The lights of the Chicago Skyway illuminated the car more than any time since the interior light had been triggered in the parking garage.

Dr. Kuzma was curled up in the space between the seat and the dash. He turned his head to look at the driver. The bum's eyes weren't the rheumy eyes of an addict. They were clear, focused. And his face, while filthy, almost looked as if the dirt had been applied. Like stage makeup. Most curious of all, he didn't smell. He didn't have that rank stench of raw humanity that clung to those who lived on the street. In fact, if the professor closed his eyes and focused, he could almost imagine the scent of fading cologne.

He had been told not to speak, but they had been traveling for close to twenty minutes in silence. He didn't believe the bum would kill him for trying to engage him. "Please, I have a wife and daughter."

The bum looked at him. "You had another child?"

And then he knew. Knew why the bum didn't move like a bum. Why he didn't rob him. Why he didn't smell. "Oh, God."

As Indiana greeted them, the professor felt certain he was being taken to a specific place. The police officer, whatever his name was—Czarcik?—had no intention of killing him in the car. "You know, for someone with such an appreciation of philosophy, I'm a little disappointed," Dr. Kuzma said.

Czarcik looked at him. The professor took this as his cue to continue.

"There are some people for whom the normal rules of society simply don't apply." He feigned disappointment. "I thought you might be one of them." Czarcik didn't respond. "People like you and me . . . we can't be burdened by these artificial constraints. These moral prisons that stifle our human and very normal desires."

The officer's mouth turned up in a slight smile. Was he reaching him? The professor continued. "The arbitrary laws of man must not be allowed—"

Czarcik's right fist shot out like a mamba. It caught Dr. Kuzma right under his armpit, breaking two of his ribs. The professor let out a feline yelp, then commenced moaning softly.

The sound didn't seem to bother Czarcik, who continued smiling.

Those who snidely refer to New Jersey as the "armpit of America" have never been to Gary, Indiana.

Even at this time of night, the toxic breath of the factories stained the cold lake air. Thick clouds of pollution hovered around the iron smokestacks, looking as solid as dirty ivory. There was no human activity. At least none visible from the highway. It was almost as if some ancient deity had declared this spit of lakeside real estate his personal ashtray.

Dr. Kuzma—sore, cramped, and increasingly desperate—tried another tack. "I'm a sick man. You must realize that?" Czarcik stared straight ahead. "You think a day goes by when I don't struggle with the urge? The urge to punish myself for what I've done? To kill myself? Take me back. Take me back, and I'll turn myself in. I'll make a statement. I'll admit to everything."

Czarcik pulled the car off to the side of the road. "Admit to what?"

The professor swallowed hard, clearly in pain. "Admit to raping Genevieve. My daughter."

Czarcik pressed the gun against the professor's knee and pulled the trigger. The man fainted the moment his patella exploded into a thousand tiny fragments.

When Dr. Kuzma came to, they were no longer on the highway. The car had stopped. It was dark and cold inside. A thin layer of frost prevented him from seeing out the window.

As if reading his thoughts, Czarcik said, "We're in the back of a paint factory that closed down years ago. This whole place is like a ghost town."

The professor felt queasy, as if he could vomit at any moment. His leg, drenched with blood, was numb. *I'm in shock,* he thought to himself.

He turned his head, which was resting on the dashboard, and looked at Czarcik. "Why me? Why after all this time?" he asked.

It was his first genuine reaction since Czarcik had accosted him. The first time he wasn't trying to rationalize or justify.

"Because ever since I saw your daughter's face in the newspaper, I haven't been able to sleep. She haunts my dreams."

"That bitch," the professor said. He closed his eyes and turned away from Czarcik. When he heard the driver-side door open, then close, he flinched, but didn't look back.

Czarcik walked away from the car, the gun at his side. An unlit cigarette in his mouth. With his free hand, he reached into his pocket and pulled out a book of matches. Ran a match against the flint with his thumb. Lit the cigarette.

Back in the car, the professor thought he had been given a reprieve. *They'll find me. If I can only last the night, they'll find me,* he thought.

Czarcik took a drag, dropped the cigarette to the dusty ground, and snuffed it out. He raised his gun, leveled it, aimed.

The bullet struck the gas tank.

A fireball exploded into the still night air as the agonizing screams of someone being burned alive echoed through the abandoned wasteland.

The next night, for the first time in years, Czarcik slept like a baby.

TWENTY-EIGHT

Czarcik needed to get from Tennessee to Olmstead, Florida, home to Crystal Lake Ranch, a reform school for boys the system had given up on, as quickly as possible.

He considered taking a plane, as Chloe had done, but with the ticket purchase, airport security, and all the other hassles air travel entailed, he figured it was probably just as fast to drive, an almost straight shot down I-75.

He called Chloe once he was on the road. Told her when he was planning to arrive. She said she was going to find a motel close to Crystal Lake Ranch and wait for him.

Although he still had half a tank of gas remaining, he decided to stop at the nearest gas station. He figured he should eat, even if he wasn't hungry. Food would metabolize the drug faster than water alone, and besides, he needed the energy.

A dishwater blond whose nametag read Me'Chelle watched him place a package of peppered beef jerky, a banana, and a lemon-lime Gatorade on the counter. He asked her for two packs of unfiltered Lucky Strikes, which he hadn't smoked for years. For what lay ahead, he needed the strong stuff. She found them behind the counter, scanned them, and bagged up all his items.

"I used to smoke those too," she offered.

He paid with a credit card and took the bag from her.

"Good for you." And he was back on the highway.

As volunteers gave way to peaches, the highway signage became more overtly religious. Catholic charities offered safe and confidential options for young women in need, while tiny congregations spent ungodly sums to warn motorists about the infernal dangers of aborting an unwanted fetus.

Some billboards displayed nothing more than a series of numbers. No text, but Czarcik figured anyone familiar enough would already know to which Bible verse they corresponded.

There were also an inordinate number of advertisements for alligator farms, although from the pictures on the signs, it was hard to determine which ones rescued and bred gators, and which ones slaughtered them for meat or clothing.

Having polished off a quart of Gatorade, Czarcik's bladder was calling. Rather than lose time, he pulled over to the side of the road. As he stood there, pecker in hand, the steaming urine darkening the roadside dirt, he had an image of a massive semi plowing straight into his car. Like a scene out of a Stephen King novel, the possessed truck, animated by an ancient evil, would reduce the Crown Vic to a husk of burning metal before continuing on its quest to sow death and destruction along the blacktop.

Only a few cars drove by, however, giving him a wide berth. He zipped up and got back in the car.

As soon as he was again on his way, he called Chloe. "Where are you?" she asked him. He found it slightly disconcerting that they didn't need to identify themselves. He blamed it on caller ID, not on their growing familiarity.

"I'll be there before dark. Where are you?"

"At a Motel 6. Around a lot of people. Website says this is the most popular place to stay for tourists exploring the Everglades. It's less than three miles from the reformatory."

"Good . . ." He felt the need to say something.

"I'm scared, Paul," Chloe admitted after a few seconds. "I can feel him. I know it sounds crazy, but I know he's already here."

"You just stay in your room. Stay in your room, and keep the door locked. You'll be fine," he reassured her, doing it badly. "Try to get some sleep. I'll be there as soon as I can." He ended the call with nothing more to say.

At the gas station, he had taken the hollow can of shaving cream out of his bag. Now, while driving, he unscrewed the bottom and tapped some coke onto the side of his hand. Seconds later it was gone. He'd needed that. He needed to concentrate.

Something was bothering him, and he didn't know what. After all, despite Daniel still being alive, Czarcik had been extraordinarily effective in tracking him. There had been no wrong moves on his part. Although Daniel had remained one step ahead, this was due to circumstance, not intuition. Czarcik had beaten him to Father Dyer's house; he had just been unable to protect the priest.

Both his abilities and his reliance on Chloe had served him well thus far.

Chloe.

It was because of her that he was this close to Daniel. He accepted that. And yet, he still didn't trust her. Not completely.

She had found the folders and delivered them right to the authorities. She had told him the truth about the insurance money. She had been accessible when needed, but hardly obtrusive.

Yet there it was. Doubt, which made no logical sense. And still he was unable to ignore it.

As soon as Czarcik hit the state line, he pressed harder on the gas, as if the arbitrary boundary somehow increased his urgency. He turned the radio to a local news station, but there was no mention of a massacre, or any disturbance, at Crystal Lake Ranch. With time to ruminate, Czarcik wondered whether he was making a mistake. Everything thus far had been linear, with only minor deviations from Daniel's original plan. But now Daniel was aware he was being followed. True, he had still continued to Tennessee after the episode in the diner, but that was for a single man. This was something bigger. A lot bigger. The grand finale of his sprawling opera.

Then again, maybe this was the genius of it. He was a serial killer who exhibited none of the defining characteristics. While most mass murderers pined for recognition, Daniel accepted anonymity, even preferred it.

The radio melted into white noise. Real estate ads, Rays scores, deals for Walt Disney World and Busch Gardens. There was a shoot-out at a nearby trailer park, but the cops on the scene had already classified it as "gang related."

The distance between strip malls grew as the first hint of the Everglades, with its distinctive foliage, came into view. Until now, Florida might as well have been New Jersey, or LA. Someone once described the entire state to Czarcik as a giant sponge with the Everglades in the middle. It was a description he now found apt.

Years ago, back in Chicago, following a tryst with an Asian escort when he was so high on coke and uppers that he was practically bouncing off the ceiling, he had tried to relax by watching a documentary on the flora and fauna of southern Florida. What he once assumed was nothing more than a vast wasteland of mangrove swamps and a dump zone for the Florida mob was in actuality one of the most diverse ecosystems on earth. Home to a menagerie of colorful birds, endangered panthers, pythons, and a rodent the size of a small pig, which supposedly made for good eating. It was also the sole habitat of the Florida manatee, the gigantic aquatic mammal that gave birth to the mermaid legend, and was a favorite feeding ground for bull sharks, one of the most aggressive shark species, which thought nothing of visiting fresh-water estuaries to find a meal.

From the car, none of this was evident. The huge cypresses that bordered the road were excellent sentries. The highway was nothing more than an ugly scar, man's incursion into God's country.

His BlackBerry rang. He picked it up without looking and held it against his ear. "Almost there."

"You want to tell me what the fuck is going on?" *Parseghian.* His voice caught Czarcik completely off guard.

"Just doing my job, boss." He tried to sound casual.

"Tell me you're still in Illinois." Czarcik didn't answer. "Goddamn it, Paul," said Parseghian. "I get a call from the lady sheriff of some Podunk county across the state line in Indiana. Seems they got a fucking bloodbath down there at some orphanage. They're still trying to make heads or tails of what the fuck happened. She remembered talking to you. Said you just disappeared. She's wondering if you might know anything that could help them."

"OK."

"OK? OK?" repeated Parseghian, incredulous. "You want to tell me what the fuck all this has to do with your case?"

The Motel 6 sign beckoned from above the tree line.

"Can't right now, boss."

A sigh. "Where are you, Paul?"

"Can't tell you that either."

"I could have Corrine trace the call."

"Knock yourself out. I'll be back in a few days."

Czarcik ended the call and then pulled off the road into the parking lot of the Motel 6. His phone rang again. Parseghian. And then it kept ringing some more.

Chloe walked out of the motel office and across the gravel parking lot to meet him.

She kissed him firmly on the lips. "I was worried." He nodded, then kissed her back.

"You got directions for me?"

She held up a piece of paper. "Only a few miles west of here. Maid at the motel said it's a single road."

"You know I don't want you coming."

She smiled. "And you know I couldn't give a shit. I'm not leaving you. Not again. Not now."

He knew there was no use arguing. "You ready now?"

She nodded. But she didn't look it.

As he was driving, Chloe took the cigarette from between his fingers and took a drag.

He looked at her. "Since when do you smoke?"

She shrugged. "I don't. But I really needed that."

"Were you able to get on the internet at the motel?"

"I was."

"Find anything interesting?"

She shrugged again. "Nothing that wasn't in the file. Paul, this place is evil. There have been hundreds of complaints over the years. And not just the usual stuff you hear about in juvenile-detention facilities. We're talking torture, solitary confinement, assaults, maybe even murder. I mean, if I wasn't a cynic before . . . Investigations have never proved anything. Witnesses won't talk, or they disappear. It's like East Germany."

"It's worse. It's Florida."

Some say the world will end in fire,
Some say in ice.
From what I've tasted of desire
I hold with those who favor fire.

Fire. His brain was on fire. Just last night, for the first time, he had soiled himself as he lay in his motel bed. He would not let that happen again.

This was the point at which he knew he should be taking stock of his life. But he had already taken care of that months ago. To do so now would seem almost . . . indulgent. He wasn't sure that was the right word. And then, the more he thought about it, the more he thought it was absolutely perfect.

He wished he had the answer for the question that everybody would want to know: How much were his actions the result of a purely physiological condition, and how much was choice?

But he didn't have the answer. Or if he did, he was in no condition to retrieve it.

The best answer, he thought, was the second half of that Robert Frost poem.

> But if it had to perish twice,
> I think I know enough of hate
> To say that for destruction ice
> Is also great
> And would suffice.

Czarcik slammed on the brakes. Walking along the side of the road was a young boy—fifteen at the most—wearing standard-issue reformatory pants and no shirt. He looked dazed. Czarcik pulled up and rolled down the window. He leaned across Chloe to talk.

"You OK, son?" The kid looked right through Czarcik. "It's OK. I'm a police officer." Czarcik realized how ridiculous he sounded considering where the kid had come from. "You want to tell me what happened?"

The kid scratched his head. He didn't appear injured. He didn't even appear particularly frightened. What he did appear was completely and utterly confused.

"There was some shooting, man. Lots of screaming and lots of shooting. And then they came. The guards. And started letting us all out." He looked at Czarcik, and his eyes focused for the first time. "Letting us out." It was as if he wanted Czarcik to explain it to him. Then he continued walking down the road.

Czarcik turned to Chloe. Neither one of them said anything. They drove on.

The enormous and immaculately maintained lawn in front of Crystal Lake Ranch looked like a scene out of *Night of the Living Dead*.

Hundreds of boys wandered aimlessly around the grounds. A handful of guards were there but looked as if they didn't know what to do either. There were a couple of fights, which no one seemed interested in breaking up, and a few boys lying facedown on the grass, either unconscious or dead.

A small dirt road, big enough for a single vehicle, hugged the west side of the lawn and led up to the ranch's main building.

Czarcik pulled to a stop. He pointed his finger at Chloe. "Stay here in the car, and keep the doors locked. And don't argue with me." He took his gun from the holster and handed it to Chloe. "You know how to use this?"

"Just point and pull the trigger?"

"Exactly. But only if someone tries to get in. Otherwise, just sit tight. I'll be back soon. But if they do . . . don't think twice."

She nodded. "What about you?"

He reached over and popped the glove compartment. Inside was an untraceable revolver. "I'll be fine."

The air smelled of madness. There was no other way to describe it.

On the steps leading up to the main building sat a young black man, seventeen or eighteen years old. In his hands he held a wooden nightstick, dripping with blood.

At his feet, sprawled out on the steps, arms and legs twisted at wrong angles, was a middle-aged man in an officer's uniform. The entire left side of his head was caved in. Blood and bits of hair everywhere.

The young man looked up as Czarcik approached. "He raped me. And his buddies raped me. And the chick guard raped me with her nightstick because, well, you know . . ." He didn't seem angry. Or sorry. Just . . . lost.

Czarcik nodded in quiet understanding and walked up the few steps to the main door. "I wouldn't go in there," the young man called out to him.

Czarcik motioned to the building with his gun. "What's in there?"

"Hell," he replied.

When he opened the door, the smell inside was easy to discern. It was the distinct and overpowering scent of gasoline. The room reeked of it.

And as soon as Czarcik stepped inside, he saw why.

There were a dozen guards, ten men and two women. They were all completely naked and spread out equidistantly around the room.

He couldn't figure out why they were all just standing there, until he noticed that each of them was standing inside a circle of gasoline. On closer inspection, they had all been thoroughly doused. The women's hair was soaked. The liquid dripped off their bodies, from their breasts to their feet.

All the circles were connected to each other by a line of gasoline.

"Who the fuck are you? Help us!" screamed one of the guards as Czarcik entered the room.

Another guard cried out, "He said if any of us move, if any of us try to escape, we all go up like candles."

Czarcik tried to reassure them with his calm demeanor. "Where is he?"

A female guard pointed to a door in the back of the room. "He took the warden in there about half an hour ago. We heard screaming."

Czarcik followed the trail of gasoline that led to the back office. Daniel wasn't fooling around. One dropped match, and a river of fire would engulf the building and turn everyone inside into human torches.

He reached for the doorknob, trying not to step in the gasoline pooled underneath the door. "Daniel, it's Czarcik. Don't shoot. I'm coming in . . ."

The warden didn't look good.

He was probably in his late fifties—closely cropped, steel-gray hair, Stalinesque mustache, pale-blue eyes.

But this wasn't why he didn't look good. He didn't look good because his left hand was missing all its fingers.

They were on the ground in front of him in a pool of blood, but not a pool as big as Czarcik would have expected. Then he saw why. Daniel was holding a small blowtorch; he had cauterized each of the finger stumps after removing the digit.

The warden was tied to a chair, his injured arm hanging listlessly at his side. Minus fingers, it looked weird. Like the thalidomide hand of a boy with whom Czarcik was friends in elementary school.

Czarcik looked at Daniel and shook his head. "My god, Daniel. The fuck did you do?" Gestured around. "This is not revenge. This is . . . chaos."

As he waited for a response, he realized Daniel didn't look good either. His eyes were shadowed and seemed to have retreated deeper into his skull, like two caves. He appeared thinner than he'd seemed in Tennessee, if that was possible. And his skin looked bad. Waxy. Like a mannequin's.

Daniel tried to wet his mouth. It was hard for him to speak. "You know what this man has done. What his subordinates have done. You've read the stories. Even if only a fraction of it were true . . ."

Czarcik pointed the gun away from Daniel and held up his hands. A gesture of surrender. "Daniel, listen to me. The other ones . . . the judge was a piece of shit. The Fernandezes deserved to die. So did Father Dyer. Many times over. Between me and you, between me and you, Daniel, in some ways you're a hero. Because we both know that the system wasn't going to punish those motherfuckers like they deserved to be punished." He paused. Looked around, disgusted. "But this . . . this isn't justice. This is mass murder."

Daniel smiled. "A rose by any other name . . ."

At that moment Czarcik realized that Daniel was no longer fully sane.

The warden moaned softly. Drool dripped from the corner of his mouth. Czarcik looked at the warden, then back up at Daniel. He had tried logic, threats, sophistry, and a little of the old reverse psychology. Now he looked into Daniel's eyes and tried one final approach. "Daniel, I'm begging you. For Chloe, please don't do this."

Daniel stiffened. He fought back tears. He held the blowtorch over the line of gasoline that led to the main room. "Make sure my story is told. Let the world know why. Only you can do that." He swallowed hard. "And tell my wife I love her."

Czarcik knew this was the end. He watched as Daniel tried to light the blowtorch.

And then he leveled his gun and blew Daniel's brains—along with the tumor—right through the back of his skull.

For a moment, after the echo of the gunshot faded into nothing, there was silence.

Then screaming from the other room. The naked corrections officers had no idea what the fuck was going on. Just that someone had been shot.

Daniel hadn't managed to light the blowtorch—or the screaming would have been much, much louder—and now it just sat there, a lump of cold metal, in the pool of gasoline.

The warden began to cry. Halting, snot-filled sobs. He looked down at his hand. "That son of a bitch . . . he *maimed* me."

Czarcik looked down at the man. In the warden's eyes, he was the cavalry. An ordinary cop who had arrived to save the day. "All those things this lunatic was saying, what was he talking about?"

"Fucking people don't know what it means to run a jail," the warden said. He ran his remaining hand across his nose, wiping away the snot. "These aren't kids, they're animals. And you need to treat them like animals. Fucking people don't understand that." His strength was slowly returning. Anger was replacing fear, now that his life was no longer in imminent danger.

But the warden was wrong about that.

He just didn't realize how wrong until Czarcik shot him in the face.

TWENTY-NINE

If it were like this every day, then everybody would want to live here.

That was the running joke among Chicagoans. Unfortunately you could only use it a handful of times each year.

But today was one of those days.

Czarcik wasn't outside enjoying the weather. He wasn't at one of his favorite watering holes, hourly motels, or shaking down a low-level drug dealer for some good dope.

He was sitting in Eldon Parseghian's office, in the leather chair across the desk.

Parseghian had Czarcik's report in his hand. He shook it in the air. "This thing has more holes than Swiss fucking cheese."

"It wasn't a traffic stop, boss."

Parseghian dropped his head into his hand. He massaged his temples. Finally, he looked up at Czarcik and shook his head. "I'm going to have a shit ton of cleaning up to do. Not just Chicago PD, the AG, and the governor. But interstate agencies, the feds. This is going to be a clusterfuck of epic proportions. You understand that, don't you?"

"It's a good thing you don't have political aspirations."

Parseghian couldn't help but smile. Then grew serious. "When this all shakes out, even if we come out smelling like a rose—or at least not like a stable full of horseshit—I still don't know where that leaves us. Leaves you."

Czarcik stood up and pushed in his chair. "I always knew that."

He was nearly out the door when Parseghian called to him. "Paul?" Czarcik turned around. "We got our man, right?"

Czarcik reflected for a moment, was ready to answer, and then decided to walk out the door.

The dust settled. Like it always does.

And for a while, despite his best intentions, Daniel Langdon was front-page news.

At first he was placed on a pedestal. The vigilante with a heart of gold. He even achieved something of folk hero status when an Austin-based bluegrass trio wrote a murder ballad about his exploits.

The inevitable backlash followed. Who was this deranged gunslinger operating outside the rule of law? Some kind of neofascist? In one of those News of the Weird stories, out in Berkeley, some talk show host died of a cerebral hemorrhage after screaming uncontrollably into the microphone, "Charles Bronson isn't real! Charles Bronson isn't real!" It was assumed he was referring to the character of Paul Kersey, played by Bronson in the *Death Wish* films, since Charles Bronson himself was very real indeed.

A few in the medical establishment latched on to the story in order to plead for increased funding into gliomas.

There was some talk that a big-name lobbyist was going to make a presentation to Congress using the case to support his argument.

Nobody could remember what that argument was, but everybody agreed that it was a terrible idea.

The murders of Luis and Marisol Fernandez were considered closed. There was no direct evidence linking Daniel to either the Fernandezes themselves or the scene of the crime, but even less will within the department to continue looking for a suspect everyone knew was dead.

The laundromat and all their remaining assets were sold, with the money going to the foster children. A silver lining.

The murder of Judge Robertson was more problematic. Because he was, well, a judge. But that was down in Texas. Aside from a few phone calls with Lance Ringland, who always seemed unnaturally cheerful and didn't appear particularly upset about the judge's death, Czarcik didn't have much to do with it.

The wife and kid—the one with MS who was beaten by the judge—made the talk show circuit. Both demonstrated the requisite amount of sorrow and toed the company line: Judge Robertson was a bad man, but one who didn't deserve this ending.

Carlee Ames eventually killed herself. One night, while watching an old Audrey Hepburn movie on TCM, she unplugged her breathing tube and never woke up. Life had simply gotten too hard. Her mother wept uncontrollably and then endured, never once admitting to herself that this was best for the both of them.

Edgar Barnes died without ever knowing how close he came to being killed. He never returned to Duluth and never saw Mona Travers again.

His death wasn't caused by Daniel but just a little bit of good old-fashioned cosmic justice. Changing a tire on the side of I-76 out of Denver, he was struck by a semi on its way to an Amazon distribution center in Des Moines. According to highway patrol, pieces of him were found smeared on the highway for miles.

Miriam Manor was closed for good, and its remaining buildings completely razed almost as soon as the last interviews were conducted. The land reverted back to the county, which turned it into a soybean field. Best forgotten, was the general consensus—especially by the authorities who had turned a blind eye for so long. But even the girls thought so, except for a hardened few who returned every year to piss on the graves of Reverend Bradley and his family.

Czarcik took some heat for Father Dyer, mainly because the crime scene was such a mess and his recollections about what happened were so hazy. His hair and DNA were everywhere—from the attic, to the bathroom, to the living room—and some local sheriff who wanted to make a name for himself was screaming to the powers that be in Nashville that there was some kind of Yankee cover-up. But in the end, no one thought it was a good idea, for any reason, to come down on the side of a prolific pedophile.

For his handling of the Crystal Lake Ranch Massacre—as the press dubbed what transpired at the reform school—Czarcik was lauded as a hero for preventing an even greater tragedy. The official story was gleaned from the surviving guards, expanded upon by Czarcik, and corroborated by investigators who had no reason to think differently.

Daniel had arrived at the property and immediately taken the warden hostage. He ordered the release of the prisoners and then demanded the guards strip. To show he meant business, he sliced off the warden's thumb. Other digits followed when his demands weren't immediately met. Like the White Knight, Czarcik arrived in the nick of time. Although he was unable to stop Daniel from killing the warden, he was able to incapacitate him before he could light the gasoline that would have incinerated the guards. He then killed Daniel with Daniel's own unmarked gun.

A mass murderer was dead at the hand of a law enforcement agent. All was right in the world.

Nobody bothered dusting the gun for prints. Wouldn't have mattered anyway. After shooting Daniel and then the warden with the unmarked gun, Czarcik placed the piece in Daniel's limp hand and squeezed his fingers around the metal. Then he left the gun on the ground.

Chloe had been waiting for him outside. Despite his warning, she had gotten out of the car. She met him coming down the steps, right by the body of the dead guard who had been brained with the nightstick, and the two of them walked off into the sunset.

THIRTY

They lay in bliss, their bodies covered in sweat and other fluids.

They had no reason to move. Neither of them had any other place to be.

The sounds of traffic from outside his window drifted up from the Kennedy. It was late afternoon; rush hour imminent.

"There is no word for it, is there?" she asked.

Her head was on his bare chest, and he looked down at her. "For what?" He was still drunk with sex.

"For the fact that I just made love to the man who killed my husband."

"At the last moment, before I pulled the trigger, I saw his eyes. It's what he wanted. You have to believe that."

"I do," she admitted. "It's just . . ." She laughed. "Like I said, there's no word for it."

"Salvation," he offered.

"That's good enough for now."

"I'm going to take a shower."

Chloe slipped out of bed nude, stretched, and began picking her underwear up off the floor.

Czarcik sat up in bed, against the headboard, and reached over to the nightstand for the remote. He began flipping through the channels, mainly out of habit, not really wanting to watch anything.

Chloe was on her way to the bathroom.

He stopped when he came across a badly restored version of *Horse Feathers* on a local public access station. He began to laugh.

Chloe came back into the room. "What is it?"

He shook his head. "It's nothing. Just . . . oh, man . . ." He took a deep breath and sighed.

Chloe glanced at the TV, watched for a few seconds. Gave a little chuckle of her own. And on her way out the door, with a mixture of relief and regret, said, "I guess it really is goodbye."

She paused. No more than a split second, as if she forgot something, or made a mistake, and then continued to the bathroom.

Czarcik shot up in bed. Heart racing. Blood pumping. The synapses firing on all cylinders. He could barely breathe. The Rush.

The sound of the shower from the bathroom.

Think, think, think . . .

But he couldn't think. It had hit him too quickly. All at once.

"My God . . ." he said out loud, watching the open door as if he expected Chloe to materialize at any moment.

"She *knew* . . . she fucking knew . . ."

A half hour later, after a shower as hot as it was long, Chloe walked into the bedroom to find Czarcik fully dressed and smoking a cigarette.

They locked eyes as she went over to the bed and began to dry herself off. "Just tell me how long. From the beginning?" he asked.

Her body was wrapped in one towel and her hair up in another one. She took the towel off her head and began to dry her hair. "Of course."

"It was Daniel's idea?"

She put the towel down next to herself. Her wet hair fell across her shoulders. "Do you really want to do this?"

Chloe had slipped up. And then the pieces had fallen into place. While she was in the shower, Czarcik had worked through it.

Chloe had recognized the relevance of Groucho. But how? He had never mentioned it to her. In fact, he had made a concerted effort to keep that part of the story secret. But she knew anyway. And there was only one other person who could have possibly told her.

"So where should we begin?" she asked him.

"How about when you first came to see me. At the office."

She nodded.

"Daniel told you to?"

Again she nodded.

"But why? You still had his folders. What could possibly have made him think that I was on to him?"

"You connected the judge and that Hispanic family from Chicago. That *really* freaked him out. He couldn't imagine how you could have done that." She lay down on the bed and propped herself up on her elbow. "How *did* you connect them?"

"I didn't. IDA did."

"Ida who?"

"Not who, what. The Integrated Database Aggregator. Sort of a supercomputer that analyzes crime scene evidence. Daniel used the same type of knot in both those crimes."

A smile played at the corner of her mouth. Czarcik was unsure which of them she was impressed with, him or her husband.

"So you knew he came to see me," he confirmed.

"I knew. He came away . . . impressed. But uncertain. He wasn't sure that you would listen to him. That his threats would be effective. So he needed a way to keep track of you."

"And who better to do it than the one person he trusted above all else," Czarcik finished.

Chloe rocked her head from side to side. Her still-damp hair smelled like Czarcik's own shampoo. Not like hers. He surprised himself by already recognizing her scent.

"What I don't understand," he continued, "is why he—why you both—allowed me to get close at all. To figure out the correct pattern. Why not send me on a wild goose chase?"

"I don't think you give yourself enough credit."

"Hmm?"

"Daniel was afraid that if I simply misled you, you'd quickly lose faith in me. He needed you to trust me completely. And the only way to do this was to ensure that my information was accurate. That it was helping you." She took the cigarette from his fingers. Took a drag and returned it. "Daniel said that the only thing worse than having you on his heels was not knowing where you were."

Czarcik's eyes went wide. Remembering. Playing with the time line in his mind.

"You . . . you never really went back to Chicago after Indiana, did you? You went to Tennessee. To the priest's house. And from there, Florida. You were there the entire time. Waiting for me."

"The ranch was Daniel's Waterloo. He knew that. But I had to make sure that he could finish his work."

There was one more thing that Czarcik wanted to ask.

And then the Rush brought him the answer. It was so incredibly simple and yet so profound.

They were back in Dnieper, the Ukrainian restaurant they'd gone to after they had first met. Chloe had leaned across the table and said to him, ". . . you'd do *anything* for the one you loved."

And with that, he understood.

Czarcik was silent. He ground out his cigarette in the ashtray on his nightstand. "You know, I never really trusted you," he said finally.

"And you shouldn't have. Almost everything was planned out. Preordained."

"*Almost* everything?"

She said nothing. She didn't have to. He looked into those blue eyes. And both of them knew exactly what she meant.

Czarcik felt as if he were on an existential game show.

Behind door number one was truth. Behind door number two was justice. Behind door number three was reality.

Czarcik was forced to balance his needs against his nature.

"Well?" Chloe asked him.

"You knew about his crimes. Well ahead of time. You helped him plan them and were intimately involved with their implementation. At the very least, that makes you an accessory to murder."

She wasn't remotely afraid. She looked at him, defiant. "You have a decision to make."

Czarcik considered this. He considered why he had pursued Daniel so tirelessly. He considered the crimes of those whom Daniel had selected. And he considered his actions at the end of the standoff at Crystal Lake Ranch.

He took her hand and pulled her toward him. The towel fell from her body. She stood before him. He looked up into her eyes and smiled.

"Actually . . . I made that decision long ago."

ACKNOWLEDGMENTS

I wrote the first draft of *Rain Will Come* on my own, with no help from anybody else. And the truth is, it wasn't something you would have wanted to read.

Now it is (hopefully), thanks to the following people.

My incredible agent Anne-Lise Spitzer, who is as smart as she is indefatigable, as well as everyone else at the Philip G. Spitzer Literary Agency, especially Philip Spitzer and Kim Lombardini, who provided me with early and indispensable advice.

My entire team at Thomas & Mercer, including Jessica Tribble, for whose enthusiasm and counsel I'm eternally grateful; Laura Barrett; Sarah Shaw; and Mike Heath.

My editors: Clarence Haynes, Wanda Zimba, and Valerie Paquin. They are truly the unsung heroes of this book. So here, it's time to sing their praises.

Maybe most importantly, Jane Friedman, without whom all of this would never have been possible. She was the very first to believe and I can never thank her enough.

And finally, my family. For their love and support. Always.

ABOUT THE AUTHOR

Photo © 2015 Kristin Reyer

Thomas Holgate has written feature films, television movies and series, nonfiction books, and countless magazine pieces published under a different name. *Rain Will Come* is his first novel.